Parched

Part One

By Andrew C. Branham

Man's nature is not essentially evil. Brute nature has been known to yield to the influence of love. You must never despair of human nature.
Mohandas Gandhi

Contents

Chapter 1

The sun no longer shone canary yellow. It hadn't done so for years. Instead, it glared down, obstinate, punishing—beet red, like the garden tomatoes that no longer existed. It stood guard over the desert-dry water taps that had likewise fallen prey to the relentless heat, even in mid-October. Livermore, California, had been a town set on rolling hills, swathed in green grass and fragrant orange poppies. Now, each day played out like the one before it: sun, heat, illness, death.

On that particular day, relative calm engulfed them. Only a few trails of smoke rose up in the distance toward the west and the Oakland Hills. Usually it was worse—the smoke was more like the dense cloud of marine fog that used to roll in daily. Now, the arid air, once fresh with coastal mist and the scent of eucalyptus trees mixed with wild lavender and rosemary, smelled like burning hay. The sun's transition from an earthly asset to man's most vicious foe had been going on for decades, but you would never have known it. It had caught humanity ill-prepared. Those who once had awaited its daily arrival now despised its very existence.

Scientists had a word for it; scientists had a word for everything. They called it a Red Giant, a star that had exhausted the supply of hydrogen at its core and had switched to thermonuclear fusion. As a result, the Earth found itself baking, its waters evaporating, and humanity's extinction imminent. No scientist or politician could explain why the sun had made such a drastic transformation; nor did it matter.

In the distance, the sound of a laboring sixteen-wheeler lumbering up the road startled James as he popped up from his sleep. Scanning the room, he breathed out his relief. *Everybody's okay*, he thought, checking out their California king bed. For a brief moment, he recalled his dream, in which he had been frolicking with his brother along the beaches of Lake Erie, near where they had grown up. But, instead of laughing, shouting, and swimming in cool waters, he was perspiring. Sweat soaked the bed and stained his shirt and underwear. His mouth felt pasty and dry.

What's the truck doing here at this hour?

The clanking of the massive tires hitting the potholes brought him back to reality. Rising cautiously, he kicked into the nightstand and let out a yelp, awakening their infant, who began to cry.

"What is it?" his wife asked.

"Nothing. Just the water truck. Go back to sleep."

1

His thirteen-year-old son, Silas, was now awake as well and was scanning the room with his eyes. His long blond hair was matted down against his boyish face and, despite his sleep, he still looked fatigued. He was irritated not only at the unrelenting heat and his sister's cries, but also that he woke up in the same depressing room where they almost always stayed. Sometimes he hoped his life was just a nightmare that he would someday wake up from. Looking around, he saw walls stacked with cardboard boxes, dirty clothing on the floor, and dirt-stained sheets on the bed in which he was lying. The two windows in the room were covered in a thick film of dust and sand. A loaded rifle and handgun were on a box next to the bed.

"Can someone keep her quiet?" Silas grumbled as he looked toward his crying infant sister, Charlotte. "It's impossible to sleep around here."

Already dressed, James grabbed his shotgun and several plastic gallon water jugs, which he had strung together with nautical rope, and sprinted down the steps, the jugs thumping with each step. He pushed aside the heavy desk and chair he had used to barricade the door and scrunched down to peek out through a two-inch crack he had opened.

He saw the truck that had stopped in the middle of the road. As he struggled to focus, he smelled the burning air and saw the heat waves reflecting off the cracked and buckled asphalt. He made out several residents emerging from their deteriorating townhomes, guns and jugs in hand, walking toward the truck with its distinctive Red Cross logo. The sound of his baby crying and the rustling of his waking family echoed through the empty stairwell.

Already his body was screaming for drink as the heat immediately kicked in the dreaded feeling of thirst he so desperately tried to ignore. Once a natural resource as common as vegetation, water was now like an endangered species that was on the verge of complete extinction. Having a dry mouth had become almost as common as the blinding sun itself.

Sensing no imminent danger and knowing that a truck carrying such priceless cargo would be there for only fifteen or twenty minutes, he crept from his home and stepped out into the debilitating daylight, along with his neighbors.

"Thank God," he said to one as the man emerged in pajama bottoms and a polo shirt. The neighbor looked at him coldly and did not respond. As the driver connected the hoses to dispense the potable water, several of the neighbors rushed the truck. Off to one side stood a guard. As chaos threatened to erupt, he pointed his gun in the air and fired several rounds. Any thoughts of a riot came to an abrupt halt as the neighbors stared at the two men at the rear of the truck.

"Listen, and listen carefully," one of the men shouted. "There'll be peace and order here or the truck'll move on. Plain and simple. Form a single line and have your bottles ready and open. This truck is only scheduled to be here for 30 minutes, and then we move on. Any further disruptions and we leave. Understood? And, just so you know, the FEMA tent has been relocated to Livermore Labs." He paused and gave the crowd time to contemplate his warning. "Now, one at a time. Quickly! Form a single-file line and move off to the side."

Howling winds peppered the crowd with dust, and James pulled from his pocket a wrinkled handkerchief to cover his face. His mouth was as dry as the ground below his feet, his body craving moisture. Having been fortunate enough to fall into line near the front, he fought off a fleeting thought. *Just raise and cock the gun and start firing. Then grab the truck and drive it around the back to unload. All 11,000 gallons!*

He shook off the thought. Once a man of faith and a respected member of the Catholic Church, he pondered what had become of mankind. He knew if push came to shove and the safety of his family was in doubt, he wouldn't hesitate. All of the principles he had valued so dearly for the past 40 years of his life were fruitless in a world where three gallons of water could buy you a running car. Fair or unfair, he was a man of God—or had been. Now, he was merely another vigilante tasked with the job of protecting those he loved.

The driver turned the spigot on the tank and, as the water flowed, the man in front of James filled a ten-gallon container before moving on. James brushed his forehead across his shirt sleeve. He guessed the temperature was 120 degrees F. and climbing.

When it was finally his turn before the spigot, James got to claim as much of the precious commodity as possible within 30 seconds. The gallon jugs, strung together with rope wrapped around his body, proved an innovative system. Once they were filled, he slung the rope around his shoulders, secured his shotgun, and hurried back to his home. *Mission complete. We'll have at least a few more days of water.*

At home, James carried the water in, soaking up the relative coolness of the foyer. When he turned on his heels to climb the stairs, he locked eyes with the stranger looking back at him in the mirror—sunken face, scraggly salt-and-pepper beard, wild long bushy hair, and his once bright blue eyes now red and dry. With his bounty in hand, he slowly climbed the steps to share his largesse with his family.

He headed up and past the bounty of stored canned and dry food that lined every square inch of the home. There were boxes of supplies stacked in every direction, leaving only a walking path through the cluster of stockpiled goods. The six gallons of water made his skinny frame sluggish as he climbed the steps. He was greeted by his seven-year-old Boxer, Brownie, named by his eldest son when Silas was six years old. He attempted to pat the friendly dog on the head, but the overwhelming heat and weight of the water made him destined to reach the top of the stairs.

"James, is everything okay, honey?" his wife called from the third story.

He tried not to sound too winded. "Yeah. I got the water. Everything's okay."

Fighting off the overwhelming urge to drink, he placed the jugs near an open spot on top of several boxes of food and made his way upstairs.

"Si? Where are you, son? I need your help bringing up the jugs."

The boy—thin and lanky—came in, looking annoyed. Still in puberty, the child had long blond hair like his mother, bright blue eyes like his father, and sharp, angular features. His squeaky voice fell somewhere between boy and man.

"Right now, Dad? Come on. It's so hot!"

"And it's going to get hotter without this water. Come on now. Get down here."

The boy followed his father down the stairs, and together they carted the water up to the third floor, where it would be safe. The third floor was also where they lived and, more importantly, housed their guns. James locked eyes with the wife he so devoutly loved. Just as they had on everyone, the conditions had left their mark on her as well. Her once golden, flowing hair had become dry, bushy, and streaked with gray. Her frame was far too skinny, her torn and soiled clothing appeared to be four sizes too large, and her eyes had large dark circles around them along with wrinkles that would usually come only to the elderly. Yet, in his mind, she was still as beautiful as the day he married her.

By that time, thirst had ceased to be an issue of urgency in the family's lives and had become, instead, more of an annoyance. Electricity had been erratic for years and had finally gone out totally soon after the water dried up. There was little to do except sleep and read from one of the books lining the shelves. Or they could sort the food, or play with Brownie or baby Charlotte. At four months, she was small for her age, weighing around ten pounds. Her future written long before her inception, the child was destined for a difficult and short life. Yet, despite knowing her fate and the likelihood of her never knowing the beautiful Earth that her family had once taken for granted, everyone treated her as if she had a rosy-bright future. No one, James had resolved, would take away their hopes and dreams.

Charlotte, despite her slight stature, was strong and healthy. Her life, confined to the three-story condominium they called home, seemed happy. She knew only what she had—a family that loved and nurtured her.

That evening, with the setting of the sun, the temperatures dropped to a more tolerable 95 degrees. But with darkness came terror. Crime by night ran rampant in the streets of the waterless world. While Lexie spent her evenings feeding Charlotte and warming their canned dinners or military MREs (Meals Ready To Eat), Silas and James prepared the house for lockdown by stringing cans around the stairs, near the windows, and by the door to alert the family of any intruder. It was the closest thing they had to a security system. Once the house was secured, James checked to be certain the guns were locked and loaded on the third floor and ready at a moment's notice. He'd never before needed them, but he instinctively knew that, when the time came, he'd have to act fast.

Silas looked up from a dinner of canned chili warmed by two Jesus candles. "This sucks," he said. "I'm tired of chili. Can't we eat something else?"

Lexie looked up from feeding the baby, her long golden-blond hair falling from her brow. "You know we have to be careful with our food. We're lucky to have what we have. Most people don't have anything. Count your blessings."

"Guess you're right, Mom," Silas sighed. Despite his complaining, any chance to eat and drink was truly a luxury. He savored every bite and the feeling of food, any food, hitting his stomach was a remarkable feeling. Even more incredible was the sensation of any beverage on his pallet. With thirst always a burden, the water Silas was drinking tasted as good as anything he had ever had.

Our blessings, James thought, as he wiped one of his pistols clean of oil. *That's a laugh.* He heard sounds coming from Selby Lane, quiet, distressing sounds. The sounds of people making their way out of their homes and onto the streets in search of anything of value. Darkness so black and void of any unnatural light, the stars lit up the sky unlike anything seen prior to the blackout. The only light besides the moon and stars was the slight flicker of candles in a few select homes in the large subdivision. Those who did walk the night were most likely those one would prefer not to meet. They were probably looting the little remaining items left behind as more and more families fled their homes in search of food and dreams of lands with water. Many had left that afternoon in search of the FEMA (Federal Emergency Management Agency) tent near the Livermore Nuclear Laboratory.

Lexie turned toward her husband. "What are you thinking?"

"Hmm?"

"You look preoccupied. I was just wondering what you're thinking."

He shook his head. "Just the usual. Just how we're going to make it through one more night safe and sound."

She smiled and continued with her chores.

With dinner behind them and the heat beginning to lift, James started

5

to nod. He looked around, his eyes falling on Silas, sprawled out in his boxers next to Brownie, who was having a series of doggie-mares and jumping in his sleep from time to time. Lexie had likewise fallen asleep, with Charlotte cradled in her arms. Minutes later, the entire family was snoozing by the light of a single dwindling candle and an ancient oil lamp.

Suddenly, several loud thumps, followed by the shattering of glass, awakened James.

"What was that?" Lexie whispered, her eyes still heavy.

James strained his ears. "Sounded like it came from downstairs." He paused, thinking. "Probably nothing. Just kids throwing rocks at the windows again. I'll go check it out. You go back to sleep." Charlotte stirred in her mother's arms. "I'll try to be quiet."

Shit, he thought, pulling on his shoes as Lexie rolled her head to one side, her chin nestled against her daughter's hair. The clanging sound of tin cans followed by the heavy sounds of footsteps on the stairs suddenly split the night. He grabbed for his shotgun and double checked to ensure there was a shell in the chamber.

Fuck! Looters. And they're in the goddamn house.

"Silas! Son!" James whispered. "Wake up!"

Before he could react, the door flew open as two men, camouflaged and armed, burst in. Lexie let out a scream and Silas popped up from the floor. The dog yapped several times before turning and ducking behind the sofa. The men, with bushy beards and stringy hair, had painted their faces with camouflage. James looked past them into the hallway where he spied a string of empty cans, betraying their means of access to the house.

Shit. Now what? He realized that desperate men act unpredictably desperate in times such as these. No time for indecision. Lexie was continuing to let out a bone-chilling scream.

"You!" one man growled at Lexie. "Stop yer whining and sit still." He shifted the muzzle of his pistol toward her. "Or else!"

"Wait a minute, wait a minute, wait a minute," James said, moving the muzzle of the shotgun in small circles. "Okay, nobody needs to get hurt here. Nobody needs to die."

Lexie was doing her best to muffle her sobs, her shoulders rising and falling with each desperate breath. The man shifted his gun back to James, who stood his ground, shotgun pointed directly between them.

"This is a no-win situation, guys," he added softly. "You don't wanna do this. You really don't."

The men looked baffled, caught off guard by a family that was actually armed. James guessed that was a first. Finally, the leader waved his gun at him. "That's right, that's right, motherfucker! It's a no-winner for sure. That goes for you and yer family. Now, drop the fucking gun before I shoot the shit out of yer wife and take yer baby."

James glanced at Silas and winked, hoping the boy wasn't too frightened to catch the signal. James had coached his son many times before that "the wink" meant serious business. The boy knew what he had to do. James turned back to his assailant. "Please. You can take all the food we have and go. Just leave me and my family alone."

"Fat chance, asshole. What's going to happen is that you're going to walk down the stairs and leave. I'm the new husband now. This is my bitch and this is my house. So you got about three seconds to make up your mind. Drop the gun and go. Now!"

The man's partner had a crazed look on his face, not knowing how to react. Obviously, the other man was winging it.

"You got to the count of three before we open fire."

James wracked his brain for a plan.

"One…"

The man's partner took several slip-steps to his right, making it more difficult to hit the two men with a single shot.

"Two…"

The second man stopped in front of a picture window overlooking the sleepy little hamlet James's family called home.

Before the man reached three, a shot rang out and the man flew backward before hitting the floor. His partner whirled to face him, stunned, before James sent a second shot that caught him in the shoulder, sending him hurtling backward against the window. As the glass gave way, the man let out a blood-wrenching scream before disappearing from sight. They could hear his body hit the concrete below.

Silas lowered the gun to his side. He stood there, stunned.

"Dad…I did it just the way you said to. Did I do good?"

James crossed over to him and grabbed him around the shoulders. "Just the way I said. Just the way we practiced. You did good, son. You saved our lives."

"Is he…" Lexie had settled Charlotte into the chair. "Is he dead? For sure?"

James crossed over to the man, still clutching his .45, and knelt down beside him. Blood trickled out from a hole in the left side of his head, staining the carpet.

"It was your choice, motherfucker," he whispered.

James stood up, went to the window, and looked outside. In the soft, distant glow of the haze on the horizon, he saw the second man prone on the ground, shards of glass surrounding him.

"Let's check the hallway, son. Make sure no one else is in the house."

The boy, holding his gun high, did as he was told, slipping silently through the doorway and out into the hall. James followed.

"James!"

He turned toward his wife.

"What's going to happen to us?" Lexie asked. "What are we going to do?"

James threw his arms around her. "It's okay, baby. It's all over. It looks as if that's all for now. We'll move them tomorrow, dump them in the field. And that will be that."

"No, I mean, what's going to happen to us? To our future?" She looked down at their daughter, who had once more fallen asleep against the cushion. "How can we go on living like this?"

For once, James didn't know what to say. He forced a smile and, squeezing her arms, took several steps toward the door before turning back. "I'd better go help, Si. We need to board up the window and reset the alarm system. We'll be back soon as we can."

That night, there was no sleep for anyone in the family. James did his best to console Silas who was still shell-shocked from having to shoot a man for the first time in his young life. Charlotte cried most of the night from the ruckus and Lexie rocked her and stroked her back. James held his arm around Silas as Brownie curled up next to them. Silence filled the remainder of the night.

James looked around the room. *How the hell did I end up here? From an usher at St. Anthony's, a youth minister, a prayer-group leader—to this!* He shook his head and dropped his hands. They had moved to a smaller bedroom adjacent to the sitting room, dragged the corpse down the stairs and outside next to the man's partner, and cleaned up the mess as best they could. Now, once again, Silas snoozed next to Brownie, and Lexie nestled with their daughter in her arms. It was all like a bad dream, a horrendous side trip through the bowels of hell. Sure, he felt like a hero, a protector of his family, and he felt proud of Silas. But the Bible was no longer the ruler of his life; instead, it was but a distant memory. The world had changed—and changed him.

I know one thing. I will fight to my last dying breath to protect my wife and my children, no matter what. Three of the best, strongest, most loving people in the world. Three people who deserve better than this. And I'm going to see that they get it!

Chapter 2

The night dragged on. Sporadic gunshots rang in the distance, screams echoing from the street. The usual eerie feeling that accompanied the darkness was unusually strong on this night.

For years, scientists had been baffled by the changes in the sun, its color, and the increase in ambient temperatures. The red phase of the sun was not supposed to have occurred for billions of years. Yet, all the signs pointed to it right there and then. While scientists argued, climate-change activists preached that they'd been right all along, as if it really mattered. While world leaders pondered various solutions, the sun grew hotter. Not only hotter, but also larger and more intense. And it was doing so more rapidly than anyone could have guessed. Any scientist or politician, at least.

As the Earth continued to bake, the military and FEMA began to plan for the worst. Lexie's sister, Karen, was a high-ranking FEMA official. For years leading up to the water stoppage, she had warned the family of the looming calamity. She exhorted them to prepare for the worst, to stockpile shelf-stable food, to buy guns and start hoarding ammunition. She told them to fill the house with bottled water and to put in a supply of first aid and emergency equipment. The family had believed she was overreacting, but they listened to her nonetheless. Pretty much. This was America, after all. The water would never actually "stop running." The government would find a way to make things right.

Still, they had heeded some of her advice. James had purchased a 12-gauge shotgun, a .45 revolver, and a .306 rifle—just in case. He ordered a pile of ammunition from various websites and stockpiled it in the garage. He had taken Silas to the local gun range so many times that the boy was now a better shot than he.

It turned out to be a wise decision. As conditions continued to deteriorate, people began to panic. Most pundits believed the West Coast would run out of water first, and the Eastern Seaboard shortly thereafter. For many years before the power went out, the government-run news network aired pictures of the miles of dried dirt and sand that had once been the mighty Mississippi, Lake Tahoe, and the Colorado River. As the waters of the Great Lakes receded, the shoreline communities relocated closer to the new shore, leaving behind desolate, cracked, and parched ground. It was common to see boats, ships, and freighters mired in a pile of sand, as if frozen in time.

The once-thriving lakes, known for their bounty of fish, had become warm baths of decaying matter surrounded by the rotting smell of death. Nearly all of America's other lakes, rivers, and reservoirs had long since succumbed to the Red Giant, becoming nothing more than a piece of history.

In fact, with the exception of the extreme North and South Poles, very little fresh water remained anywhere on the planet. In the absence of water, agriculture ceased. With no agriculture, there was no grain or produce. With no grain or produce, there was no livestock. Since there were no resources with which to manufacture food, the food that remained on the planet was all the food there was—forever.

Governments around the globe tried to build desalinization plants to create fresh water. But the plants took years to construct and were outrageously expensive. They also consumed massive amounts of natural resources that were sparse. The governments had waited far too long to build the plants, nearly all of which lay uncompleted. By the time the few that had been built were operational, the conditions had deteriorated so badly that the owners could not find enough people to run them. Moreover, the cost to produce a single gallon of fresh water was a hundred times greater than the cost of natural water. Strapped financially, not a government in the world had enough resources even to dream of building more plants or taking care of the few that already existed.

Even more alarming were the rising ocean levels on both coasts due to the rapid melt-off of the polar ice caps. The ocean levels had been rising for years, and newscasts had often shown footage of the water engulfing many of the cities on the East Coast. Much of Florida was already under water, and the citizens of New York City had been retreating farther inland for months.

In the West, water levels had taken a toll on many coastal communities. San Francisco—virtually submerged—was known as The Islands of San Francisco, while San Diego, completely submerged, was simply the Bay of San Diego. Even Los Angeles had mostly succumbed to the rising seas, as the coast had crept inland by several miles when the ocean reclaimed some of L.A.'s most populated parts of town. It had been some time since James's family had seen a news report. So, as far as they knew, the oceans had already consumed a large chunk of both coasts.

Images from the Rexcon Telescope showed that Earth had evolved to Mars-like conditions, with barren cracked craggy land devoid of trees or any other greenery. Just as on Mars, the ground was pocked with large dry gray craters in nearly all countries that were formerly lush with lakes, rivers, and streams. A few stands of dead trees remained, but most had collapsed long ago, toppling to the scorched earth below.

What were once meandering lakes had become spiraling canyons. What were once rolling hills alive with livestock were now desolate boneyards. Cold ocean waters had turned hot. Snowcapped mountains had withered into deserts. Playgrounds and parks stood silent as rust slowly decomposed their metal structures. Most dogs, cats, and other household pets had long since perished. Life—once vibrant and abundant—had quickly transitioned into death.

In August, against all agency rules, Lexie's sister forwarded a classified email to the family. In less than a month, the government predicted, the municipal water supply serving the entirety of the West Coast would be gone—the aquifers dry, the rivers turned to dust, and the reservoirs drained to dirt pits. The water being pumped in from other states had dried up and, with no rain, there was no hope. Without hope, the email warned, they could expect widespread looting, anarchy, and roaming bands of outlaws—not to mention rampant thirst and starvation.

The email estimated that electricity would last roughly one week before panicking Americans brought the country to a grinding halt. The agency predicted that, within days, nearly all citizens would abandon their jobs to care for their families and attend to their own basic human needs—for as long as they could. The U.S. government would collapse, and all services would disappear for good. There would be no police, no fire department, and no hospital care. Planes would no longer fly, gas stations would no longer pump fuel, and even the military would collapse.

James and Lexie believed it. After what they had already witnessed, they decided to use the last of their funds to stockpile shelf-stable food, all the water they could find, all the medications they could beg, and whatever other supplies they felt they might need. They stuffed the house and garage full until they could hold no more. They purchased several drums that they filled with gasoline and stored in the garage. When their house was full, they filled a nearby storage locker. The only space that remained was inside the old SUV that James had purchased in exchange for several gallons of water weeks before. Their electric car, now completely useless, sat abandoned on the street below.

Shortly thereafter, the water had ceased to flow and there was a nationwide permanent blackout. A very small percentage of the population had solar power, but there simply were not enough panels to make a big impact. Companies that made solar power panels did not have the enormous amount of resources required to keep up with demand. When society began to crumble, the solar companies closed their doors along with the rest of the businesses. Even those panels that existed struggled to tolerate the extreme heat.

Just as FEMA had predicted, America collapsed into chaos. Many of the unprepared, the weak, and the sick perished of starvation or thirst.

Many of those who were better prepared wished they had perished. Life, taken for granted for eons, now toppled on the mountaintop of extinction. It was no longer a matter of if but when. Most animal and plant species had already become extinct. Now the clock was ticking on modern Homo sapiens. The only help still existing came from the dedicated volunteers of the Red Cross, FEMA, and a small group of patriotic retired military men and women who continued to dedicate their lives to protecting whatever remained of the country.

James thought back to that eventful October day when the tap water had gone from cool and clear to warm and murky. Finally, the tap ran dry, belching only air. The look on Lexie's face was one he would never forget—and never hoped to see again.

While they were more prepared than most Americans, the idea that there would likely never be running water again seemed incredible. James reached for his wife and squeezed her as they quietly sobbed together. Mostly, their tears fell neither for themselves nor for the millions of others who would die, but for the future that Silas and Charlotte would never know. There would be no prom or college for Silas. No flowers, days at the park, or swimming in the pool for Charlotte. What hurt the most, though, was the realization that neither child would likely survive to see adulthood, or the world that James and Lexie had known as children.

Their children's destiny was far removed from what they themselves had known. It was a destiny not made in heaven but, rather, carved out of the molten fires of hell.

Chapter 3

As the red rays of the sun rose above the foothills ringing the Livermore Valley, the light was already too intense to look into in the east. The smoldering wildfires throughout the countryside had turned the skyline a muddy reddish-brown. They consumed everything in their path—from fallen trees to entire housing developments, schools, businesses, and factories. With no means of stopping the flames, humanity was helpless. Vegetation was only a remote memory. Fire was always a major danger to anyone at any time and, without water to fight the blazes, man was helpless.

Exhausted from their night of terror, the family moved slowly, carefully cleansing themselves with a few wet wipes from the pile of packages they had stockpiled. As usual, they grabbed the first clothes they could find that weren't caked with dirt or full of holes. Then they went down to breakfast. With mouths as pasty and dry as cotton, they would try anything in their power to ignore the thirst and hold out for a few more hours before taking any water.

Doing whatever he could to keep his mind off his thirst, James set about nailing some wooden strips he had scavenged from their broken furniture to reinforce the boarded-up windows from the previous night. Sweat from his head landed in puddles at his feet. Lexie had changed Charlotte's diaper and was feeding her another bottle. She sang to the child as she rocked back and forth, tears welling in her eyes. James pretended not to notice, choosing to focus on the windows instead.

Silas, too, was busy preparing for the day. After wiping himself with a dry rag and throwing on his shoes, he went down to the first floor to visit "The Bucket." That's what his father called it—a five-gallon container that was the closest thing the family had to a working toilet. Every couple of days, James carried it out to the garage and dumped the contents down the storm drain. He worked as quickly as he could, the sweat rolling down his face, so he wouldn't have to breathe in the noxious odors until he was well clear of the building.

At first, relieving oneself in a five-gallon bucket had been a humiliating experience. But, in time, The Bucket had become the "new normal." Silas himself avoided the garage at all costs.

For the boy, boredom had become Public Enemy Number One. Without any music, television, computers, or video games, his only escape was reading. At thirteen, he'd already had a taste of what he felt was a normal life back when electricity had provided him a few hours a day of fun. Now, he had only Brownie and his books. And most of them he'd already read. Of course, he loved his baby sister, but she was still just that—a baby—and often more of a nuisance than someone of any conceivable entertainment value.

Finally relieved, Silas pulled his pants up and cinched the belt around his waist before he and Brownie made their way back up the stairs to the safe haven of the third floor, where James had finished boarding up the windows. Sitting down to a breakfast of crackers, boxed juice, and Spam, Silas gave Brownie half a can of his favorite dog food, of which he never seemed to tire.

"Si, don't open that can of Spam please," James said.

"Why? I'm starving!"

"Because I said so. That's why. We need to ration our food. Crackers and juice is plenty for breakfast."

"Man, this sucks. I'm always starving. It's not fair."

"Enough, Silas!"

The family felt full after the light meal as their bodies had adapted to the times and hunger was much more easily satisfied. It did not stop them from daydreaming of hot pizza, steaks, or juicy hamburgers from the famous West Coast fast-food chain, In and Out. The juice, however, was more precious than anything in the world and the satisfaction it brought as it slowly entered the mouth and trickled down the esophagus was more gratifying than could be described.

It was not long ago that sex, love, money, companionship, and fine dining were the things humans craved the most. The world had become a land of extreme drought and previously desired feelings were replaced with only one—the drive to find food and drink. As the family completed its morning ritual, James looked up.

"What's that?"

From outside came the sound of a vehicle speeding down the street. As the roar of the engine grew louder, James jumped up and hurried to the window.

"What is it?" Lexie asked.

"What's going on, Dad?"

James looked out at the truck that had come to a stop several dozen feet from their home. Four men, armed and dressed in military fatigues, spilled out onto the street. With rags covering their heads to protect them from the heat, they split up and headed off in different directions.

More looters!

James watched as one group pounded on a neighbor's door. No response. He knew the owners had fled several days earlier in search of

14

the FEMA tent, desperate for supplies. He doubted they had made it. They had run out of fuel for their car, so they had to make the trip on foot.

The looters drew their guns and kicked the door in. They were inside for only a few minutes before they reemerged.

Well, they didn't find anything there. Now what?

The men moved on to the next neighboring home, also abandoned. Again they pounded on the door, received no answer, and burst in. They were inside for several minutes, leading James to believe they'd found at least something of value.

Won't be long, he thought, his heart racing. *Gotta be ready for anything!*

He sprinted up the stairs. "Lexie! Silas! Take Charlotte and the shotgun and get into the SUV in the garage."

Silas's face went white with fear.

"Come on, son. No time to waste. Fill up all of the gas cans you can find and put them in the hatchback."

"What about me?" Lexie asked.

James breathed out hard. "Grab all the food and water you can fit into the car. And be quick about it!" He grabbed a rifle, a handgun, and a canvas bag filled with ammunition.

"What's going on?" Lexie frowned.

"We have visitors. Unfriendlies. And we need to leave now. Fast. Listen up! Do what I say, you hear?" He paused, looked into two confused faces, and took another deep breath. "Now!"

Racing down to the garage, Lexie made Charlotte comfortable in the car and began working with Silas to load it with food and water. The boy filled several large gas cans, grabbed five ten-gallon cans that were already filled, and carefully placed all of them in the back of the vehicle. They were extraordinarily heavy and he struggled to lift them into the back of the SUV. He was sweating profusely. With no ventilation, the air in the garage soon seemed swollen with the fumes from the open drums and the trails of gas Silas had spilled. He and his mother worked frantically until the car was filled to capacity.

Upstairs, James slowly opened a window looking out onto the street. He remained quiet as he peered down at the men exiting the neighbor's home with a few boxes of booty they had claimed. The men threw the boxes into the back of their truck before turning their sights on James's home. They walked casually down the street, one man joking with the other, both men laughing out loud. They had unkempt wispy beards and skin so black with dirt, it was impossible to tell their race. James knew from their thick southern accents that they were not native to the area. More likely they were violent looters who would do anything to survive another day. These were the most dangerous of bandits—the ones who had nothing to lose.

When they were only steps from James's front door, he slowly lifted the rifle and rested it on the window sill. Using the scope, he locked onto one of the men. He fired a shot that whizzed past him, shattering a porch light across the street. The men ducked, peeling off in separate directions, diving for cover behind some parked cars. Pulling their side arms, they looked around, clearly puzzled as to where the shots had come from. James stood up with his back to the wall and slowly craned his head around the window frame, just enough so he could project his voice outside.

"Hold your fire! Don't shoot. We're a family of peace!"

The looters turned toward the house, and two shots popped off as James ducked back away from the sash. One bullet made its way into the home, hitting a box, and the other hit the exterior stucco.

James's mind flew into overdrive.

"We have a house full of food here! And plenty of water. It's yours. It's all yours. Just let us leave in peace."

The men responded with a litany of shots aimed in the general direction of James's head.

"We ain't gonna hurt y'all. Not what we want. Just let us in and we can work 'er out," the tall skinny man said. James knew better.

"That's not going to happen! So, hold your fire and we'll leave peacefully and everything in here is yours. You have no risk."

The men turned toward one another, nodding, before raising their weapons and unleashing a hailstorm of bullets toward the house. Dust from the bullets hitting the drywall in the room filled the air.

Shit! These guys are serious! Only one thing left to do.

James took the .306 and began peeling off shots in the general direction of the men. The looters, caught off guard, crab-crawled farther from the house, taking up new positions offering more safety. They thought. James continued firing.

The other two looters, several doors down, had heard the commotion and made their way cautiously toward the scene. James placed the rifle at his feet, loaded his revolver, and fired off five quick shots in the direction of the first two men, still crouched behind the abandoned cars. He reloaded the gun, tucked it in his jeans, and grabbed the rifle once again.

"Okay, okay," he yelled. "You win. I surrender!"

He took no time to look back to see their reaction. Grabbing all the guns, ammunition, and whatever else he could, he ran down the stairs to the garage where his family was already waiting in the SUV.

"Oh, thank God!" Lexie cried. "We heard the shots. I thought you'd been…"

James shoved the ammunition bag and water jugs into the back of the SUV. Silas and Lexie looked on as he opened the lid to a gasoline can and kicked it over. The gasoline rushed out, soaking the floor. He slid into the driver's seat, put the keys in the ignition, and motioned with his finger for his family to be silent.

What James had not planned for was an upset baby. Silence was the key to his plan and Charlotte was beginning to cry lightly as the unfamiliar fumes filled the air. Lexie knew all the tricks to keep her comforted and she slowly rocked her, blew lightly on her face, and put her favorite pacifier in her mouth. At least for now it did the trick. Brownie sat quietly in the back as if he knew he had to be silent.

It was only a matter of moments before the looters had rushed the house and were banging at the front door. Then James heard them kicking at it. Shots followed as the men pushed their way in. Listening to the footsteps, James could tell they had rushed up to the third floor. As he had expected, the men ignored the door to the garage and he could hear them running quickly and violently up the stairs. The family heard the shouts from the men, screaming for them to come out of hiding. Doors were being kicked open, shower curtains opened, and the yelling continued.

"All right," he said, turning the key in the ignition. "Hang on, everyone, here we go."

He threw the car into reverse, barreling through the garage door, sending pieces of metal flying. Slamming on the brakes, he pulled a Zippo lighter from his pocket, ignited the flame, and rolled down the window.

"Dad, what are you doing?" Silas cried. "No, Dad, don't do it! Please don't kill any more people."

Ignoring him, James tossed the flame onto the gas-soaked garage floor. With a loud whooshing sound, the gas ignited in a violent eruption of flames. James put the car in drive and sped down the street. Rather than speeding on, James had one more stop. He screeched to a halt next to the military truck, pulled out the handgun and shot out both the front and rear tires of the passenger side. He put the SUV in drive, hit the pedal to the floor, and the family sped off down Selby Lane.

Hearing the massive explosion, James, Lexie, and Silas all turned around and saw their home engulfed in flames. The fire had the entire first floor ablaze and was already making its way up to the second floor. It was agonizing for the three of them to see their home of many years in ravaging flames. Everything they owned, including irreplaceable pictures, photo albums, and keepsakes was now being taken by the fire. Silas broke down into a hysterical crying fit and neither Lexie nor James could do anything to soothe their kind and emotional boy.

As they neared the on-ramp to I-580 East, James knew he had both won and lost that battle. On the one hand, the bandits were trapped in the burning home and unlikely to survive. If they did, they'd end up with none of the possessions James's family had spent their life's savings accumulating. On the other hand, they had just given up the only advantage they had over the rest of the desperate population—their home, stockpiled with supplies. Once, they had taken pride in knowing they were far better prepared than most Americans to face adversity. Now, they had little more than a negligible advantage—a car full of food, a few boxes of baby formula, and some water. Of course, they had escaped. And they'd brought with them their all-important guns and ammo. So they had that going for them.

James slammed on the brakes and the car came to an abrupt halt. He grabbed Lexie and Charlotte and gave them a huge hug. Both were crying and he rocked with them while rubbing Lexie's back.

"I love you all so much! I won't allow you to be hurt!"

Tearing up yet again, Lexie sobbed, "Thank you, baby! Thank you for saving our lives!"

"It wasn't just me, Lex. That was a total team effort," he said with a smile.

With the car still running, he jumped out and into the back seat where Silas was surrounded by boxes and supplies.

"I love you, son. I'm so proud of you. You were so brave and so strong back there!" He gave him a big, manly hug and Silas blushed.

"I love you too, Dad. Wow, that was close!"

"We're all safe now."

"Okay, now let's get the fuck out of here!" Silas said with a smirk.

Despite the situation, Silas's choice of language was not amusing to Lexie. "Watch your mouth, young man! You will not use that word ever again," she snapped.

"Whatever!" he shot back. Brownie poked his nose out from the back of the SUV and gave both Silas and James a happy lick. Silas, from the back seat, chuckled. "Hey, Dad, at least there's one good thing about all this. I won't have to clean my room."

"Or use The Bucket," James said, smiling.

"Thank God." He wiped his face in his sleeve. "Can you turn on the air conditioning? It's getting hot already."

The three of them took a moment to laugh at Silas's observation, but James had to quickly remind him that the air conditioning used gas and they had to save every precious drop.

"Fan only, son! You should be used to the heat."

Silas slouched in his seat with a big pout on his face. "Man, it would feel so good. Just for a few minutes?"

Always thinking of the safety of his family, James would not budge. "I'm sorry, buddy. No can do! That sucks gas like a vacuum." *And God knows what lies ahead...*

Chapter 4

As the family wound their way east, Silas settled back against the seat, and Lexie stared out the window, contemplating their surroundings.

"It wasn't long ago," she said, "this time of year would have meant rolling, bright green hills, mountains filled with wildflowers, the air sweet with floral scents." She paused, looking out over the horizon. "Remember how the rainy season was our favorite time of year?"

"Before the red phase? I remember," James sighed. "But, even then, Livermore was so hot. Not like San Francisco. The climate was so different, with hot dry long summers. Endless summers."

"All those months that'd go by without a drop of rain, the hills turning brown. And wildfires. And then came October and the rainy season when temperatures were nearly perfect and the sun was hidden behind the clouds for days at a time."

James, eyes glued to the road, nodded. "I remember."

"And the children in the neighborhood waited for the wet weather and, when it came, they played for hours on end, frolicking in the mist. In a matter of days, the brown hills came to life again. Green and bright as Ireland. Wild orange poppies. Yellow fields. Purple lavender. All those heavenly scents just everywhere."

She paused again, realizing that Silas had never known those days of rain and he never would. Charlotte, she thought, would likely never even see a natural body of fresh water.

James pushed on toward the FEMA tent the Red Cross volunteer had told them about. Lexie's sister had advised them many times to go and register their names in the FEMA database in the event of a national emergency. That would allow her to know the family's whereabouts and provide whatever assistance she could to them. FEMA had computers that were still operational—with electricity from generators—so they could provide medical help, food, and water.

From what James and Lexie knew, it was the only government agency still functioning. Their new location at the Lawrence Livermore National Laboratory, run by volunteers, offered hope that the family could get into an underground bunker that retained many modern conveniences. Some folks had said that the labs had built bomb-proof bunkers into the mountains, where a group of people could live for years in the event of a nuclear crisis. Although never confirmed, it was a warming thought, a shred of hope. If the facilities could survive a nuclear holocaust, they could surely survive a year or two in a waterless world! And to James and his family, a year or two seemed like an eternity.

The heat in the SUV was nearly intolerable and James, for a split second, considered the air conditioning, but knew it would be wasteful. The red sun was vicious that day and his eyes burned from having to drive without sunglasses. Thankfully they were heading east and not west.

Their dehydration was evident as their throats burned, their mouths were dry, their heads ached, and their lips were chapped like leather. Beyond the dehydration, the chronically chapped lips were the biggest burden as they often cracked and bled in a painful manner. Not to mention their skin, which was dry as a catcher's mitt. It wasn't as if you could just pop down to the nearest Walgreens to get a bottle of lotion.

As they exited Vasco Road, they found themselves only a mile or two from the labs and the FEMA tent. James was certain he would find some sort of help and resources for his family. The idea of a safe place to live, protected from the bandits roaming the countryside, would be a dream come true.

In the distance, he spotted the white tops of the FEMA tents. "There it is!" It was a good sign. Or was it? The closer they came, the more disturbing the scene grew. Masses of people had converged on the area. Like an outdoor rock concert, a crowd of thousands swarmed the grounds.

Shit! Has this all been a pipedream? Just a fantasy? I know one thing, James thought, *I'd be crazy to put the safety of my family in the hands of that mob!*

He would be crazy, too, if he hadn't realized the place was overrun with people just as desperate as they—or more so.

As they made the final turn off the highway, they saw large groups of people lying in the dirt.

"What's going on?" Lexie asked. "What are they doing? It's 130 degrees outside. Why are they lying in the dirt?"

"Oh, my God, Mom," Silas called. "They're dead!"

"What?"

"They're dead, Mom. They're not moving!"

No sooner had Silas made the observation than the stench of death entered the SUV through the vents. Immediately they all cupped their hands over their noses.

Beyond the dead, thousands of people swarming the main tent waved their hands, pushing and shoving in a vain attempt to claim what few emergency supplies remained.

"He's right," James said, shaking his head as the car snaked its way toward the tent.

"Oh, my God. Silas, don't watch!" Lexie pulled Charlotte closer to her and looked out across a field where hundreds, maybe thousands, of dead bodies lay baking, decaying beneath the sun. "Put your head down!"

"Everybody roll up the windows!"

James looked from side to side at women with dead babies in their arms, men with hands still clutching empty jugs, children nestled up to their deceased parents. It was a scene from the pages of Dante.

"I can't believe it. I've never seen anything like it...never even imagined anything..."

"I think I'm going to be sick," Lexie groaned.

"Here." James fished a handkerchief out of his pants pocket and handed it to her. "Breathe through this."

"Let's get out of here!" Silas cried, his head buried against his knees. "The smell is awful. Come on, Dad, let's go back. Hurry!"

It was a hellish sight and yet another testament to how far society had crumbled. It was no longer man helping man...it was every man, woman, and child for themselves. The days of generosity, helping others....hell, even the Golden Rule were long gone. James pondered just how fast all of this happened. It felt like only yesterday he was sitting in his office, watching the Browns' game, or having a picnic in the park with Lexie. It was almost inconceivable how quickly society had fallen into the clutches of evil.

"Silas, just don't look, baby," Lexie said through the handkerchief. "Just close your eyes." Silas didn't argue, and he didn't look. But James did, and so did Lexie. The closer they got to the tent, the less promising things appeared. Only a few FEMA volunteers toiled away at crowd control.

The tent was being run by only a handful of diehard volunteers. It was anyone's guess what had happened to the remainder of the FEMA team, but James assumed that many had died, some had deserted, and some simply went home to their family. Regardless, the few volunteers that remained were trying without success to maintain control of the situation.

The crowd began to descend on the medical tent where patients were being treated by two volunteer physicians. They were much more interested in food and water than they were Band-Aid®, gauze, and iodine. The doctors continued to treat the many patients in the tent despite the pandemonium that was only a few steps away. For the most part, they were treating dehydration, heat stroke, severe sun burns, and flesh wounds. They only had a very limited supply of IVs and it was wearing thin. In an hour, there would be nothing left to treat the sick and injured.

As James and Lexie watched the chaos from the SUV, the little order that was still intact in the tent was quickly disintegrating. Several large trailers full of food and water were directly behind the tents. The

23

volunteers would pull out the boxes, open them, and hand out bottled water and MREs to the distressed citizens who were pushed aside and asked to move on. The desperate people would begin to argue with the volunteers, begging them for more and pleading their case as to why they needed additional rations. Women begged on behalf of their children, fathers for their kids, kids for their dying parents, or the elderly simply seeking help.

Like a mosh pit at a heavy metal concert, the crowd continued to push forward until the people in the front were nearly on top of the volunteers. As a result of the moving crowd and the pushing, people began to topple over in droves. Once they had fallen, their fate was sealed as the uncaring crowd trampled over them, precipitating their ultimate demise. The horde continued to push forward, more and more people were falling, and now the volunteers were also being pushed and pulled in all directions. The tables fell over, the boxes of supplies spilled, and the gas generators were knocked over.

Before long, the crowd had overtaken the volunteers and were now serving themselves by taking as many boxes as they could carry directly out of the semi-trucks. People would grab several boxes and begin to run away from the crowd and would then be purposely tripped or tackled by those who were toward the back. On dropping the boxes, they would be picked up by another person or family who would begin running off in another direction. Sometimes they would make it and other times the cycle would repeat itself as they were knocked down by someone taking the provisions.

It was hard for James to watch, but he could clearly observe the tent beginning to rock, ultimately falling down and draping itself over the top of several hundred people. Those that were trapped under the heavy white canvas were then trampled over as the horde of people began moving forward toward the trailers.

Seeing the uncontrolled mob, those in the medical tent abandoned their patients and made a quick exit toward their waiting FEMA trucks and cars. Leaving everything behind, the vehicles sped away down the street, leaving the complete and utter chaos behind. It was an all-out evacuation for all of the volunteers that were still standing.

The scene at the former tent was something that James and Lexie could not believe. As large masses of people entered the trailers from all sides to get the boxes, the trailers began to sway due to the weight. It looked as though they would tip over and fall at any moment. Many people were sensing the danger of the mob and were now running in the opposite direction. Those still near the front were in an all-out brawl and war for the remaining supplies. Boxes were being torn open as people grabbed at them from all sides, spilling the contents onto the ground.

24

Fights were breaking out throughout the entire area and more people were now falling than standing upright.

"My God, what are we going to do?"

James shrugged as several men and women in white lab coats hopped into official FEMA vehicles and sped off, tires spinning, gravel spitting up like buckshot in their wake.

"We're sure as hell not getting out of the car, I'll tell you that!"

Unable to bear the noise without knowing what was happening, Silas peeked up over the front seat and flinched at the chaos engulfing them.

"Can we go? Please, Dad, let's get outta here before something happens to us!"

We're not going to get any help here. "Don't worry, we're getting out of here, son."

Lexie grabbed his arm. "But my sister! Karen—she won't know where we are, how to find us, how to help us, if we leave without registering!" Panic quivered in her throat.

"Registering? With whom? Them?" He motioned to the crowd, people crawling over the top of the trailers and rocking them in a desperate effort to overturn them, so they could more easily rifle their contents.

"Please, Dad! Before they come after us! We've gotta go now."

James looked over at Lexie, saw the fear in her eyes, and patted her on the thigh. "We'll be okay. We'll find another way to get word to your sister."

She hesitated, looked down at Charlotte, and nodded, holding back the tears of frustration that had been welling up for hours, days, and years.

"All right," she sighed finally. "Let's go."

James and Lexie knew no help was going to come from FEMA and, when guns shots began to fill the area, followed by screams, they turned the car around and headed back in the direction from which they came. The pandemonium and bedlam had forced people to run onto the road, making it difficult for James to navigate the SUV. There were walls of people blocking the way as they scattered about the area. James was aware that, if he hesitated, his family's safety could be compromised, so he knew he had to simply press forward and hope people cleared the way. If he were to stop, the SUV would be overrun with people and they would likely be casualties of the mob themselves.

Silas was in the back seat, eyes as wide as saucers, and was beginning to weep in fear. James was sure his window of opportunity to escape safely was now or never. He pressed down on the horn and held it as the SUV moved forward at a leisurely fifteen miles per hour. People were veering out of the way at the very last moment and James was doing his very best not to strike any pedestrians. Rocks and debris were being thrown at the SUV and James was quickly losing control. He grabbed the hand gun, rolled down the window, and fired off shots in the air. People screamed and darted out of his path. In front of him, James could now see a clear path ahead and he floored the gas pedal, thrusting them forward as their heads were pushed against the headrests from the force.

Now safely on the road, with the intense scene behind them, the family breathed a sigh of relief. Silas momentarily calmed down as James sped down the road back toward the highway.

"James, should we drive to the other side of the labs to see if there's any type of safe haven or bunker? Remember what Karen said?" Lexie asked.

"It's not safe, Lex. The crowd'll no doubt make their way through the entire complex if they haven't already. The whole area's a death trap."

"But, Dad, what if there really is an underground bunker? What if it's our only chance?" Silas asked.

James thought for a moment, briefly considered the idea, before saying, "It's not safe. Even if there is a bunker, there are thousands of people trying to get there. I'm certain the doors have long since been closed and sealed if it exists. Those places aren't made for normal people like us. If the bunker was truly there, then government officials and diplomats would have already been placed inside and there would be no way in." Lexie and Silas knew he was right and their hopes of a safe haven were now just dreams. With their heads down and hope shattered, they continued forward and back toward the freeway.

Years ago, James had read a book about America in a post-nuclear war society. In it, nothing remained but death, destruction, crime, and anarchy. He remembered thinking the book was entertaining but completely unrealistic. In his mind, regardless of the crisis, man would never sink to those levels. Eventually, life would return to normal. Now, after witnessing the horrifying scene, he again questioned all that he believed. Man was ruthless...a bloodthirsty killer that would stop at nothing on a quest for individual survival. The evil people were the ones prospering. The world which he once loved was nothing more than a black abyss of crime, evil, and debauchery. A tear ran down his face as he realized he would be forced to be a part of that black abyss for the sake of the safety of his beloved family.

As daylight slipped into night, James drove along in silence. Lexie had given Charlotte her evening feeding, and Silas and he had swallowed something that resembled spaghetti. As the others nodded off, James let his mind wander. He'd always believed in having a backup plan for every conceivable occasion—sometimes several of them. But the events of the day had placed him in a situation he had not been in for a very long time. He had no plan, no ideas, no strategy to save his family. Where would they go? What would they do? How would they survive with only their car, several boxes of food, and six gallons of drinking water? How far could they travel on that?

But to what end would he travel in that abyss? How far would he go to survive? Would he riot? Would he steal? Threaten someone's life, perhaps even at gunpoint? To just what end would a person go to ensure his family's survival? To what end would he?

How about to the ultimate end? He thought as he steered the vehicle deeper into the night. *How about murder?*

Chapter 5

James and Lexie had met in Cleveland, in the suburb of Lorain on the shores of Lake Erie. They had grown up there and were one of few couples who met in high school, dated exclusively, and married. They were each other's first and only love.

As their high school's most visible couple, they were soul mates. They attended Ohio State together and, much to their parents' dismay, spent nearly every night together for the next four years. Lexie majored in business administration, while James pursued a degree in computer science. After graduation, Lexie was offered a position in Chicago with a large Fortune 500 firm, so the two moved to the Windy City. Before long, James, too, found a job. Only months later, they announced their wedding plans to friends and family.

But Chicago was not destined to be their Happily Ever After. With each new promotion, Lexie was forced to relocate, and James along with her. From Chicago, they moved to Atlanta, Pittsburgh, and then finally Livermore. Wherever they hung their hats, James always found a good job—computer science professionals were in high demand.

The focus on Lexie's career finally shifted when they relocated to the San Francisco Bay Area and the epicenter of the computer science and Internet start-up industry. While Lexie was doing well, James hit the jackpot with a high-profile social media company. As his income skyrocketed, the couple decided it was time to start a family. Once Lexie was pregnant, she put her career on hold for the benefit of the baby. She had every intention of returning to work when the child was older—if necessary. But she was more than happy to be a stay-at-home mom. That was just about the time that major changes in the sun and the atmosphere had begun to unfold, changes that would alter their lives forever.

Despite the problems on Earth, Silas had brought a joy to their lives that they could never have imagined. Even as the sun transformed the Earth's surface into a blistering inferno, they made every effort to give their son a normal childhood.

As he grew, Silas expressed curiosity in almost everything. When he started school, his teachers were impressed. But, while he thrived academically, he struggled socially. He had a difficult time making friends and socialized only with girls. James and Lexie could never put their finger on it, but they always felt Silas was just different from other boys his age. He didn't excel at sports and didn't even care to play them.

His biggest fear was gym class and he would always make up any excuse to try and get a free pass for the day. His only extracurricular interests were in drama and dance. His teachers told his parents that their son was remarkably talented and that he had a special gift—Silas, they said, never seemed happier than when he was on stage performing with other kids his age.

And then they said something that disturbed them—he showed frequent signs of depression. James and Lexie thought that was due to the classroom bullies who had targeted him from his elementary days on. James had to intervene with school officials several times. But all that ended when food supplies and water had become so scarce that businesses shut down, followed soon after by schools and nearly everything else. Although Silas missed his drama classes, he seemed happier at home with his parents.

And Brownie.

And then, one day, Silas came up to his parents in tears. He had something important to tell them, but he didn't know how. Both Lexie and James knew what was coming, but it was still a shock when they heard the words. Their son was gay. As they listened, it became evident that unburdening himself was like having a stone lifted from his chest.

Afterward, as his parents contemplated his coming out, Lexie seemed confused.

"How can a twelve-year-old boy who knows so little about sex possibly know he's gay?"

James shrugged. "I don't know. Something inside him, I guess."

"I mean, he's never had a relationship with another boy." She paused. "At least, I'm pretty sure he hasn't. He's only twelve, for heaven's sake. How could he?"

"Yeah, I don't think he has either."

"Could he be wrong? Maybe he's just confused, just…just going through a phase. You know how tough it is for a boy his age. And with everything that's happening around us…"

James shook his head. "I'm not so sure. When you think back—his childhood, growing up, his problems at school—it kinda makes sense. He's different from most boys his age."

"More sensitive than most, that's for sure. Still, I don't know how he can be so certain."

"How can a straight child be so sure of his sexual identity? It's something that's just ingrained within each of us, I suppose."

"How old were you when you first started being attracted to girls?"

"Me?" He paused. "I don't know. Three. Four maybe."

"That young?"

He shrugged. "I just found everything about them exciting."

30

"Well, that's one thing that hasn't changed!"

He chuckled. "I was a little horn dog, that's for sure."

"Was?"

James laughed. "Some things never change."

"So you think our son really is…" She stared at him, searching for the word.

"Gay," James said. "Homosexual. It's just a word. You can say it."

"I know. I just…"

"Whatever he is, he's still our son. And we still love him."

She grabbed his hand and squeezed.

It was tough for Lexie to realize that Silas would likely never have the opportunity to fall in love or have a life partner as he grew older because of the state of the environment around them. She didn't have a problem with the thought of her son loving another man. She worried about him. She worried about diseases. She worried about how others would treat him. She wondered if he would be bullied or abused.

And then it struck her. But if he's never had a chance to act on his feelings, he's never really even tried anything! He can't possibly be sure.

After all, there wasn't a person on Earth who could say he never had an impure thought. Never lusted after someone or something in his heart. That made her feel better.

James, on the other hand, had a completely different view. He loved his son, even if he still had difficulty picturing him in a physical relationship with another man. He took some amount of solace in the fact that the boy would most likely never have that opportunity—would never date, explore his sexuality, or fall in love. Never experience the heartbreak of losing a lover. And Silas would never succumb to the rash of pornography that once thrived on the Internet. He was still James's little boy, pure of heart and mind. And that would never change.

Back on the road, and with absolutely no plan in mind but dwindling hopes, James merged east on the highway, while trying to create any possible strategy that made sense. The further he drove toward the east and the less populated valley, the fewer the obstacles there were in the road. Once he was over the Altamont Pass, he was cruising at 60 miles per hour and felt safe doing so. As always, it was a stifling hot day and he could see the waves of heat coming off the asphalt. Beads of sweat dripped down from his head and onto the steering wheel.

There is no plan! He realized, panicking. *And no plan means no hope!*

He fought off the urge to despair—no need to frighten the rest of the family. Merging east onto the highway, he goaded his brain into action. There had to be some way, there had to be somewhere to go to find water.

He looked in the rear-view mirror at Silas, staring out at the passing landscape.

"Where are we going?" Lexie asked.

"I don't know, baby. I'm thinking…" He turned to his wife and nodded toward the bundle in her arms. "She all right?"

Lexie looked down. "She's just fine. What a little trooper. Must be because she comes from good stock."

James smiled.

And then he stopped smiling, his mind whirring.

Good stock. Yeah, that's it. That's the answer.

Quickly calculating the amount of fuel they had onboard, the gas mileage they were getting, and the distance they would need to travel, he felt his heart begin to pound.

"Good stock, that's it!"

"That's what?" Lexie asked.

"We'll head for home. I think we can just make it."

"What are you talking about—home?"

"Lake Erie. If we can somehow make it home to Lorain, we'll find water. I know we will!"

"But Lake Erie's drying up, too. Remember the last newscasts we saw? How the water was receding from the shoreline?"

"Yeah, but it can't all be dried up. And even if there's no water left in Lorain, we can head farther north to the new shoreline. And all the water we need."

James knew the plan was far from perfect. It meant traversing thousands of miles of dried-up barren desert filled with outlaws and ringed with danger. It meant embarking on the most challenging venture of their lives. He also knew they would need to find some additional gasoline at some point.

"How long will it take? We've only got a few days' supply of fresh water. We have plenty of food, but not much else."

"Well, we'll just have to find water along the way. Somewhere."

Silas looked puzzled. "You mean drive all the way to Ohio? In this heat? When we don't even know what's there? We could die, Dad! This is ridic!"

James knew there was some truth to that, but he could think of no other plan. Lake Erie was their best hope.

"Nobody's going to die. I have it all figured out."

He peered into the mirror as Silas dropped his head, his shoulders hunched forward, a single tear creasing one cheek. James shifted his attention back to the road.

"Let's think about this for a minute," Lexie said. "We could head north toward Calistoga and see if the geothermal waters are still there. If not, we could drive down the coast and try to find a desalinization plant that's still working. We could stop at every store along the way and see if anything's left behind. We have options, James. We really do."

James hesitated only a second. "But, since all the aquifers are dry, don't you think the geothermal waters will be dry, too? And while I love the idea of the coastal drive, there's no electricity, remember? So how could any desalinization plants still be running? Matter of fact, most of them are underwater now. The idea of checking all the stores is smart, but I'm betting everyone and his brother has already ravaged everything worth taking." He checked the rear-view mirror again. Silas was wiping his eyes on his shirt sleeve. "No, I think the best thing to do," he added, looking back out over the road, "is to keep on driving."

"Well, when you put it that way, I guess that does make the most sense. I suppose heading east is the best hope we have right now."

"Hey," Silas said, his voice turning from soft to excited. "We'll get to see Grandma. And Poppy and Grammy!"

For Lexie, it was a bittersweet thought. It had been over a year since she'd heard from her parents. With no way to communicate, she had no idea if they were even alive. Silas had only seen his Grammy and Poppy a few times in his life, although he once Skyped with them weekly. Despite their geographical barriers, Silas felt close to them. In fact, Poppy was the first person he told about being gay. His trust and love for the man ran so deep that he never for a moment thought he would make a big deal of it. When the time came and Poppy finally appeared on the computer screen, Silas broke down and cried. Eventually his Grandpa did the work for him. He gave Silas a big smile.

"Look, boy, if you're trying to tell me you're gay, I already know."

Silas stopped sniffling. "You know?" He ran the statement through his memory banks and came up empty. "How?"

"Doesn't matter, son. I don't think any differently of you. I love you just the same. Grammy, too."

Lexie wondered what fate had befallen her family. James already knew what had happened to his mother. She had fallen ill with congestive heart failure and was placed in a hospice and, with the collapse of the healthcare system, he presumed she was dead, although he had yet to share that thought with Silas. James's father had passed a decade before.

The family drove on, approaching Stockton. Lexie turned to her husband.

"Remember, we have to check out the stores. Better get off here."

"I told you—" he said.

"I know, I know. But we can't take any chances. We just might get lucky. Besides, it will give you a break from driving."

Exiting the highway, James pulled into a large shopping plaza. Abandoned cars that were completely covered in dust peppered the lot of the once upscale grocery store that now stood windowless and looted. Large piles of sand drifts coated the buckling black asphalt. Like an old Western movie, the occasional tumbleweed whirled past them. James had no intention of leaving his family alone.

"Okay. Everybody come with me," he said.

As they all emerged, Silas looked toward the store. "It's toast."

"Toast or not, let's go."

Slowly, they entered the store. Both James and Silas had their guns drawn. Brownie charged ahead as if scouting the building for them. As they moved past the entranceway and around the piles of shattered glass, James whispered, "This is a lost cause." He looked around. "There's nothing here but empty shelves." And he was right. With the exception of some cell phones, cleaning products, and frozen foods that had probably been rotting for over a year, nothing of use was left.

"It stinks, Dad," Silas scowled.

"Yeah," James sighed. "Let's get back to the car."

After pulling back out onto the main road, they traveled a few miles farther, finally pulling off into the parking lot of another grocery store that appeared very similar to the first. This one had been looted much more heavily. Aside from rotting food, not a single item remained in the store. The place was in such shambles it looked as if a tornado had passed through.

"Jeez, this is a complete waste," Silas groaned. "Let's go."

"Let's check the back room first," Lexie said, leading the way through the double-door entranceway.

Inside, the shelves were bare, with the exception of discarded cardboard and broken wooden pallets everywhere the eye could see. Just as they were about to give up hope, Silas spotted what appeared to be an unopened box teetering on the edge of a shelf. He went to investigate and tried to lift it off.

"Man, this is heavy!"

"Here, let me help," James said. Together they got the dusty box down to the ground and quickly ripped it open. Inside was an unopened case of bottled store-brand clam juice.

"Yuck!" Silas said as he pushed the box aside. "It's no wonder people left it."

Lexie glared at him. "It's not yuck, son; it's liquid! And with liquid comes water. It may not taste like Coke, but it'll sure help. Anything liquid will help right now. It's a blessing."

"Well, you can have it all for yourself!"

They exited the store and stepped back onto the asphalt parking lot. It was so hot that their shoes began to stick to the ground. With nothing else left to take, they used their hands to wipe the dust and peered through the windows of the abandoned cars.

"Maybe we'll find...something of value."

And, Lexie thought, *maybe not*. She was right. They made their way back to the SUV and hopped in. Charlotte was fussing and it soon turned into a tantrum. Silas covered his ears with his hands. "Please, shut her up, will you, Mom? Do something. Give her a bottle!"

Lexie grabbed one of the cans of formula and prepared a four-ounce mix, adding a box of juice to the powder. As soon as the bottle touched the baby's lips, she grew quiet.

Lexie could never forget the scorching summer afternoon when she first suspected she might be pregnant. She had missed her period and she woke up with morning nausea for weeks. Without any contraceptives, she and James had been very careful; they didn't want to bring a child into their fading world.

Lexie had made her way to a retail store that still had some inventory and found a pregnancy test. At home, she sat by herself in the upstairs bathroom, sobbing as she saw the "+" on the stick. James kept knocking on the door, asking if she was all right; if there was anything he could do for her.

What's the matter with me? How could I bring an innocent baby into this dark hot lawless world for a few minutes of pleasure? What's going to happen to him? For a split second, she felt her conservative values fly out the window as she contemplated ways to end her pregnancy. Coat hanger? Some morning after pills? Whatever, she just couldn't think about delivering another child. Not now. Who would do it? James? Silas? Without any hospitals or doctors around anymore, she'd be completely on her own. And the child, doomed to death. Doomed to a life of misery. Doomed to a life that would never know true happiness.

When she finally found the courage to emerge, she told James the news.

"What?" His eyebrows arched nearly to his hairline. "A what?"

She nodded.

"Are you sure?"

She nodded again and, as he saw the pain in her face, he took her into his arms.

"We just can't have another child now," she said, tears bursting from her eyes. "I'm going to have an abortion."

"You're going to do no such thing! It's our baby! Yours and mine. Why would you ever say something so ridiculous?"

"What can this world possibly offer a baby? Searing heat? Crime? A constant struggle for food and water? What kind of life will he have? We don't even know if we'll be alive tomorrow, let alone twenty years from now! I'll be damned if I'm going to bring a child into a world that's getting more disgusting by the hour!" Then, softening her tone, she added, "Even if the baby survives the birth, what will happen in a few years? All of the things a baby needs—we can't provide any of them."

"We'll make do with what we have. We always have. We'll provide love and nurturing for our baby. We'll find a way to make it work. It isn't our choice as to whether or not our children live or die!"

"How can you possibly say that? Nurturing? With what? What's more evil—bringing a baby into a world where there is no good, or sparing him from ever having to experience it? Think damn hard and I think you'll come up with the right answer. The answer is pretty goddamn clear, James."

"We'll give the baby whatever happiness we can provide in the time we have with it. It isn't our choice, Lex." He looked into her eyes, she into his. He wasn't sure what to say, how to convince her. And then the words fell from his lips. "Please, think about what you're contemplating. This is a human life we're talking about here. A precious human life! We'll get through this, no matter how bleak you may think things look. We will. I promise you. I'll protect you and our children."

Lexie knew deep inside that she could never take the life of their unborn child, regardless of her feelings or the conditions of life on Earth. Still, she couldn't escape a deep sense of sadness inside her. Her child would never know any of the beauty that the world once offered. All the wonderful joys that she remembered from her childhood would never be for this baby. It was truly a depressing thought.

Chapter 6

On the road, James watched the brown ugly world go by. Nothing to look at but death, dust, and destruction. Past Sacramento and on toward Nevada. His mouth was dry and his body craved drink, but he knew they needed to ration all of their supplies. As the red sun loomed just above the mountains, he knew they needed a safe place to sleep.

But where?

Sleeping in the car would only be an invitation for roaming groups of bandits so, when he saw the Nevada exit sign for its desert capital of Carson City, he veered off onto the ramp.

"Are you looking for a place to spend the night?"

James glanced at Lexie. "It'll be dark soon."

Charlotte began to squirm as Lexie tried to coax her into taking her pacifier. "Good. I have to feed the baby, and my legs are so cramped."

Once a town of more than 50,000 people, Carson City had become a ghost town. James drove through the downtown area, careful to avoid the buckling pavement and potholes.

"This is like a time warp," he murmured. "Like someone beamed everybody up to the mother ship, leaving all their stuff behind."

"Maybe we can scavenge something of value."

They passed cars parked in the streets and shopping centers, a local theater with the show times still listed, several historic hotels and casinos with VACANCY signs out front.

They drove past the local Walmart and considered stopping to see if the looters had claimed all of the merchandise.

"Let's check it out tomorrow," James said. "We need to find a place to sleep."

They passed several hotels, nearly completely destroyed, before coming across an old Holiday Inn Express that looked to be in better shape than the others.

They pulled up to the front entrance as if they were checking in, grabbed as many of their belongings as they could, and walked through the front doors into the lobby.

"Should I ring for service?" Lexie asked as Brownie charged ahead, sniffing everything in her path.

This place looks like Bagdad after the Gulf war! James thought. He turned to Lexie. "Let's not leave anything in the car. There might be looters around."

Due to the broken glass, the hotel lobby was engulfed in dust and debris. Inside, it was extremely hot, stuffy, and smelled stale. There were several old newspapers lying on the ground along with scattered tourist pamphlets from years ago. Grabbing a luggage cart, he and Silas unloaded the car while Lexie tended to Charlotte. Once they'd loaded whatever they could carry, they pushed it past the front desk, down the hall, and past the abandoned pool, and finally to the second-to-last room on the right. James found the door ajar. He drew his revolver.

"Anyone here?" he called, pushing the door farther open with his foot. When he was satisfied it was safe, he motioned for his family to enter.

Silas stopped short, sniffing the air. "What's that nasty smell?"

James looked around and, peeking into the bathroom, saw the toilet bowl filled with feces.

"Never mind. We'll just keep this door closed and open the windows. It'll go away."

"We're on the first floor," Lexie said. "We can't open the windows."

"You want to look around for another room?"

"This is disgusting, Mom. We can't sleep here!"

She shook her head. "They're probably all the same. We'll just have to make the best of it."

"Great," Silas said, fanning the air with his hand.

"Just pretend we're camping."

"If we were camping, we'd have tents, fresh air, sleeping bags, and s'mores. This isn't camping! We're trapped in a poop-smelling room that's 130 degrees."

The dark of night had taken over the city and the bright desert stars shone down so clearly that it felt as if they were inside the most stunning planetarium that ever existed. Lexie had already fed Charlotte who was asleep on the top of the couch in just her diaper. It was stiflingly hot and they had stripped down to the essentials of shorts-only for the men, and shorts and a T-shirt for Lexie. Brownie had already devoured his can of dog food while Silas was pulling out three MREs for their meal. He was clearly excited when he pulled out his favorite—spaghetti and meatballs. It wasn't much but, to Silas, it was heaven as he devoured the preservative-filled meal in seconds.

"This is so good! I could eat three more."

"Well, that's not going to happen," James said. "We need to ration."

"I know, Dad. I know," he said, rolling his eyes.

When all three were done eating, Silas sat patiently, waiting for Lexie and James to give him the cookie that came with the meals. With a smile, he held out his hand like a child asking for a lollipop. As all parents do, they both caved in and gave him the sweet treat.

With the door securely locked, James lay down by the window with his guns by his side. Lexie and Charlotte took one bed and Silas took one to himself. James passed the revolver to Silas who took it reluctantly with a roll of the eyes.

"You can never be too careful," James explained.

"This place is like a ghost town, Dad. The only thing here is ghosts," he sarcastically snickered.

"Ha-ha-ha," James said.

Lexie snored with Charlotte carefully by her side, Silas dreamed while talking in his sleep, Brownie lay with his eyes half open, and James dozed off next to the window. At some point in the middle of the night, James heard the voices of several men. He could not make out what they were saying, but they got progressively closer. The town was apparently not completely empty and they had unexpected guests. The voices got closer and closer until James could almost make out their words. He was getting nervous and did not want his family to become sitting ducks inside the hotel room.

He sat silently and waited with his gun locked and loaded. Just when he thought the men were nearly right outside his window, he heard a car pull up. The sound of the car stopping, the doors being opened and then slammed shut, was music to his ears. He then heard the most delightful sound ever—the screeching tires of the sedan as it pulled away with the men in it. Whatever they were doing, whatever they were looking for...it did not matter now. They were gone and, for now, the family was safe. James was not able to fall back asleep, but daydreamed of better times. Water, Lake Erie, turquoise pools, waterfalls, and ice cold beer filled his head.

As the sun slowly rose, the temperature of the hotel room began to climb and, listlessly, the entire family rose from their sleep. Brownie was up and about, sniffing around and looking for a way out of the room to relieve himself. James got up, slowly unlatched the door, peered around the hallway, and let Brownie out to do his business. Charlotte was awakened by the stirring and began to cry for her morning bottle as Lexie rubbed her back. Silas, in no mood to wake, opened his eyes, observed the situation, and then tried to go back to sleep. The heat had caused him to sweat through the dirty sheets and had him lying in a pool of moisture. His mouth was as dry as the sand outside the room, and he had a thirst like a marathon runner crossing the finish line. Reluctantly he forced himself out of bed.

"Oh, God," Lexie said. "I feel as if I just got to sleep."

"Come on, everyone, up and at 'em. We need to hit the road. Time's a-wasting."

Silas let out a groan.

"We've got to check out that Walmart today. Charlotte's running low on diapers."

"We'll find some, don't worry. Either diapers or some towels or something we can use in their place."

"Don't count on it, Dad. This place is nothing but dust."

After a quick breakfast of crackers, peanut butter, and water, James and Silas packed up their things and rolled the cart out to the car. While it tasted great, Silas hated eating the peanut butter because all it did was intensify his already pronounced thirst. The wind was already blowing up, the dry parched air carrying sand and grit along with it, the heat, stinging like a jolt from a blast furnace. As they finished loading up, James got behind the wheel and slipped the key into the ignition.

"Everyone here? Silas? Brownie? All set?"

"Let's hit it, Dad!"

James pulled out of the hotel and onto the main road and, before long, they came to a strip mall, where they thought they might find some diapers. Ten minutes later, James and Silas returned empty-handed.

"Nothing?" Lexie asked.

"There's plenty of broken furniture and glass," Silas shrugged. "Not much of anything else."

After continuing down the street, they spied the Walmart they'd seen the day before, but it, too, proved to be a disappointment. The shelves were empty, the place was ransacked, and the back room was bare.

"This is pointless," Silas sighed. "All the stores have been picked dry."

"Well, son, if Mohammed won't come to the mountains, the mountains will just have to come to Mohammed."

"Huh?"

James veered off onto a side street, heading for the residential part of town. Before long, they found themselves in an upper-scale section of town with newer homes, evaporated swimming pools, and three-car garages—all abandoned and decaying. Drifts of sand replaced what had formerly been green lawns. Children's playsets sat abandoned in the yards. Cars covered in dust and debris sat idle on the cracking driveways. Regardless of their former color, all of the homes were brown from dust, with windows too dirty to see through.

"There's one over there," Lexie said, pointing. "That big one behind that gate. Looks perfect."

As he pulled in, he saw a sign that read THIS HOME IS PROTECTED BY AHS. The sign, faded and cracked, stood in a pile of sand outside the front door.

Pulling to a stop, he turned to Silas. "Okay, let's be quick about this. In and out! Understand?"

"I'm coming, too," Lexie said as she picked up Charlotte.

James motioned them forward but, when they reached the door, he found it locked. He pounded a few times on the door to see if anyone was living there.

"No one's home, Dad."

"Maybe there's a back door that's open," Lexie suggested.

"Maybe," James said and, with one sudden karate kick, he popped the door free. "Oops. Seems like this one's open after all."

Brownie ran in, sniffing around and running from one room to the next.

"Hello!" James called. "Is anyone home?" He received nothing in return. "Okay, come on in. It's safe. Let's see what we can find."

They rummaged around the house, where Lexie found several pillowcases and some towels to use as diapers. The remainder of the home had been stripped bare, so they moved on to the next house. It was a massive two-story stucco home that looked as if it was once quite luxurious. Like all the homes, it was in shambles and two dust-covered cars sat in the driveway. Finding the door unlocked, they followed Brownie in and stopped short in the foyer.

"What is it?" Lexie asked. Brownie had stumbled on a dark mass in the middle of the floor and was busy checking it out.

"Holy shit," James exclaimed.

"What?"

"What is it?" Silas said, going up to it.

"It's a dog," James said. "It's mummified."

"Oh, gross!"

"It's still got a collar on." He stooped down for a closer look. "Buddy. Please Call (775) 555-5555."

"Don't touch it, Silas."

He looked up. "Are you kidding?"

"Must have been here for years. Poor little fella. The family probably abandoned him when they left."

"It's gross," Lexie wrinkled her nose. "Let's check this place out and get out of here. It gives me the creeps."

James pointed down a hallway. "That looks like the kitchen down there. Why don't you take a look around, and I'll go upstairs—"

Before he could finish, Silas let out a horrifying, high-pitched scream.

"Oh, God. Mom. Dad. Come here. Quick!"

"What?"

"What is it, son?"

They followed the sound of his voice into a family room adjacent to the kitchen—complete with family.

"Oh, my goodness," Lexie cried.

"Wow. Look at them."

"They're all just like the dog!" Silas said, stunned. There, on a leather sofa facing a large-screen television set, sat the mummified remains of a man slumped forward, his teeth standing in marked contrast to the chocolate brown of his leathered skin. A woman, her long dark hair still in place, lay curled up on the opposite end of the sofa. Two smaller children were sprawled out on the floor, one in a fetal position and the other with one hand stretching toward the sofa. A small bassinet sat adjacent to the couch. Even from afar, Lexie could see the shriveled body of what had been their new baby lying in the bed.

"Oh, dear Lord, why?" she said softly.

Silas, near tears, looked up. "Let's get outta here. This is just too gross! I'm scared."

For a moment, Lexie and James stared at the corpses, driving home the reality of what life had become. Life for others—and very possibly life for themselves.

"How could this've happened? Why'd they all die together?" Silas asked.

"They probably ran out of food or water and just couldn't fight anymore," Lexie told him.

"Maybe," James said, scowling, "they just gave up on this evil world."

"James! Don't say those things. You know better than that. Times are bad, yes. But you can't just give up. It doesn't work like that."

James cut her off with the throw of a hand and, as if on cue, they turned to leave. Before they departed, he quickly rifled through the kitchen cabinets. Nothing. The only thing that remained was an old glue mousetrap, complete with skeleton. They stepped outside and into the stifling heat. The hot winds whipped up, sending dust and debris flying. Nearly gale force.

"I can't see!" Lexie called.

"Hold your hands over your eyes. Here. Give me your arm, Silas!"

"I'm following Mom," the boy mumbled, his chin buried in his chest.

When they reached the SUV, they closed the doors and windows and sat for several seconds, absorbing the horror they'd just seen. James looked at Lexie, her face as white as the pillowcases in her arms.

"Where're we going now, Dad?" Silas asked, his voice cracking.

"Back to the ramp, son, and back on the Interstate."

Chapter 7

The winds howled like the souls of the dead as James edged the SUV north toward I-80 East. The temperatures had climbed to 127 degrees, and it wasn't even noon yet. Everyone was drenched in sweat, and their bodies were all craving water. The intensity of their thirst was almost too much to stand. No one spoke a word for the first hour of the drive. Finally, Lexie broke the ice.

"We're getting low on supplies. We're going to need some things before long."

"What things?" James asked.

She thought to herself. "Well, we only have one package of baby wipes, three diapers, plus the towels and pillow cases. I think we still have four cans of powdered formula, one box of premade, one case of juice boxes, one case of clam juice, one case of MREs, maybe ten cans of dog food, and one box of assorted canned foods."

"Well, we're not desperate yet. We'll need to cut back even more. Step up our rationing."

She turned toward the rear seat. "Silas, check out the water supply. How many gallon jugs are left?"

She watched as he reached over the back seat, moved some items around, and looked back at her. "Three."

She paused. "Three! Are you sure?"

He checked again. "Yep. That's it. Three."

She turned to James. "Did you hear that?"

He tried to look as though he'd known it all along. "Yeah, why?"

"Why?" she settled back into her seat, pulling Charlotte down into her lap. The baby was awake and chewing on a teething ring. "Three gallons won't hold us more than a couple of days! We've got to find some more."

"We'll...yeah, I know. We will. We'll find more soon. When we get to Salt Lake City. We'll find more water there."

"And what if we don't?"

"Yeah, Dad, what if we don't? We die of thirst."

"We need food, formula, dog food, and diapers, too," Lexie said.

"I know, I know. I know all about what we need. When we get to town, we'll keep searching until we find everything. These roads seem pretty safe. We should be in Salt Lake by nine tonight if we drive straight through."

"If you ask me, we're screwed," Silas said. "I'm going to take a nap."

"Thanks, son," James grimaced. "I needed that."

Silas shrugged and lay down, his head resting on a box to his left, and was dozing almost immediately.

The winds were gusting so forcefully that they were causing James to veer off the road and the drive was becoming tiring. He was exhausted from the night of no sleep so he and Lexie decided to switch to have her drive through to Salt Lake City. They pulled over, quickly switched sides, and she took over the controls of the SUV.

James immediately rested his head on the window, closed his eyes, and did his best to try and get some sleep. The hot air blowing through the vents and into his face felt like lying next to a heating vent in his old home in Lorain. It was making him nauseated, but the complete fatigue of his body quickly overtook him and he was fast asleep with his mouth open and snoring loudly within twenty minutes.

As she navigated the highway, Brownie asleep in the back and Charlotte beside Silas, Lexie couldn't turn off her brain. What if they didn't find what they needed in Salt Lake? What if they actually ran out of water? Would someone, years later, stumble across them in their SUV, shriveled up like the family they discovered in Carson City? Her hands still clutching the wheel? Brownie a mere solidified puddle in the back of the car?

What are you doing? Why are you doing this? Why are you letting all these thoughts get the better of you?

She even considered a subject that no one ever wanted to think of— what would happen when they were so low on supplies that they had to choose between themselves or Brownie? He was a member of the family and she knew that, but could she allow her children to suffer in order to save the dog? As sad as it was, she knew she would be forced to make a terrible but necessary decision. Silas would be devastated as Brownie was truly his best and only friend. She did not know if she could do that to him as he would never forgive her. The best case scenario would be that they found enough supplies in Salt Lake City to last them for quite some time.

As she drove along the barren roads, she daydreamed of food, water, shelter, safety, and hope that there was still some form of society remaining near Cleveland. Lexie continued the drive northwest through Nevada, dark reddish-brown clouds looming ahead.

Uh, oh. Trouble.

The winds began to pick up, forcing the car back and forth as she struggled to maintain control. Several small dust devils spun off over the desert, picking up dirt and debris, swirling around and getting larger and more intense, as were the dark clouds ahead.

She focused her eyes and realized they were driving into a massive dust storm. Suddenly, the car hit a bump in the road, jolting James awake.

"What is it? What happened? Trouble?"

She turned on the windshield wipers to cut through the dust. "Wind's picking up."

"Well, slow down. Slow way down."

Silas popped his head up.

"What's going on?"

"Hang tight, buddy," James said.

Through the dust and flying debris they could see the green road sign, LOVELOCK EXIT 1 MILE. It was no longer simply dust and tumbleweeds blowing, but now large chunks of debris, branches, and sticks were whirling around too.

"Let's get off at Lovelock and see if we can find some shelter until the storm blows over."

"The wind!"

"What are you doing?"

"I can't...the wind is so strong, it's hard to control."

"Just slow down!"

Suddenly, the SUV hit a large object in the road.

Thump!

"What the hell was that?" For a split second, Lexie's hands flew off the wheel as the vehicle veered over the shoulder into the desert.

"Look out!" Silas screamed.

"Hit the brakes!"

The car bucked forward, slowing nearly to a halt. James felt a rhythmic pounding coming from beneath and heard the unmistakable klunk-klunk-klunk of a blown tire. The SUV listed to the right and came to a grinding halt.

"Wow!" Lexie said, sweat pouring off her brow.

"Yeah, wow." James wiped his head. "Everybody okay?"

Silas let out a cough. "Yeah, except for all the dust in here."

James looked out. "Can't last long. Use your handkerchief."

"Look," Lexie said, pointing. "We're right at the exit! Let's just drive the rest of the way and find some shelter."

James shook his head. "Can't risk it. If we ruin the rim, we're screwed. We'll have no backup at all." He motioned to Silas. "Give me your shirt and any rags you can find in the back. I'm going to change the tire."

Silas removed his shirt and handed it to his father, passing along several dirty rags he found in the supply boxes. James wrapped them around his head so that only his eyes were exposed. He jumped out of the SUV and grabbed the lug wrench from the rear. The spare tire was secured on the back of the vehicle and James wasted no time undoing the lug nuts and removing it. He struggled as he was pelted with dirt, sticks, and flying debris while his eyes were watering and burning as if he had been splashed with a toxic acid. He fell to his knees, dropping the lug wrench which skipped off several feet in front of him. Seeing his father struggling helplessly, Silas ignored his fears, grabbed two of the newly-found pillowcases, wrapped them around his head, and began to exit the SUV.

"Silas Morgan Deforio, get back in here right now!" his mother yelled.

"Can't hear you!" he called, slamming the door. As he rounded the rear of the vehicle, he called out. "Dad. Dad!" He waved his hands in front of his face, unable to see even inches in front of himself.

"I'm right here," his father yelled. Silas followed his voice to the opposite side of the car, the dust thicker than dense San Francisco fog.

"The lug wrench," James said. "I can't find it. It's got to be right here. Somewhere. Search with your hands. It can't have gone far."

"This stings like fire!" the boy cried, coughing, gagging on the grit swirling around them.

"Feel around with your hands."

Silas lowered his head against his chest and closed his eyes as he groped around for the tool. "Got it, Dad!" he yelled.

"Good!" James called, grabbing the tool and heading for the wheel while Silas held onto his shirt tail.

In the SUV, Lexie covered her face with a rag and did her best to shield the baby, who was crying. "I know, honey. It won't be long. Daddy's going to fix everything soon, and we'll get out of this storm."

Outside, James tightened the last of the nuts and jacked the vehicle back down. He motioned for his son to grab the flat tire. "Put it in the back," he said. "And then get in the car."

Silas rolled the tire to the back and, as he struggled to lift it up, James threw the jack in and helped hoist the tire. Lexie slid over to the passenger side as James climbed into the driver's seat. "My God! You're both just covered with grit!" Instinctively reaching for a gallon jug, she poured a cup for each of them. "Are you okay?"

"Okay," James said, peeling the last layer of cloth from his face and grabbing the cup. She watched as he drained it, before starting the engine and putting the car in gear. "Let's get the hell out of here and find some shelter before this storm gets worse." He looked back. "You okay, Si?"

"Let's get the hell outta here," the boy replied.

James inched the car slowly back to the exit ramp and it hobbled into Lovelock, the storm all but preventing them from seeing farther than a few feet. Lexie, coughing to clear her throat, was cradling Charlotte, who had stopped crying and was struggling to catch her breath.

Not good, James thought. *If we don't find some shelter soon...*

Just as he'd begun to give up hope, he spied what appeared to be a large public building. For a moment, he saw the outlines of concrete columns and steps. *Looks like the town hall—or maybe a courthouse!* He veered the vehicle in that direction and came to a stop at the front steps.

James grabbed Charlotte from Lexie and slipped the handgun beneath his belt. Silas, Brownie, and Lexie ran up the steps to the large wooden double doors. The wind, howling out of the west and whipping around in circles, nearly knocked Lexie off the stairs. James caught up to them, pushed the doors open, and took a quick peek around. He motioned for his family to follow.

The wind made it difficult to close the wooden doors, but James forcefully slammed them shut and the loud wind abruptly went silent. Their grim expressions evaporated once they were out of the elements and into the safety of what they now learned, thanks to a wall plaque, was the Pershing County Courthouse.

James, with his back against the doors, allowed his body to slowly drop until he was sitting on the tiled floor of the entryway, panting in exhaustion. Lexie observed her family whom she could now barely recognize. Silas, as skinny and lanky as he was, looked like a brown skeleton and was completely covered in sweat and dark brown dirt. Charlotte's once blond hair was caked with a thick brown film.

What worried her the most was James. He looked far too skinny. He, too, was covered in dirt and he was also making a loud wheezing sound as if he were having difficulty breathing. He began to cough violently and wheezed in between coughs in a lame attempt to collect air. Lexie rushed over to his side while Silas looked on in horror. She was rubbing on James's back as he hacked up load after load of dark brown mucus which he spat onto the floor.

"You need a drink of water. I'll get a jug from the car."

"No!" he called, wheezing while struggling to catch his breath. "No. No water. I'll be fine in a minute or two. We have to save the water."

"Don't argue," she said and, opening the doors, disappeared back out into the storm.

"Once she makes up her mind..." Silas said, shrugging.

"Your mother can be a stubborn woman." He bent down and set Charlotte on a small throw rug several feet from the door.

"I know," Silas said. "So can her husband!"

Leaving the peace and comfort of the courthouse lobby, Lexie stepped back out into the dust hurricane and made her way back to the SUV. She was trying to hold her breath, but had to take a gulp of air, which caused her to cough violently. Quickly, she sorted through the boxes and was able to grab one box of MREs and the box of clam juice. She awkwardly held the heavy boxes in her arms as she climbed the concrete steps and

47

made her way back inside. She slammed the door shut and placed the boxes on the ground. "Mission accomplished!"

She ripped open the corrugated cardboard and grabbed one bottle of clam juice which she opened and handed to James. He took it without hesitation and drank the entire bottle in a matter of seconds. To him, it was the most amazing thing he had ever tasted and it did not matter for a moment that he was drinking such an undesirable beverage. Petty things like taste, color, smell, and texture mattered not in a world where finding a drop of liquid was more important than nearly anything else.

"That's frickin' nasty!" said Silas, with a look of disgust on his face.

"You know what, son? It was the best thing I've ever had the pleasure of drinking," James said with a smile.

Lexie had found a janitor's supply closet and was thrilled to find a large industrial plastic jar of sanitizing wipes. While it was not perfect, it would be ideal to clean the layers of dirt and grime off their bodies. She proudly walked back to the lobby and showed the family her gift. Before the crisis, she practically had to force Silas into the shower or bath, but now he was lunging for the wipes to clean himself.

Having had almost no privacy for the past year, the family had no modesty as they stripped down nude to commence the makeshift bath. Silas was wiping himself head to toe as layer upon layer of dirt was removed by the cloth wipe. It felt incredible and, before long, his pale white skin had returned. His skin was still smooth and not hairy like his father which made cleaning himself much easier.

James was still struggling, so Lexie performed the bath for him as he held his arms in the air so she could reach all areas. Silas put his shorts back on and proceeded to lightly wipe off Brownie who was not appreciating the gesture and nipping at his hand. Trying to be mature and make himself useful, he then went over to his baby sister and began to clean her off as well. James and Lexie were pleased to see him do something selfless without having to be asked.

By the time they had gotten cleaned and situated their belongings, the sun had begun to lower in the sky. James decided to have a closer look around the building before darkness engulfed them.

"Wanna come, anybody?"

"Why don't you wait a couple minutes? I'm going to finish feeding the baby," Lexie said. "Then we'll break out some MREs."

James nodded and turned toward the back of the building, honeycombed with doors. *Where should we begin?* Spying an especially elaborate door, complete with antique leaded glass, he thought, *I wonder what's behind Door Number One...*

Chapter 8

Lexie had finished with the feeding, and the three of them had each eaten dinner. After putting Charlotte down for the night, James grabbed a flashlight and slowly pulled himself to his feet.

"Okay, time to check this place out."

"You want me to watch the baby?" Silas asked.

Lexie bent over the bundle swathed in old clothes and rags. Feeling Charlotte's head, she smiled. "She's asleep. She'll be okay."

As the family moved from the main courtroom to one auxiliary room after another, they passed beneath a wood carving that read BE JUST AND FEAR NOT.

"This was a beautiful courthouse at one time," Lexie said.

"Like the one in *To Kill a Mockingbird*," Silas exclaimed.

James pointed out the gold crown molding, a large painted mural, and the decorative rotunda dome designed to look like blue sky and clouds. A sign on one wall read AD 1920.

James motioned with his head. "Come on, gang. Let's check this one out."

As they entered a meeting room, Lexie opened the closet door and looked inside. "Nothing much of value here."

She was about to close the door when James stopped her.

"What?"

"What's that on the shelf up there? That bottle?"

He reached past her and grabbed it.

"What is it? Whiskey?"

James grinned. "Not just whiskey. It's Maker's Mark whiskey, one of the best."

"What do we want with whiskey?"

He flashed her a big toothy smile. "Guess."

She waved him off as he set the bottle in a large duffle bag he'd brought with them.

"That's the last thing we need, a family of drunks when we should be relying on our wits to see us through!"

"Shhh," he said.

"Don't you shoosh me. I think—"

"Quiet." He held up his fingers, straining to hear.

"What?"

"I thought I heard something."

Silas turned toward the door. "There. I heard it too. Some kind of rustling coming from the main courtroom."

Lexie's face turned white. "Charlotte!"

"Get that gun ready, son, and follow me."

As they reentered the courtroom, they heard the noise again, this time accompanied by some whispers. James motioned toward the judge's desk. "You stay back. I'm going to sneak around to the side."

Lexie peered in, saw the bundle at rest in the middle of the room, and let out a sigh. "Be careful," she whispered to Silas, who was holding the gun in trembling hands.

"Okay, who is it? Who's there?" James demanded. "Show yourself right now. I know there's someone back there!"

The rustling suddenly stopped, and James turned to Silas, motioning him down to the floor.

"What is it, James?" Lexie murmured.

"Stay back. Get back. Someone's in here!"

James leaned toward the desk, his gun locked and loaded. He heard movements and some whispering.

"Who is it?" Lexie asked.

"Okay, show yourself!" James yelled once more.

Suddenly, Brownie came bounding into the room, heading straight for the desk. "Brownie, get back here!"

The dog ran past him, barked twice, and sprang. Two young children let out a yell and leaped up.

Brownie was dancing around on his hind feet, licking at the children. The girl, whom James figured to be around six, let out a shriek. "Don't let him bite me. Don't let him…"

"He's okay," James said. "He won't bite."

Dressed in yellow and without shoes, the girl had a face caked with dirt and she clutched a pink teddy bear. The boy—James guessed he was her brother—stooped down to pet the dog. He looked to be nine or ten, extremely small and skinny, and had greasy shoulder-length hair. He wore shorts and no shirt and he, too, was covered in grime.

"Are you okay?"

The two stared back at him.

"Where are your parents?"

Silas pulled himself up to his feet, his eyes bulging. "Jeez, Dad, they're just a couple of kids."

The children stood silent, the boy smiling, the girl confused.

"I'm not going to hurt you. None of us will hurt you," James told them. The two looked from one to the other. "What are your names?"

At first, the boy hesitated. His lips quivered before beating out, "My name is Devin." He turned to the girl and nodded. "And this is my little sister, Ava."

"Are you alone? Where are your parents?" James asked again.

"They're in the back room, but they're sick. Real sick," Devin spilled out the words through downturned lips. Ava started to cry.

"Oh, honey," Lexie said, hurrying to comfort them. She took Ava in her arms as the girl rubbed at her eyes. "It's okay. Nobody's going to hurt you. We're here to help."

"Okay," James said, "show me where they are."

Devin took his sister's hand and led them through a door in the back of the courtroom. Silas stopped in the doorway of the judge's chambers as James wiggled past him. There he saw two adults lying on the floor, each clinging to the other.

"Are they...are they...?" James couldn't bring himself to say the word. He knelt beside them and tried to wake them. The father opened his eyes for only a second before clamping them closed again. James prodded him, and he let out a bone-chilling moan. He had a full scraggly beard and wild flying hair. Dressed only in boxer shorts, his stomach was concave and his ribs were clearly visible. His wife was in her bra and shorts. James shook her; she failed to stir. She was covered in dirt and had filthy blond hair as dry as straw. She was thin, and her eyes were rimmed with dark circles. There was one empty can of fruit cocktail on the floor.

Lexie had heard the commotion and looked in. "James," she said, rushing to his side. "What's happening here? They look as if they're dying."

"I'm afraid they are."

"Well, we have to do something!"

"Like what?"

"Give them some food, some water."

"Are you kidding? We don't have enough for ourselves."

"So what? We're just going to leave them here to die?"

He shrugged.

"What's come over you?"

"What's come over me? I'll tell you what. We have to survive, remember? Do you see what's going on right now? We're living from day to day. This is a dog-eat-dog world we're living in, for Christ's sake! Anything goes! And you want to give away the last of our food and water?"

Silas was on his knees talking to Devin and Ava. He had taken Ava's pink bear and was pretending it was talking to her. He picked her up and was holding her as he joked around with Devin. Neither child realized the seriousness of their parents' situation.

"Dad, there's no way you can just let them die. Mom, can't we get them some food and water so they don't die? We can't just leave them here."

"Are you two fucking serious? We have three goddamn gallons of water and a few days of food and you want to give it the hell away? What's wrong with you, anyway?"

"No, the question is, what's wrong with *you?* Have you lost your heart? Have you lost all sense of humanity?" Lexie turned to her son. "Silas, go get them something to eat and a carton of juice and bring it back. Quickly."

Silas ran through the courtroom and back to the lobby, where they had set their rations. He grabbed two bottles of clam juice, two boxes of fruit juice, and two cans of spaghetti. Picking up two MREs as an afterthought, he rushed back to his mother. Lexie popped open the clam juice as Silas prepared the fruit juice for the youngsters. Then he opened the canned spaghetti for them. They devoured it cold.

"Not so fast, kids. You'll get sick."

Lexie poured a small amount of clam juice into the man's mouth. He opened his eyes and began to suck the liquid down. Coughing, he focused on Lexie. His eyes expressed gratitude as he continued to drink.

"Please! Please," he said after several minutes. "Help my wife."

"James, I could really use your help here!" Lexie said. He did not react.

Silas came to her side. "You go help his wife. I'll stay here with him," he said.

"Thank you, Silas," she said, glaring back at her husband.

Lexie grabbed more juice and tilted back the woman's head, but she simply coughed the juice out. Lexie shook her, tried to get her to sit her up, and slapped her face lightly, but nothing seemed to wake her. Grabbing her wrist, she was shocked to find nearly no pulse.

"James! She's going into a coma!"

Lexie tried moving her to the sofa across the room, but the woman was too heavy. Silas stopped what he was doing and reached down to help, just as James bent down and grabbed her torso. Together they set her limp body on the couch, balling up a blanket to support her head.

The man managed to finish the clam juice and had dragged himself to a sitting position. "My wife is dying," he said bluntly.

Lexie knew he was right, but held her tongue. "She's very sick."

The man lowered his head and called out, "Devin? Ava?" The children came running to their father, throwing their arms around his neck. "I love you both so much," he said, weeping. "I wasn't sure if I'd ever see you again."

"What about Ma?" Devin asked.

"I don't know yet, son. Nobody knows."

Devin and Ava went over to their mother and looked on as she lay with her eyes closed. Her breathing had become more labored and she was wheezing very loudly. It was clear that she was suffering. Devin stroked her arm, tears trickling down his cheeks. Ava appeared unsure of what was happening. "Mommy, why don't you wake up?"

"Silas," James said, motioning with his head.

Lexie turned to her son. "Take them out into the courtroom. Get them some cookies or something. I think there's some in my bag. And see that your sister is all right." Silas took the children's hands and led them back out.

James turned to the man. "I'm afraid there's nothing more we can do for your wife."

The man did not respond, but he crawled over to them, put his hand on his wife's head, and kissed her on the lips, tears streaming down his face.

"We've been married for twelve years," he said. "I never thought it would end like this."

Lexie grabbed James's arm. "Why don't we leave him alone with his wife for a while?"

"Hmm? What?"

"We can go in the other room and give them some time alone."

"Oh. Yeah. Yeah. That's a good idea." He took Lexie's hand and followed her back out to the hall. "Where's Silas?" he asked.

"He's entertaining the children."

James nodded, a peculiar feeling of emptiness washing over him. Outside, the wind continued to blow, whipping up the sand and debris, sending the tumbleweeds skittering across the parking lot.

"We're going to have to spend the night here," Lexie said.

"I know. That would be the safest thing to do."

He looked over toward Silas, doing his best to distract the kids with a game of hide-and-seek. Devin appeared bored, but Ava was giggling each time Silas covered his eyes and began to count. She kept running to hide behind the same chair.

"Let her win now and then," Lexie called. She turned to James, who pointed toward a large desk.

"Give me a hand here, will you?"

"With what?"

She led him into one of the offices. "Let's move this desk out to the lobby and push it up against the front door. Just to be safe."

Together, they slid the mammoth piece of furniture across the marble floor and into place. Then James spread out a large rug and stacked their supplies next to it.

"How long do you figure we'll stay here?"

James shook his head. "Not long. That woman in there isn't going to get any better. I think we'll leave first thing in the morning."

"You're right about her, I know. But what about the man? And those poor innocent children?"

"Once the woman passes, it's every man for himself. He'll have to find a way to care for his own kids."

"What will they use for food?"

He shrugged. "I don't know. Maybe they'll…"

"Well, we can give them something, can't we?"

"What? We can't give them our supplies. We'll die!"

"But that seems so…harsh."

James shrugged. "Survival of the fittest."

"But if we let those innocent children die, is survival really worth living for?"

He set his shotgun on the ground next to him and looked up at her, surprised. "Yes. Yes, it is. Every day we're together is precious." He looked down, hesitated, and looked up into her soulful eyes. "Look, honey. We don't know how much time we're going to have together. We have to make the most of it."

The man had emerged from the chambers, walking shakily. His children ran up and hugged him before returning to Silas.

"I don't know what to say other than thank you," the man said.

"You're very welcome. What's your name?" Lexie asked.

"Jonathan," he said. "We were on our way east when we ran out of gas. We were hoping to find some supplies in this town, but it's nothing but dust. We've been here for over a week with no food, hardly any water. Now even that's gone."

"Do you have a car?"

"Yeah. It's parked a few blocks down the road. It's useless."

"I'm so sorry to hear that," Lexie said. "And I'm very sorry about your wife. I'm sure this is very difficult, what with the children and all."

He shook his head. "Toughest part is, I don't know what I'm going to tell them about their mother."

"Why don't you come with us?" Silas blurted out. "We have lots of supplies left."

"Silas!" James snapped. "I'm afraid that isn't possible, son. We have no room at all in the SUV and we have only a few days' worth of supplies. I wish we could help more, but we can't."

The man's eyes dropped.

Lexie reached out and squeezed his arm. "We can at least share a meal with you. It looks like it's been a while since you had one. Then tomorrow we'll have to be on our way. We hope you find some help in town once the storm dies down." She paused. "Or somewhere," she added softly.

As night fell, Lexie lit several candles. They reflected brightly off the walls and ceiling of the lobby. Jonathan had gone back to the chambers to be with his wife while everyone else gathered around for a meal. The little boy and girl shared a can of chili while the rest ate MREs. They each had a small cup of water, reducing their supply to a little over two gallons. Once the children had finished eating, they looked around for more.

"Mom, I don't understand how we can just leave these kids without anything. It's not right. What if they die?"

"It's complicated, baby. It really is. Things are different now. We have to look out for ourselves. Jonathan will find a way to get food and water for them."

"Doesn't the saying go that it's better to give than to receive? Or that whoever is generous to the poor will be repaid for his deeds?"

James's eyebrows rose involuntarily. "We have only enough for ourselves, and we barely have that. It's pretty much as simple as that, Silas. We can't give away what we don't have."

That night, as Jonathan and his children retired to be with their wife and mother respectively, James had trouble falling asleep. The heat was still oppressive, and the old building was poorly insulated.

"Dad?"

James stirred. "What is it, son? I thought you were asleep."

"It's too hot, and Brownie keeps rubbing up against me."

"Well, go on and try, anyway. Just try."

There were several minutes of silence. "Dad?"

He sighed. "Yes?"

"Could you tell me a story about the days when you were growing up? You know, when you had all that water you used to play in, and the sun wasn't red, and…"

"I don't think so, son. Not tonight. We don't want to wake your mother."

From across the room, Lexie stirred. "Are you kidding? Who can sleep in this heat?"

James lifted himself up on his elbows, rolled his shirt into a ball, and wedged it against the blanket he used as a pillow. It smelled like scorched earth.

"Okay," he said, settling back down on his back. "I'll tell you about all the great times we used to have swimming and fishing in Lake Erie, and all the waterslides we used to go to, and the trip we took to the Caribbean, with those magnificent turquoise beaches everywhere you looked."

"Great."

So James started relaying his history once again—for the tenth or twelfth time?—and Silas interrupted every now and again for clarification. And then the interruptions came less often. And, finally, not at all.

About time! If only we could all get to sleep so easily.

He turned toward his wife. "Lex?"

He heard a small spurting sound from her mouth. And he wondered how he would get to sleep. And then it struck him. Sitting next to his sleeping area was the bottle of Maker's Mark.

Hey, who deserves it more than I do?

Pouring half a glass from the bottle, he downed it quickly, the fiery liquid stinging his throat all the way through to his belly. He set the cup down and screwed the cap back on the bottle.

Why not? He mused.

Picking the bottle up again, he refilled the cup and, this time, drained it more slowly, taking time to taste the years of work involved in creating the golden liquid. And by the time he'd finished the third glass, he felt his eyes grow heavy and nestled his head down against his "pillow." He dreamed of better days past—and more hopeful days to come.

Chapter 9

From the distance, a dog whimpered. Cried. Growled. James opened his eyes, blinking to clear his vision. His head pounded as his body was clearly no longer used to alcohol. The headache, combined with the heat, had his brain feeling foggy.

"Brownie! What is it, boy?"

Oh, shit, he thought, grabbing his head. He looked up, looked around, and bolted.

Lexie turned in her sleep. "Honey, what is it? Is everything all right?"

Everything wasn't all right. All of their boxes had vanished during the night, along with one of his rifles. He reached for the keys to the SUV which he had placed under his head for safekeeping. Gone!

How could I have been so fucking stupid? My family's lives are at stake and I decide to drink my woes away. If all of our supplies are gone, I may have put the nail in my family's coffin.

"Damn it," he mumbled.

"What is it?" his wife asked again.

He pulled his loaded revolver out of his pocket and crept up to the front window. He could hear soft voices and saw Jonathan putting his finger to his lips, signaling Devin and Ava to be quiet. He had loaded the SUV with all their possessions and was helping the children into the back seat.

"That bastard is going to steal all our stuff!" James cried.

"What? Who is?" Lexie said, sitting up. "Who are you talking about?"

"Our good friend, Jonathan, that's who!"

She looked around. "Are they gone?" She paused, her eyes opening wide. "Oh, no. Not our car!"

"He's just about ready to steal everything we fucking own!"

"That's not possible. There has to be another explanation."

"Yeah, and Christmas comes once a month. Here. Take a look out the damn window and you can see for yourself. The damn bastard left his dying wife, too. I'm going to kill him!"

"James, don't do that. Don't say that!"

James had no time to argue. "Silas, wake up, son."

The boy popped up, bleary-eyed. "What? What is it, Dad?"

"Grab the shotgun. Jonathan's trying to steal our stuff. The bastard even took my rifle."

"What?"

"Grab the shotgun and watch out the window, just in case."

"Are you sure?"

"Just do it!"

Silas grabbed the 12-gauge and crossed over to the window, still rubbing his eyes, as James ran to the far side of the building and let himself out. The day, already a furnace, was clear and bright, the storm having vanished sometime during the night. Slowly he rounded the building toward the front, with his gun drawn. He had just reached the corner, where he watched Jonathan trying to coax Ava into the car.

"God damn it, Ava, forget about that stupid bear. I'll get you another one when we get to the next town."

Ava began to cry.

"Come on, now. Be a big girl. You've got to be quiet."

"But, my bear. What about my bear?"

Jonathan had slammed the door shut as Ava tried to muffle her sobs. Devin was sitting in the passenger side of the SUV and looking around with wide eyes. Jonathan set the rifle in the back seat and softly closed the door. Just as he was about to slip into the SUV and pull away, James dashed out from cover. He lowered his pistol toward the man and then fired one round in the air.

The sound echoed off the brick building, the shell shattering the side mirror. Jonathan jumped back and, on seeing James, made a move to get into the car.

"Hold it! Hold it right there! Move one more inch and I'll blow your fucking head off! Right in front of your fucking kids!"

Jonathan froze and stuck his hands in the air. "Okay. Okay. Don't shoot. You've got me. Please don't shoot."

"Keep your hands in the air, you slimy bastard. My family helps you, and you repay us by stealing everything we have?"

Jonathan shrugged. "You said it yourself. It's a dog-eat-dog world."

"Enough!" James cried. "Now, everyone out of the car. Devin! Ava! Out!" The children jumped out and ran around to their father. James motioned with the gun. "Now, slowly walk back inside. One move and you die, Jonathan. You all die."

"Please, no, not my children. They're only—"

"Shut your fucking mouth and move!"

Silas, waiting inside, opened the door, the shotgun trained on Jonathan's chest as he entered. Lexie stood to the side, holding Charlotte, who was cooing softly in anticipation of her feeding. As the family entered, Brownie growled before backing down.

"I tried to help you guys," Silas yelled, fighting back the tears in his eyes. "I tried to help you, and this is the thanks I get?"

Jonathan looked up at him before looking down, his shoulders slumped. Lexie stood shaking her head.

Silas turned to his father. "What are you going to do with them, Dad? You're not going to kill them, are you?"

"I don't know, son." He hesitated. "Go to the janitor's closet and get me anything you can find to tie them up."

He ordered Jonathan and his kids back into the judge's chambers. Jonathan's wife lay silent on the couch. James couldn't tell whether she was alive or dead.

"Now, all of you, sit. Hands behind your back!" James paused as the three looked from one to the other. "I kid you not. One wrong move and you are dead. Now, sit!" James was still astonished by the man's audacity. Had they succeeded in his plan, James's entire family would have been left for dead. Thinking about it made him furious.

Silas came back with a roll of gray duct tape.

"Keep the shotgun on him at all times," James said. "If he tries anything at all, shoot his fucking head off!" Devin and Ava began to cry, but Jonathan showed absolutely no emotion as he stared at Silas, the boy's hands trembling.

Lexie came in, still holding the baby. "What are you going to do with them?"

"Lexie! Back outside. Now!"

"Excuse me? Don't you dare talk to me like that! Don't hurt them. You're not going to…"

"Just trust me. I'm not going to hurt anyone unless this idiot tries something stupid. Now, please take Charlotte back to the courtroom."

She turned around and retreated without looking back. James took the duct tape from Silas.

"Kneel with your hands behind your back."

Jonathan did as he was told, and James wrapped the tape around his wrists.

"Now, lie down on your side!"

He wrapped the tape around his legs.

"Right," James said, "you're not going anywhere soon."

"I'll die like this, and so will my kids. Can you live with that?" Jonathan begged.

James turned toward the little boy. "Devin, do you know how to use a pocket knife?"

"Ummm. I guess so," the boy said.

"So, here's the deal, Jonathan. I should kill you, but I'm not going to do that. Instead, I'm going to put this knife on the floor in the front lobby when we leave. Devin, you take that knife and free your father, understand?"

The boy hesitated before nodding.

"We'll die here. We have nothing to drink or eat!"

"Not my concern," James snapped. "I'm sure you'll find a way to manage. You sure didn't seem to care about stealing my family's food and leaving us for dead."

There was nothing else Jonathan could say.

Silas walked up to the man and placed one can of chili and one bottle of clam juice next to him. "Here, take this. I only wish we had more to give you."

"Thank you," Jonathan said.

"Damn it, Silas!"

The boy turned to his Dad. "But...the kids! Think about the kids." He looked as if he was about to cry.

"James," Lexie said, coming back in at the sound of her husband shouting. "Let him be." She placed Silas's head on her shoulder and rubbed his back in small circles.

"You think I'm right, Mom?"

"Of course. You're such a nice young man. So thoughtful and caring. You have a gentle soul, and I'm proud of you." Silas looked over at Devin and Ava.

James sighed. "Come on, then. It's time to go. Let's finish packing the car."

Silas and Lexie took a long look back at the family before following James out of the chamber. Most of their belongings were already in the SUV, courtesy of Jonathan. Within a few more minutes, they had exited the courthouse and climbed into their rolling oven, ready to leave. James emptied one of the five-gallon gas cans into the tank before climbing behind the wheel and turning the key in the ignition.

Within moments, they had left the courthouse and were headed downtown again as quickly as the heaving, buckling roads and wrinkled concrete would allow. Headed next for...

James wiped the frustration from his brow.

I only wish I knew.

Chapter 10

Despite being a desert town, tall trees once flourished throughout the downtown area. Once planted to beautify the area, they now stood, reaching toward the glaring sun like drift wood on a deserted beach. Many had toppled over years ago only to be consumed by the dry desert and mounds of blowing sand. The city was as brown and dead as Death Valley and was only getting uglier by the day. It had become so hot that breathing the air proved to be difficult.

At Lexie's suggestion, James drove toward the former downtown and was in search of a drugstore or general store that might still have scraps of supplies left behind. He navigated the desolate Main Street that was once the hub of the country and was now nothing but a place for abandoned cars, sand drifts, and piles of dead brush. He turned a corner and pulled directly into the parking lot of a chain drugstore. Given all of the recent troubles, James decided to go in alone and leave Silas with the revolver while he carried the shotgun.

He carefully entered the store only to find nothing but empty shelves and garbage. He perused the place in its entirety, including the back storeroom, only to be disappointed. The store had utterly nothing of value. He made an about-face to the car and the family set the course for their next destination only a block away. To his dismay, he searched the local grocery store to find all the shelf-stable foods gone, all the useful supplies vanished, and dried, decomposing fresh foods and meats stinking to high hell. Panic was beginning to set in as he went through the family's current list of goods in his mind. He knew two gallons of water would not last long and they were in a desperate and near hopeless situation.

"Well?" Lexie asked when he returned.

"Nothing," he said. "Picked clean."

"So?"

"So, we move on to the next store. They can't all be emptied."

"Jonathan said there wasn't anything but dust in the entire town," Silas said.

"Jonathan said lots of things that weren't true."

James started the car and headed back down the street and past a small medical building with a sign that read DR. MARK WOODSON, PEDIATRICIAN.

"Quick! Stop the car!" Lexie shouted. He slammed on the breaks and edged the vehicle to a stop in front of the building.

"What?"

"Formula! There could be formula in there," she exclaimed.

"In where? It's a fucking doctor's office."

"It's a *pediatrician's* office. There's a difference. Sales reps hand out samples of their products for the doctors to give to their patients all the time. If we're lucky, we'll find some in there. Don't you remember, James? Every doctor's appointment we ever went to they gave us freebies."

James looked from his wife to the building and back again, his skepticism turning to resolution.

"Well, come on, what are we waiting for? Let's go find some formula!"

"You go with Dad, Silas. Charlotte's getting fidgety. I'll wait here."

Stuffing a handgun into his belt, James led the way to the office door. "Locked," he said.

"That could be a good sign. Like maybe no one's been here yet."

"Stand back."

Picking up a landscaping rock, he threw it through the glass, reached his hand in, and unlatched the bolt. The two entered the office.

"Spooky," Silas said.

"Like stepping back in time."

"Yeah."

It looked as if everyone had rushed to get out before some major calamity struck, yet everything was well preserved. A dry water dispenser in the corner, the front desk with patients' files still open, chairs, even a small playhouse with several plastic toys scattered around the floor. There was even a dried-up aquarium with several fish corpses at the bottom.

James led the way to a janitor's closet only to find a number of empty cleaning supply bottles. *Nothing useful here.* Working their way to the back of the area, they found a large filing cabinet with a sticker on it that read PHARMACEUTICAL SAMPLES. He opened the top drawer.

"What's in it?" Silas asked.

James rifled through the supplies. "A bunch of expired medications."

"Great."

"Wait a minute! Here's something." He grabbed an emergency medical kit, still unopened, and threw it into the duffle bag at his side. He opened the next drawer. Sifting through the packages, he broke into a grin. "Pay day!"

"You mean you found it? You found some formula?"

He turned to the boy. "Not some, son. We found the Mother Lode!"

"Wow, look at it all!" Silas grinned, helping his father stuff the bag full.

"Yeah. At least one of us won't go hungry."

"That's for sure." He grabbed the last several samples and stuffed them in the bag. "Hey, maybe we could all get used to this stuff."

"Don't laugh. We may have to!"

James grabbed the bag and motioned for Silas to follow him into an adjacent examining room. Opening one of the cabinets, he found a box of vanilla-flavored Ensure® and several gallons of nursery water, which he quickly threw into a plastic sack lying on the floor.

He turned to his son. "What d'you think?"

"I think Mom is a genius!"

He smiled. "Let's go share the good news."

Before James pulled away from the doctor's office, each member of the family except Charlotte drank one of the shakes. They tasted wonderful. He opted to make a U-turn back toward the highway to begin making some much needed progress eastward. Just as they were crossing a set of railroad tracks, Silas called out, "Oh cool! A train." James and Lexie both looked toward the right and could see a stopped train several hundred feet down the track.

"That looks like a passenger train," James insisted. "It looks like it could be an Amtrak train. There could be some items of value on there."

They all three stared at the train sitting silently in place on the tracks as if someone had paused an old movie. It was evident from their faces that they were all thinking it would be worthwhile to check the train for supplies, and so James turned the SUV and headed directly down the tracks toward the train. It was easily 140 degrees and there was no sense in walking in the heat when their vehicle could easily ride along the tracks.

Within minutes, they were pulled up directly to the back car of the long Amtrak train. Silver train cars went as far as their eyes could see and enormous piles of sand drifts leaned on the Amtrak logo. The once clear windows were not only covered in a film of dirt, but they were also foggy from years of abuse from the ravaging sun.

"Let's go take a look see," James said to Silas.

"You two be careful, d'you hear? Don't take any unnecessary chances. If there's nothing of value there, hurry back so we can get going again. I'm going to stay here with Charlotte. She's looking a little pale. I think she's overheated."

James pulled his revolver from his pants. "Here, keep this with you. And don't hesitate to use it if anyone suspicious comes along."

"What about you?" she said, grabbing the pistol and setting it on the seat next to her.

"I'll take the shotgun. And you," he said, turning to Silas, "take the rifle."

"Will do, Dad."

"And check to make sure they're loaded. In fact, bring half a dozen extra shells for each of us."

"Remember what I said," she told him as he turned back to her. He saluted smartly. "Yes, sir!"

He reached his head in through the window and kissed his wife on the lips, stopping to tousle his daughter's hair. "See here, young lady, be sure to look after your mom, you hear?" He tickled her belly, and she began to laugh. He kissed Lexie again and gave her a wink. "Keep the doors locked until we get back." He turned to Silas. "Ready?"

"Let's do it!"

As they walked along the tracks, James told his son to be sure to take anything he found of value—clothing, food, medicine and, of course, water. He handed him one of the canvas satchels he'd brought along. *Hopefully they'll be full when we return.* As they reached the last of the four passenger cars, James opened the door and turned back toward Silas. He looked down to see two black eyes and a dark brown nose staring up at him.

"Brownie!" He called, turning to Silas. "What's he doing here?"

"I couldn't help it. He jumped out of the car when I opened the rear to get the guns." Silas reached down and scratched the dog's neck. "It'll be okay. He won't be any trouble."

"Well...I guess it'll have to be okay. Just stay close. Keep an eye on him and be careful with that gun. I don't want you shooting me!"

James climbed into the car before reaching down to give Silas a boost up. Inside, it was ominously dark even in daylight, the windows shaded with dirt.

"Looks like the mail car."

"Cool," Silas said, raising his head slightly. His eyes narrowed. "Uhh. Maybe not." He crinkled his nose. "What's that smell?"

James sniffed the air. "I don't know. Smells a little like gas. And something else. Probably some food or something that went bad." He looked around. "Open that window there, son."

Silas went over to the sash and searched for a lock. "I can't," he said. "It's sealed shut."

Mail car. Of course. "Come on, let's check out the passenger cars."

James led the way out, opening the door to the next coach.

Deserted. He motioned to Silas. "You check the aisle on that side. And don't forget the overheads." He nodded toward his left. "I'll check this over here."

As they moved down the aisle, working in synch—two cogs in a timepiece, one as important to its smooth functioning as the other—Silas squealed with delight.

"Hey, look at this!"

"What is it?"

"A brand new X64 video game."

James frowned, shaking his head. By the time they had reached the front of the car, they had rounded up several towels, a few diapers, three small cartons of juice, new clothing for everyone, and another emergency medical kit.

"Not much to write home about," James said.

Silas shrugged. "Looks like somebody else beat us to it."

"More likely *lots* of somebody elses." James sighed. "Let's check out the next car."

James led the way out the door and through the vestibule with Silas on his heels. As he opened the door, he took a quick step back. "Oh, God!" he cried, burying his face in the back of his hand.

"What *is* it?" Silas asked. "Oh, what's that smell?"

"Holy fucking shit!"

"What is it, Dad?"

"Oh, my God. Son, maybe you should...don't come in."

"What? Why?"

"Just...stay back."

Suddenly, Brownie bounded past them, scooting down the aisle, with Silas trying to grab him from behind. The boy took several paces before halting, his eyes opened wide, his feet frozen to the floor. "Oh, my God, Dad!"

James looked out over the seats at the House of Horrors that lay before them. He raised his hand to his temple. "Oh...no."

"What is it?" Silas cried. "Dad, what happened here?"

James's eyes traveled up one side of the coach and down the other. He felt his jaw fall slack. His pulse quickened. His eyes scoured the car. Every seat was occupied. One corpse after another sat stone-faced and rigid, upright in their seats or slumped over in peaceful repose, as if casually waiting for the train stop that would never come. Their skin shone brown-black—cracked and wrinkled leather offset by glistening white bones and teeth. Their eyes were empty black holes in the universe that had once been life. Women slumped next to their children, men huddled next to their wives, entire families sat together, their rotting hands still clasped in warm embrace.

All were dressed in their Sunday best.

"What happened to them, Dad?"

He paused, looking around for a clue. *What* did *happen?*

James's eyes looked toward the windows, the distinct smell of gasoline still trapped inside.

"Open some windows!" he barked. "Get this stench out. Let in some fresh air!"

Silas did as he was told, and the air outside washed across them, hot and repressive, but clean. As James walked down the aisle, he froze. Next to one of the seats sat a small gas-powered machine covered in dust.

"What is it?" Silas asked.

James squatted down for a closer look. "This," he said, running his hand across the dusty surface, "is a generator."

"A what?"

He looked more closely at the people, at what remained of the expressions on their faces. *They look as if they'd just...gone to sleep! They must have been trapped in this heat for days and decided to end it all in one mass suicide. They must have known that the gasoline-powered engine would emit carbon dioxide. Yet no one even attempted to open a single window to let the fumes out. It had to be intentional. They had to have made that conscious decision. Quick, easy...painless.*

"These people killed themselves, Si. They committed suicide."

"But...but why?"

James shook his head. "I'm not sure." His eyes settled on a solitary corpse in the front of the car. Dressed in the colorful vestments of a Roman Catholic priest, he clasped a Bible in one hand and a rosary in the other. An empty chalice and a gold communion dish occupied the space next to him. James leaned closer to read the writing scribbled in lipstick on the silver wall. It was a quotation from the New Testament:

John 3:16. For God so loved the world that He gave His one and only Son, that whoever believes in Him shall not perish but have eternal life.

"Everyone's holding a Bible, Dad," Silas said.

"Yeah, I see that."

James suddenly felt sorry for the children, for all the brainwashed idiots who were dead because their parents could think of no other way out. Still, their fate was probably better than a slow death from thirst or starvation. He envisioned the terror they must have felt as they turned the generator on and made their peace. *It was love that drove them to their decision. At the very least,* he thought, *they were at peace and wouldn't have to live in a world that had turned evil.*

It was a tragic fate, but there was nothing they could do now. Besides, he knew that the people were all in a better place. Wherever that might be.

"I guess we need to be thankful, huh, Dad? At least we have food and water. And a running car."

"And one another, son."

James pulled the boy to his side and held him. Tight. He could feel Silas trembling.

"Come on. Let's take this stuff back to the car. There's nothing more for us here."

James wriggled past Silas as they quickened their pace. Snaking their way down the aisle back through the mail car, headed toward sunlight and the SUV, they were soaked in perspiration. They stepped out into a cauldron of heat. In the distance, James could see Lexie and Charlotte still waiting in the car.

"Why did they do it, Dad? How could anybody do something like that?"

"Stupidity, son. Just plain stupidity. These people believed in fairy tales." He put his arm around Silas's shoulders. "Come on, let's get back to your mother and Charlotte."

As they neared the vehicle, Silas headed around the back to open the door for Brownie to jump in. As James walked around him, he stopped. Thinking for several seconds, he turned toward his son, apprehension scarring his face. "One more thing," he said softly.

Silas looked up.

"Don't tell your mother. I mean about the mass suicide and all. It would just upset her."

Opening the door and climbing into the driver's seat, James reached for the key in the ignition.

"Find anything?"

He shrugged. "Oh, a little. Not much. Mostly junk. Most of the stuff had already been picked over. We did get some new clothing for everyone."

She nodded, returning her gaze to Charlotte.

As he pulled out into the road, James pointed the car northeast once again. He was surprised Lexie hadn't pressed him further on exactly what they'd found on the train. Had she suspected something? Had she known they were withholding something from her?

"James," she said finally.

He looked at her.

"Something's wrong."

"What? What do you mean?" *She knows all right*, he thought.

And then it hit him. The unmistakable odor of methane gas and undigested formula.

"Oh-oh. Smells like someone just did something *awful*."

"I'm not kidding."

He squinted out at the road. "What d'you mean?"

"Something's really wrong."

He glanced again at his wife and child, Charlotte naked in her mother's lap, covered by only a light cloth.

"She has terrible diarrhea."

James smiled. "All children get diarrhea."

"And she's feverish."

His smile turned suddenly down. "How feverish?"

"She's hot. I think she may have drunk some spoiled formula." Lexie's face was ashen, her eyes glued to their daughter.

"It...it...it will probably pass. Just give it time. And keep giving her liquids."

He realized any illness could be devastating in this strange new world, but for a baby it would be catastrophic. If the diarrhea didn't pass on its own, they would need to find a doctor. And the task of finding a doctor who still maintained a practice would be monumental.

"I'm giving her liquids, but she's not drinking."

"Oh, Jeez, Mom. What's that stink?"

"Get your mother some of those new diapers and some of the water we found at the pediatrician's office. Hurry."

As Silas rummaged through the back of the vehicle, James couldn't help but keep a positive thought. They would keep driving east and they would find someone. Unless the child could beat whatever bug it was that had attacked her, they would need to find some help. And soon.

At least, he thought, *we have fresh clothes and food and water for the baby. At least we're prepared to tackle the next couple of days. Come what may.*

Chapter 11

By evening, Charlotte's condition had worsened. Her parents were helpless as the infant's health drained out of her tiny body. She was no longer crying; she could no longer muster the strength. Mostly she lay in silent slumber.

"That's a good sign," James said. "Her body is fighting it off." He said it, but he didn't believe it.

Neither did Lexie. She periodically tried waking Charlotte to drink from a bottle. When she did, the baby either threw up or expelled the liquid into her diaper. She had soiled so many of them that Lexie was forced to go back to using any rags or clothes she could find.

Despite the dire situation, James continued to push on eastward and, late in the evening, they began to approach Salt Lake City. While he could not be sure, he knew it was late; most likely near midnight as the family came upon the large city. He knew it would not be safe to stay in the car or to continue driving and they would once again need to find shelter. As a man who loved to be in control, he was losing his battle and there were far too many unknowns in the current situation. He needed to find a doctor for Charlotte, diapers, Pedialyte, more food and water, and shelter for the night.

"We'll have to find some help in the morning."

"I wish we could find someone tonight."

James shook his head. "It's dangerous at night. We'll have to find a safe place to sleep." Lexie looked down at the child, tears wending down her cheeks. "James, we need to do something. Right now. She's growing weaker by the minute."

"I know. Believe me." He looked into the rear-view mirror and saw Silas's furrowed brow staring back at him. "We all know."

James continued east until they saw the signs for the downtown area. As they drove through the decimated city, he was shocked to see so many people outside, roaming from one building to another, their firearms never far from view. Despite it being evening, the heat was unrelenting and most people were walking around shirtless, some even completely nude.

"There's hope," he said. "At least it isn't deserted."

In the distance, shots rang out, followed by men shouting. Several fires were burning on the horizon. As they turned a corner, an entire apartment building burst into flames, the residents standing outside, slack-jawed, watching their lives go up in smoke. Abandoned cars littered the buckling streets, making passage nearly impossible. Shady characters lurked in every corner. The vehicles, debris, and garbage peppered the streets, and potholes the size of small cars made the roads nearly impassable.

"Let's get out of here!" Lexie said.

James steered the SUV down a street leading away from the city center. *Shit. If we can't find a safe building to camp in, we'll have to risk staying in the car.*

As they drove along, they passed small makeshift camps along the road. People were standing around tents thrown together with canvas, plastic, or cardboard. The people stared at them like zombies as the family passed by.

Suddenly, a rock bounced off the roof of the SUV. And then a second and a third. James veered into the oncoming lane before zig-zagging down the road.

"Dad! Look out...they're stoning us!"

James hit the gas just as a large rock split the rear window, sending shards of glass flying.

"Goddamn it!" James yelled. He thought about pulling out the gun and firing some warning shots out the window. But if the mob began firing back, he knew they'd be in a world of trouble.

Driving as fast as he dared, he barely missed colliding with an abandoned postal vehicle as he swerved sharply to the right, mowing down half a dozen parking meters.

"Watch out!"

"What are you doing, Dad?"

James barely heard. He was in a war zone, and he wasn't about to lose the battle. He had to find a way out of the city before the car broke down—or worse. Taking a sharp right, he spied a sign pointing back to I-80. Just short of the ramp, he saw an abandoned SUV nearly identical to their own. He slammed on the brakes.

"What are you doing?" Lexie cried. "Are you crazy? Why are you stopping?"

"Spare tire's still on that car. We need it."

"What?"

He opened the door and jumped out.

"You want some help, Dad?"

"Stay in the car!"

He grabbed the wrench from the back of their car and stripped the spare tire from the other vehicle. Like a pit crew at the Indy 500, he had mounted it on their own car and thrown the jack back inside within minutes. His shirt was wringing with sweat and he was as thirsty as he'd ever been.

Climbing back into the driver's seat, he watched Lexie mop Charlotte's brow; the infant had spit up and had a bowel movement at the same time. All without stirring.

"Looks like she's sweating something awful," he said.

Lexie raised one of their daughter's eyelids. "James. Her eyes!"

"What?"

"Look. They're glazed over." She checked the other one—with the same results. "And her lips. They look like they're shriveling up. We have to get her some help!"

"Damn it!" he cried. "Goddamnit!" He banged his hand against the steering wheel, his eyes instinctively falling on the rear-view mirror. Silas's face glowed with terror.

James sighed, the heaviness of the night pressing in on him. "Maybe she'll drink some plain water," he suggested to Lexie. "We have to try to hydrate her. Force her to drink if you have to." He put the car back in gear and steered it onto the ramp leading to I-80.

Now what? Now where?

On into the night they pressed, into the black abyss of the sea around them.

"She's stopped sweating," Lexie said.

"Really? That's a good sign, then."

"I don't think there's any moisture left in her body to sweat."

Shit!

"Hang on. We'll be coming to another town soon. Hopefully, they'll have a—"

"Her breathing has slowed."

"What?"

"She's barely breathing, James!"

We're losing her. The last pure innocent being left on this planet, and we're losing her! He felt tears forming in his eyes, but pressed on, intent on finding someone to help—anyone!

Ten minutes, twenty, thirty. Who knew? All he knew was how much he loved her, that sweet innocent baby girl of theirs, and how he couldn't simply let her die.

My baby girl. My sweet little pumpkin. Playing in the sun. Frolicking in the water. Lake Erie. Fishing. Swimming. Diving. How that girl could...

"Dad!" Silas yelled. "Wake up! You're falling asleep!"

James's eyes popped open. *Holy shit!* Just as he realized he was in the wrong lane headed for the guard rail, he yanked on the wheel, the SUV swaying beneath the strain of the maneuver. Sweat poured off his brow as he stabilized the vehicle, his fingernails biting hard into the leather-

71

wrapped wheel. He put his foot on the brake and gently slowed the car down. He pulled over onto the shoulder and came to a stop.

Everyone but Charlotte was awake and staring at him.

"I'm sorry." He breathed out. "I guess I just...dozed off. It won't happen again."

He took a deep breath and went to put the vehicle back in gear.

"Don't even think about it, James," Lexie said. "You're too tired to drive. You need to get some rest."

"Mom's right, Dad," Silas said, still trembling.

James knew it, too, but they couldn't afford to take the time. He heard Charlotte's breaths coming in short, wheezing spurts.

"She won't make it much longer. We can't stop here," he insisted. "We have to find a drugstore or a pharmacy and hope there's something left on the shelves. Something."

Lexie opened the door.

"What are you doing?"

"Slide over," she said, "and you take Charlotte. I'm going to drive."

James, too tired to argue, did as he was told and, with his daughter lying limp in his arms, Lexie pulled back onto the road and headed deeper into the night.

After only a few miles, they spied an exit sign for a town called Echo. Lexie pulled onto the ramp.

"Why are you exiting here?"

"It's a town," she said. "Towns have pharmacies. We can only hope!"

"I don't think this is much of a town, Mom." She suspected Silas was right, but she also knew they didn't have much choice.

Lexie was determined and, regardless of the negativity, she continued on down the road. Coming across an old building that served as a former gas station and grimy hotel, she pulled in. The half-moon provided the only light and she was lucky to have spotted the building. The area was as dark as complete blindness, but there did not appear to be any threat to them. They all got out, Brownie found a nice gas pump to pee on, as James, Silas, and Lexie rummaged through the very old building.

With no light to see, Lexie had to leave the car running with the headlights shining through the building's windows. She had pulled out a single jar candle from one of the boxes, lit it, and carried it through the gas station for light. They all began searching for anything of use, but they soon learned the place was barren. Any items that may have once lined the shelves, filled the small cooler, or sat behind the register were long since gone with the souls that used to own it.

Still determined, Lexie wanted to search the small hotel rooms adjacent to the gas station and she made a shot for the first one. It was completely empty. James and Silas checked the next room and it, too, was nothing more than a dirty and empty space.

"Let's get back in the car and try to make it to a bigger town. I'm all right to drive now."

"We're nearly to the Wyoming border," Lexie said. "There are no bigger towns until we hit Laramie. We're in no-man's land."

"We can make it to Rock Springs in a few hours. It's bound to have something to help her out."

Lexie wasn't sure but, with no other options, she knew that was their only chance. Charlotte, breathing slower than ever, was laboring to stay alive. She wouldn't make it through the night.

They drove along, all three sets of eyes scanning the horizon for an exit sign.

"Whoa, Dad!" Silas cried. "I see lights!"

"What? Where?"

"Over there, across the desert there."

James strained to see something, anything that could have been a light. "It's probably just a distant fire. Our eyes are playing tricks on us."

"I don't think so. That's a light," the boy insisted.

"Honey, it does look like a light."

"There's no electricity. It's a fire. Trust me," James said.

"We have no choice. Pull off the road and lock in the four-wheel drive."

"We're going off-roading!" Silas called.

"Head off in that direction, James. Please. I think I see some sort of gravel road or something. A path leading up toward the light."

James locked the SUV in and cut across the field, bouncing and skittering as they drove, until they reached a winding desert road.

"This is worse than the fucking field!" he cried, jerking the wheel first one way and then the next as he dodged the rocks and sprawling drifts of gravel and sand. "Hold on, everyone!"

Picking up speed as they descended a steep decline, James veered the car around a sharp corner and up an even steeper grade. Slowing to a crawl, they picked their way along a dark and desolate road, bucking and jerking, up a winding mountain path, and onward toward the source of the light. As they approached the top of the hill, the car ground to a halt.

"There!" Silas called, pointing.

"My God!" Lexie cried.

James squinted into the night. "I don't believe it."

"Believe it," Lexie grinned.

"It's a goddamn cabin."

"A cabin with lights!"

The boy had been right. Below them, and off a hundred feet from the car, stood a small simple wooden cabin, glowing orange-yellow. A rusted old Ford sat in the driveway. Several rooms appeared to be lighted...by incandescent bulbs.

"How in the world could a house way out here in the middle of nowhere still have electricity?" Lexie asked.

"Well, let's go find out. We need to see who's in there."

They opened the doors and climbed out of the SUV, closing them again as softly as they could before picking their way down the road toward the house. James carried Charlotte along the rocky steep grade. The only light they had was from the moon and the stars, but it was enough to lead them to their goal. But the closer they came, the more confused they grew. The house was lit up like a Christmas tree, with lighting in every room.

"Solar, James! Look!" Lexie exclaimed, pointing out half a dozen large flat black panels glistening by moonlight. "They're using solar panels for electricity."

As they drew closer to the cabin, James handed Charlotte to his wife and motioned them to stand back while he took a look inside. Sneaking up to the window, he peered in at a middle-aged man—slim, bearded, and with wild locks of hair—rocking in the living room. He appeared to be carving a piece of wood. James looked around for any signs of danger before taking a deep breath and walking up to the door.

Here goes nothing.

He knocked. He waited. Through the window, Lexie saw the man calmly rise and walk to the door. When it opened, the man made eye contact with James.

"Hello, stranger," the man said.

"Hi. I'm sorry to bother you at this time of night, but my family and I were traveling east when my infant daughter became ill. We noticed your lights and were hoping for some help."

"Where's your family?"

"They're just behind me, up on the hill. I had them wait until I was sure you...I mean, until I saw if anyone was home. I think our baby daughter is...dying."

"Well, we can't have that, now, can we? Your family is welcome here. They'll be safe and protected. I'm alone and unarmed. Bring your family inside and let's take a look."

"Oh, thank you. Thank you so much. You don't know how much this...Well, just thank you!" He took the man's hand and pumped it hard several times before turning to motion his family to join them.

Lexie handed Charlotte to James as she, Silas, and Brownie came down the hill and all stood at the front door. The man stepped aside and held out his arm to welcome them into his humble cabin. The family walked in and immediately noticed that the house was at least 30 degrees cooler than outside. The man had a functioning air conditioner that was actually running and the feeling was extraordinary. It had been a very long time since they were in a comfortable temperature.

The man motioned for them to take a seat at the wooden kitchen table. Without saying anything, he went to his refrigerator and pulled out a jug of water. He retrieved some glasses, filled them, and placed them in front of the family.

"Please drink," he said softly.

James was hesitant to drink the water, wondering if it was poisoned or drugged, but his thirst outweighed his intuition. All of them quickly drank the amazing glasses of cold water as the man filled them up again. They had not had a cold drink in months and they grinned euphorically at the feel of it trickling down their throats.

"Please help yourself," the man said, pointing to the water as he went to his cabinet and pulled out a box of crackers. He opened them and set them on the table. Silas reached without hesitation and began devouring them. Again, the man walked into his kitchen, grabbed a metal bowl, filled it with water, and placed it at Brownie's feet. Brownie began lapping up the water as fast as he could.

Later, with the family settled into the cabin, the man told them he had retired some time earlier and, seeing the writing on the wall, built a cabin in the back hills and had it fitted it with a solar power supply so that he had lights, a refrigerator, a stove—even air conditioning. He began hoarding supplies and filling his water tanks for the coming apocalypse. He hadn't been wrong.

"My name is James. This is Lexie, Silas, and our daughter Charlotte," James said.

"A pleasure to meet you. My name is Immanuel. Your daughter is ill?" he asked.

"Yes, we think she's taken some spoiled formula and is now dehydrated with a very high fever. Are you a doctor?" James asked with hope.

"No. I am no doctor. Wait one moment," he said. "I'll be right back."

He disappeared into the next room. He reemerged moments later with a concoction of electrolytes, antibiotics, and acetaminophen to add to Charlotte's bottle. He told Lexie that the mixture would restore her bodily functions, kill off whatever bacteria she'd picked up along the way, and bring down her fever.

"How will we ever thank you? Can we give you some food?" Lexie responded.

"You don't need to thank me and I need nothing in return. I'm self-sufficient here in my modest home. I help people when I can. When they come to me, I give them what I have."

"Well, you're a very kind man," James interjected. "And we'll be thankful to your forever."

"There are no guarantees that this will work. I'm not a doctor. I'll pray that what I gave you will be effective. You can stay here until she's well," he said.

"There are no words to tell you our appreciation," Lexie said as she began to cry.

Immanuel pulled out several blankets and pillows from a nearby closet and set them down in the main living area.

"My home's modest, but you may make yourselves comfortable. You may help yourselves to any of the canned food in my kitchen. The microwave is no longer functioning. There's no running water, so you must use the outhouse in the backyard." He stepped over to his rocking chair, picked up his knife, and began to whittle on some wood next to his chair. It appeared he was making a bird of some sort.

While Silas and Brownie were stretched out on a small rug enjoying the air conditioning, Lexie and James began to administer treatment on Charlotte. They mixed the Gatorade with some water, a child's size dose of Tylenol, and then added a small amount of the antibiotic by opening the capsule and pouring a portion of the contents into the liquid. They began to feed the mixture to her, but started very slowly to ensure she kept it down. They would allow her to suck from the bottle for two or three minutes at a time and then they would pull it away. Letting her stomach settle, they would then put the bottle back in her mouth. They did this until the bottle was gone.

Shortly after, she did spit up a small amount, but they were pleased she had kept most of it down. She was still very warm and in the same semi-unconscious state. They set her down on a soft blanket to allow her to rest. They were hopeful that the liquids, the cool air conditioning, and the medications would have a fast impact.

Silas had wandered to the kitchen where he opened a can of beefaroni for himself and one for Brownie. An enormous smile lit up his face as he ate, overjoyed at the taste and being able to use a real metal spoon which he had found in one of the drawers. Silas was still hungry and walked back to the pantry to see if he could find something sweet. He was thrilled to find a can of pears in heavy syrup. He opened the can and devoured it in less than a minute. The taste of the sugary sweet syrup had awakened some of his senses that had been asleep for a long time. Lexie looked up and noticed Silas overindulging.

"Silas, please don't take advantage of this kind man's generosity. That's enough food."

"It's no concern. Please indulge all that you wish. I have plenty for all," Immanuel said.

"Thank you," Lexie said softly.

She sat next to Charlotte and rubbed her head as she was fast asleep and still wheezing. Silas walked into the room and plopped down next to Immanuel who was in the rocking chair.

"Hi," he said as he smiled.

"Hi," Immanuel replied.

"How'd you get all this stuff?" Silas asked inquisitively.

Immanuel placed his wooden dove down on the table next to him and turned to Silas. "Well, boy, I built my cabin with my bare hands. I had seen the signs coming for years, so I made myself very prepared."

"Wow!" Silas said. "How'd you know?"

"I just did! There were very clear signs," he said.

James interjected, "If you don't mind my asking, how have you managed to escape thieves and robbers? Your home is so brightly lit up."

Immanuel paused and gave James a puzzled look. "Well, James, your eyes see what they want to see. The righteous can see my home as I guide them here. The evil cannot see my home. They are blind to the good."

James was beginning to think the man was a religious nutcase. "So your home has never been approached by the bad guys?"

"No, never."

"Well, if I were you, I would at least have a gun," James suggested.

"I will not take part in the evil of mankind. If I die, so be it. I have faith."

Immanuel began rubbing his eyes and informed the group he would be retiring to his bedroom for the night. Just like that, he got up and disappeared behind his bedroom door. Silas and Brownie had moved back onto their blankets and curled up together in the cool, air-conditioned room. It was the first time in a very long time that Silas remembered having to use a blanket. It felt wonderful!

James and Lexie intended to take turns sleeping while the other watched Charlotte. James had a slight sense of distrust of their host as he was questioning his sanity. Some of the things he had said did not make sense and he was convinced he had been brainwashed by religion. Once Immanuel had gone to bed, James's suspicions about religion were confirmed when he found that all of the items he had whittled were of a religious nature. The table next to his chair had several pieces that he had carved…several holy crosses, doves, and tons of various angels. A single book sat next to his chair and it was a very old version of the Bible. James was getting irritated with every new item he found.

While James was snooping, Lexie was tending to Charlotte. Although there was no change in her condition, Lexie thought she would need some nourishment in addition to the sports drink. She gave her a two-ounce bottle of formula with the hopes that she would keep it down. To her surprise, Charlotte took the entire bottle and did not regurgitate any. Lexie stayed there for the next two hours simply stroking her hair and lying by her side.

At some time in the middle of the night, James came over and relieved Lexie. After feeling Charlotte's head for heat, she grabbed a blanket and lay down near a sound-asleep Silas and Brownie. James prepared another bottle of the Gatorade, Tylenol, and antibiotic mixture and fed it to Charlotte. He was surprised as she seemed to drink it effortlessly and probably would have taken more if he had given it to her. Once again, she did not spit up and was soon sound asleep. He felt her head and she was still hot, but James was optimistic that she was improving. Just as Lexie did, he lay by her side and stared at the daughter he so dearly loved.

Chapter 12

By the time morning broke, James was awakened to the smell of...he wasn't sure what.

"Lexie?" he whispered. "Lex?"

"Hmm? What is it?"

"That's what I want to know. That smell. What is it?"

"What is it?" She leaped up from the floor. "It's food!"

Sure enough, Immanuel had risen an hour earlier and was preparing a meal of corned-beef hash and reconstituted scrambled eggs, with a few buttermilk pancakes thrown in for good measure. He slipped around the kitchen as effortlessly as a porpoise navigates the ocean's waves. James grabbed a baby bottle filled with formula and was mixing in some Tylenol and antibiotics to feed to his daughter when Brownie jumped up, sniffed the air, and let out a low growl.

"What is it?" Silas asked, rolling over on his back. "What's wrong, boy?" He rose to his knees and clapped his hands for the dog to come. James watched as Lexie got up, called to the dog, and took several steps forward before stumbling nearly to the ground.

"Lex!"

The dog let out a loud moan and ducked beneath the blankets as James felt the surge beneath him—the low slow rocking motion accompanied by a hushed whisper like an air-conditioning unit that had just kicked on. And then the violent tremors.

"Dad!" Silas called.

James pulled Charlotte closer to his chest, cradling the child as he leaned over her for protection. Lexie grabbed a chair to steady herself. When James looked up, he saw Immanuel backed up against the refrigerator, steadying himself against the door. The sound of breaking glass and thunder, like a large semi-truck barreling through the living room, rattled the cabin, splitting the early morning softness.

In a matter of seconds, the earthquake was over.

Immanuel took a deep breath, shook his head, and returned to the job at hand. "Watch out for that glass," he said. "I'll sweep it up and get some boards on that window once we're finished eating."

Shaken, the family hugged together, amazed by the man's calm demeanor. After several more minutes, he motioned for them to join him at the table. James set the baby on a blanket well clear of the debris and joined them.

"Please," Immanuel said, holding his arms out to his sides. "Won't you take my hands in prayer?" James hesitated, glanced up at Lexie, and finally clasped Immanuel's hand. With the circle complete, he said simply, "Please bless this food we shall eat and the water we shall drink. May you bless this visiting family and protect the health of all. Amen."

"Amen."

"Amen," Silas added.

"Now," he said, motioning, "please eat."

Lexie reached for some pancakes and eggs, "Does that happen often?" she asked.

Immanuel looked up. "What? Oh, you mean that quake? Why, yes, happens so often I have to think twice before I notice 'em at all."

"You did seem to take it in stride."

He pointed to the syrup. "Eat, young fellow. You need to keep growing!"

"Don't worry," Silas said. "I will!" He was devouring the food, hardly chewing it before he swallowed.

Immanuel motioned with his head toward the door. "They say in the Bible that the coming of the end of the world shall be foretold by the quaking of the ground and the violence wreaked upon the earth."

James grinned. "If that's the case, California would have triggered the end of time years ago."

"James!" Lexie said.

He raised his brows. "What?"

Immanuel smiled. "That's quite all right. There are different ways of interpreting things." He paused, noticing James's embarrassment. Immanuel had seen it right off—or perhaps felt it. "Tell me something," he said to his guest.

James looked up. "Yes?"

"Are you a believer?"

Surprised by the question, James thought for several moments. He didn't want to offend their host, but he felt he had to be honest.

"Yes," he said, hesitating. "Or at least I was. I was a believer until evil took over the world. Suddenly it seems as if there's nothing much to believe in anymore."

Smiling, Immanuel looked him straight in the eye. "Ahh, James, I have heard those words before. They tell me you're still a believer. I can see it in you. You're blinding your faith with hate, shame, and fear. Open your heart and your faith will return, along with your happiness."

Unsure how to respond, James looked down, picking up a forkful of hash and sliding it into his mouth.

Immanuel poured some coffee from the percolator he'd brought to the table and, as everyone dug in, James thought about what he had said.

80

"Can I have some more of that please?" Silas asked, pointing to the hash.

"Don't you think you've had enough, young man?" Lexie asked.

"That's perfectly all right," Immanuel said. "He's a growing boy. And I have all I require for myself, and then some. Plus enough for those in need."

James, his stomach growing heavier, settled back in his chair, feeling placid, secure, sated. *It's been a long time since I've sat in a comfortable chair in an air-conditioned room. Almost forgot what it feels like! And a real breakfast with hot coffee?* He smiled his best Cheshire Cat grin. *I never thought I'd taste hot coffee again, let alone eat in such a cozy setting as this.*

He looked up at his wife, aglow, and over to Silas, wolfing down the food as if he might not eat again for a month.

"More coffee, James?" Immanuel asked, breaking his train of thought.

James nodded. "Thanks."

James and his family stayed the rest of the day with Immanuel. They stayed three additional nights, at their benefactor's insistence. And, with each passing hour, Charlotte's health improved. By the third day, she was smiling, giggling, laughing again, just as she used to do. James wasn't sure what had done the trick, but Immanuel had worked a miracle. The child was back to being her former happy playful carefree self. James was relieved and, when he looked into Lexie's eyes, he could tell she had had a huge iron cross lifted from her chest.

Cross? He chuckled to himself at the analogy. *More like stone.*

And then, on the fourth day, with the miracle of life restored to their child, James knew it was time to continue on their journey.

It was difficult for them to leave the safety of the little cabin. James had seen how much the family had bonded with Immanuel. Silas, Lexi, and, to a lesser degree, himself. But Silas most of all. He had found in Immanuel someone he could look up to, someone who would listen to him without judging. He had found a man who accepted him without a second thought. At one point, the man had smiled at the boy and said, "You're a boy who reflects pure innocence. You will bring good to this world. Of this I am sure."

By midday, James had begun gathering their belongings, which Lexie and Silas packed into the back of the car. It wouldn't be easy, leaving the air conditioning for the stifling heat of everyday life. But it was a burden they'd have to bear.

Finally, with their goods stashed in the car and the tank filled with gas, they thanked their host.

"We'll remember your kindness forever," Lexie said, hugging him and giving him a kiss on the cheek.

"Oh, that reminds me. Just one minute." He turned and disappeared into the cabin before emerging again, tugging a large box behind him.

"What's this?" she asked.

"Nothing much. A few gallons of water, some canned food, and acetaminophen—just in case!"

James shook the man's hand and thanked him for everything. Silas, fighting back a tear, gave him a hug. Immanuel patted him on the shoulder and tousled his hair.

As they said their farewells and James turned the key in the ignition, they waved before beginning down the long curving driveway.

"Good bye, and good luck," Immanuel called. "I'll see you again!"

The words echoed in James's head. *What did he mean, "He'll see us again." How? He knows we're headed for Lake Erie.*

Nevertheless, as they pulled away from the cabin toward the Interstate, James couldn't help but think they might, indeed, cross paths again someday, somehow.

As they entered the ramp to the expressway, the cabin grew steadily fainter in the distance until, before long, they could see it no more.

James furled his brow. "Did all that really happen?"

"Did all what really happen?"

"The last four days. It seems as if they've been one long mirage of salvation in a desert of dread. Like it happened only in our minds."

Charlotte let out a sudden giggle as Lexie tickled her tummy. "I know what you mean and I'd be tempted to agree," she said, lifting the girl from her lap and holding her up to her father. "Except...for this."

Chapter 13

Back on the Interstate, James couldn't help but notice that they were all in good spirits, despite the heat. The thermostat on the SUV read "Error." James had to concentrate to avoid driving over some of the asphalt that had buckled up in spots. Weaving back and forth around the obstacles like a teenager completing the cone portion of the driver's exam, he thought back to his youth, to Lorain, Ohio, when he had just turned sixteen. He was the first in his class to be eligible for his license. Like all kids that age, he begged his father to take him for the exam. And, like all fathers of kids that age, his Dad was reluctant.

"Son, you need more practice. You're not ready!" he would say. James was relentless in his pestering until his father finally caved in and drove him to the DMV. Thirty minutes later, when he came out with a huge smile on his face and holding his new license in the air, his father could only laugh.

"I'll give you this James...somehow you always find a way to make things happen. Congratulations, son."

James veered the car to avoid a pothole. *Where has the time gone? It's been 25 years since that day with my father. Now, here I am with a teenage son of my own—one who will never see the inside of a DMV station, never know the anxiety of waiting for the results of his first driver's exam.*

He looked in the rear-view mirror, craning his head to see his graying beard, the gray on his sideburns, and the gray hairs coming out of his nostrils. The reality of his age suddenly hit him. He was a middle-aged man with a family, and he suddenly realized that his time on Earth was limited. For so many years, he had taken life for granted. Yet, he could still reminisce about the joys of childhood. Silas and Charlotte would never have that opportunity. They would never get to smell the air in a dark forest or catch their first fish or jump off a tire swinging out over the waters of Lake Erie. The aroma of freshly cut grass and spring lilacs filled his brain. He wondered what would occupy the space in his children's brains.

Yet, his son was still happy, and Charlotte was too little to know any different. James realized that, as the world changes, so do man's expectations. In the old world, expectations continued to climb as the world got more complex—life, with its modern technology, more convenient. He understood that, while he had so many material possessions, he always wanted more. It was impossible to satisfy one's appetite for all those things. Now, in a world with almost no "things" at all, there were no expectations, no disappointments. What an ironic twist of fate that Silas and Charlotte would be spared that much, at least.

Silas interrupted his daydreams.

"Where're we headed next, Dad?"

"East, son. Forever east."

"I know, but east where? How much longer do we have to go?"

"It'll be a while yet. I hope to make it to Nebraska tonight. That would officially place us in the Midwest."

"That's where you grew up."

He smiled. "A little east of there," he said. "Although I spent a lot of time there, as well."

Silas looked around. "Musta been different when you were a kid."

"Why do you say that?"

"One state looks just the same as the last. Brown and dead."

"It wasn't always like that, Si," Lexie said. "Wyoming was once full of snowcapped mountains, grass-covered valleys filled with cattle, and tall stands of pine. Nebraska boasted waving fields of corn as far as the eye could see."

"Yeah, I read about that. Too bad nothing's left," Silas said.

"Well, we don't know that for sure. We haven't seen the lands to the east yet. We don't know what the earth is like there. Maybe we'll find more water, grass, trees. We won't know until we get there," she said.

"Don't count on it, Mom!" He snickered.

Maybe Silas is correct, James thought. *Maybe the only green left is in Lexie's head. At least she can hang onto the memory of that.* There was no way to know for sure what Lorain was like—or anywhere along the East Coast—until they got there. The last news reports they had heard suggested there was still some water in the Great Lakes.

"Well," Lexie said, "we have to keep our faith. And keep on hoping for the best."

As night settled over the baked earth, James found a stretch of highway still in decent shape. That helped them make better time. Occasionally they passed cars traveling in the opposite direction, heading west. James wished he could have flagged them down to tell them they were heading toward nothing but barren wasteland, but he doubted they would have believed him.

As they drove on, James noticed a large truck getting closer to them.

"What is it?" Lexie asked, noticing him looking in the mirror.

"Look back."

She paused, before craning her head around. "At what?"

"That truck. It's been gaining on us for the last several minutes. Driving awfully fast."

She whirled back around. "You don't think…"

"Bandits? Could be."

"Well, maybe we should pull off the highway, find an exit, and make a run for it."

"And then what? Have them catch us, rob us, and kill us?"

"Well, what will we do? They're still getting closer."

"Here," he said, pulling the revolver from his belt. "Give this to Silas and have him pass the shotgun up to you. I'll keep the rifle next to me."

She turned to Silas, who was dozing. "Silas? Silas, wake up."

He jumped up. "Yeah, what is it? Are we there yet?"

"Take this," she said, handing the pistol to him. "There's an old truck right behind us. Your father thinks it might be bandits."

Silas grabbed the pistol, opened the chamber, and closed it again.

"Keep calm," James said, "Everybody just look forward. Like we're not looking for any trouble."

"Slip the shotgun up here, Si."

Lexie set her daughter on the floor between her legs and took the gun from her son as an oversized green military truck pulled up alongside them as if to pass. James instinctively slowed the car down just as the truck slowed to keep pace with them. He glanced to his left to see three burly bearded rough-looking men peering back at him blankly. James was certain they would pull ahead of them, get directly in front of them, and force them to stop. That's when he'd pretend to go along with them until they got out of the truck, after which he'd floor the accelerator and leave them standing in the dust.

He hoped.

With any luck, he'd find an exit and pull off before they managed to regroup.

"What's happening?" Lexie asked.

James let out a deep breath as one of the men threw them a friendly nod before the truck accelerated, leaving them far behind.

No one spoke a word. *They're just one of the few friendly bands of people left, people doing exactly what we're doing—looking for a better place to live.*

As they drove on, a sign came into view: NORTH PLATTE 270 MILES. They had nearly made it to the middle of the United States and were halfway toward their goal. Nearing Laramie, Wyoming, James figured they could easily make it to Nebraska before late night—and even more danger. As they passed the town, Silas pointed to his left. "That's where Matthew Shepard was killed! We read about that in school."

Lexie squinted at him.

85

"Remember? He was killed for being gay and his story made national news. It was one of the first times America stood up for a gay kid. It started everything!"

"Yes," she said. "I remember. That was such a tragedy."

James could tell Lexie felt Silas was beginning to become more comfortable in his own skin—a good thing. She was happy he felt comfortable talking about his sexuality. For months, Silas seemed embarrassed whenever the subject came up. As time had moved forward, however, Lexie and James had noticed a new sense of self-confidence and self-worth in him. They were also impressed that he would have remembered a historical event that had taken place so long ago. They knew it must have been important to him. James turned to his wife, smiled, and nodded.

Pushing on, James continued down the highway and was making extremely good time as the road continued to improve. He was not sure why the road was in a better state, but he assumed it was due to such little traffic that came through this rugged part of the country. As they drove on, James saw flashing emergency lights in the distance.

Emergency lights? Why would anyone want to draw attention to himself at this hour of night? Unless...

"I don't like this," he frowned. "We should pull off somewhere."

"And go where, James?" Lexie asked. "There's nothing else here."

"We could find some side roads and still make our way east. We don't need to attract attention."

"Dad, just drive!" Silas said. "It's probably just an abandoned car."

While that was entirely possible, James thought it unlikely that anyone would turn on their hazard lights if they had abandoned their car. As usual, James slowed the car to a stop so that he could prepare for a possible attack. The first thing he did was hide as much food in the SUV as there was space in case they were going to be robbed. He pushed cans under the seats, in the seat pockets, in the electrical box, and in the glove compartment. He wedged several jugs of water under the seats and in the space that formerly held the jack and tools.

He then exited the SUV, popped the hood, and loaded as many cans and water bottles as he could fit without causing damage to the engine. Once he had filled as much as possible, he moved back to the rear of the SUV and began filling the gas tank with the fuel from the cans. Finally, he got back into the car and made sure both Silas and Lexie had loaded firearms that were ready to go.

"James, isn't this a little much?" Lexie asked.

James simply shot her an irritated look as he fired up the ignition and began driving toward the flashing lights. As they approached, they could see it was an old red Jeep Wrangler that was pulled off the road and onto the shoulder. James slowed down slightly when they were almost next to it and the family did their best to look inconspicuous as they pressed past. James and Lexie stared straight forward without ever taking a glance. They had overtaken the Jeep without incident and were driving beyond it when Silas alarmingly yelled out, "STOP THE CAR, DAD! STOP! STOP! STOP!"

James let out another sigh. *Another!*

"Stop the car, Dad! Stop! Stop!"

James, suddenly frightened, hit the accelerator. "What d'you mean, stop?"

"Dad, there are people back there that're hurt. They need help. We've got to stop and help!"

James put his foot on the brakes, slowing the SUV down.

"What? What are you talking about?"

"There was a woman in the passenger seat. She was crying. She was holding a small girl. They were yelling something to us as we drove by. There was a man, too, but he was lying on the ground. We've gotta go back."

"No. No, Silas, not a chance. It could be a trap."

"Dad, please! They need help. We can't just leave 'em."

James hesitated, confused.

"James, it can't hurt to go back and take a look," Lexie said. "We have guns and they can't rush all of us. If they really are in trouble, we should try to help. After all, look at what a complete stranger did for us. It's the least we can do. Do unto others!"

"Shit!" James spat. "Just when we were starting to make good time!"

"Time we have. They may not!" Lexie cried.

"Great. Fine. We'll go back and check it out. But if we get robbed, don't say I didn't warn you. Both of you!"

He ground the SUV to a halt and threw it into reverse. Backtracking for nearly a mile, he brought them close enough to the Jeep to see the woman through the rear-view mirror. She looked Hispanic. She was hugging a girl and mouthing the word, "help," to them. The driver's-side window had been shattered. The woman was crying while she rocked her daughter and shouted out.

"Alright," James said, slipping the shifter into Park. "Stay here in the car!"

He opened the door and slowly emerged, eyeing the family closely. He heard the woman yelling frantically in a thick accent.

"Please, sir, please help us. Please. My God, please help us!"

As James approached the driver's side, he saw that blood was splattered everywhere. A man was lying face down on the shoulder.

James held up his hand to the woman and squatted down to see what was wrong. He found a bullet hole the size of a golf ball in the back of the man's head. He took two steps backward when the woman began to beg.

"Please, sir, they shot my Lorenzo and took everything! They siphoned our gas. Please, sir, please help us! We're stuck. We have nowhere to go."

She was completely disheveled and looked as though, at one time, she had probably been pretty. The years of sun and stress had taken their toll on her. Her dark skin was now wrinkled from years of exposure yet, like her daughter, she still had striking eyes and dark brown shoulder-length hair. The small girl in her arms turned around and looked up at James. She was stunning, with dark hair, large brown eyes reddened from crying, and lips swollen from drought.

And then she stirred.

"Mister, can you please help my mommy?" She said it almost robotically, presumably in a state of shock.

Silas, no longer able to control himself, jumped out of the car and ran over to the Jeep.

"Okay, tell me what happened," James asked.

The woman hesitated, gasping for breath.

"I...I..."

"It's okay. Easy. We're here to help."

"We...we...we were driving along the road. And then...then, a truck pulled up in front of us and made us stop." She began to sob.

"Okay, okay, I know this is difficult. But if we're going to help you, you have to calm down. What happened after that?"

"We stopped the car. They got out and told us they were with the Red Cross and were there to help. We trusted them."

"Okay, I understand. And what happened next?"

"But before we even knew what was happening, they drew their guns on us. They ordered Olivia and me out of the car. They had us kneel on the side of the road. Lorenzo was just about to get out of the car when we heard the shot. Before he could even get out, they had shot him in the back of the head. He wasn't even armed!" she cried, weeping. "My poor Lorenzo. My poor, poor Lorenzo! And for Olivia to have to see it! We meant no harm to anyone! We were only doing as they asked."

Lexie, moved by the woman's pain, emerged from the SUV and opened her arms to her.

"Okay, it's going to be okay!" she said as she hugged her and then her child. "We're here now. Nobody is going to hurt you. No one will harm you anymore." She pulled the woman and child closer. "Where did the people who did this go?"

"They sped off down the road with all of our food. They took our water. They took our gas. Olivia and I will die tomorrow when the sun comes up—we will die from heat and thirst. Please, can you please help us? They killed my husband. They killed Lorenzo."

"We only have enough for ourselves…" James started to say.

Lexie looked crossly at him. "Of course we will. Silas, get them some water."

Silas hurried back to the car, grabbed a jug of water, and returned to his mother's side. Lexie offered the water to them, encouraging them to drink. She held the woman's hand in an attempt to comfort her. "Now, what's your name?"

The woman looked up over the jug, lowering it finally to her side. "I am Maria and this is Olivia." The girl lifted her head when she heard her name. She was holding a brown teddy bear in her arms.

"Hi, Olivia, sweetie!" Lexie said, reaching out to the child. "Everything is going to be okay now. We're going to help you. I promise."

Great, James thought. *We can't spare any gasoline or food or water, but my wife is taking in boarders. Great news!*

He realized they couldn't simply abandon a helpless mother and daughter, leaving them to certain death. He knew Lexie was right. Had the man in the cabin not helped his family, who knew where they might have ended up. His only option for now was to put them in the SUV and hope to find them some help when they arrived in the next big city. While it was far from ideal to have two more mouths to feed, it was the only solution James could come up with on the spot. Besides, it was only temporary.

His more immediate concern was where the bandits had gone. Had they left for good, or were they still lurking nearby, watching their every move?

James grabbed a soiled sheet from the car and covered the body as Maria and Olivia looked on in tears. James had Silas help carry Lorenzo's body into the desert. When Silas lost his grip, James continued on, dragging the man through the sand and gravel to the edge of the desert.

"We can't just leave him there! My poor Lorenzo. We can't just leave him in the desert!"

Olivia burst into tears. "Daddy! Why?"

"There is nothing we can do with him, Maria," James said. "There is nowhere else to take him, no place else to put him. And we have to get moving before the bad guys come back after us."

Maria sobbed softly, her shoulders heaving with every breath, her head nodding, before asking for one last moment with her husband. Lexie escorted them from the Jeep as James set out to transfer anything of value to their SUV.

Nothing! He realized. *They picked it clean, the bastards. Left them to die as sure as they took Lorenzo's life, the poor bastard.*

In the desert, Maria bowed her head. "Oh, Lorenzo, my love," she said as she rubbed his blood-matted hair, the tears falling from her eyes. She washed her hand across his face and closed his eyelids. "We'll never forget you, Lorenzo! We'll fight even harder for you. I know you will be in heaven waiting for us. The wait won't be long."

Olivia raised her head enough to take one last look at her father before she tucked her head back into the comfort of her mother's arms. "Bye, Daddy! I love you." Maria bowed her head, a prayer on her lips. Silas looked on in tears as he imagined how he'd feel if his father had been in Lorenzo's shoes.

With Olivia still in her embrace, Maria covered Lorenzo with the sheet and slowly backed away. She blew a kiss toward him, turned around, and walked back to the SUV. Lexie helped them into the vehicle. The car was packed tight, with Silas, Brownie, Maria, and Olivia occupying the back seat. James was just about to pull away and head back onto the highway when Maria made a request.

"Please, sir. These guns…"

James looked back. "What?"

"Can you possibly put them in the back? After what just happened, Oliva is afraid."

James looked at Lexie, who smiled lightly and nodded. James passed the rifle and the shotgun back to Silas, who stowed them behind the seat.

"There you go," James said. "All gone. But I'm keeping the revolver up here. Just in case."

"Do you have to, sir? I'd really appreciate it if there were no more guns."

But James was persistent and would not cave in to her requests. "Sorry, this is staying up here with me. To protect us all." He became slightly suspicious of her repeated attempts to move the guns, but he was certain it was simply her nerves from the traumatic events.

For more than an hour, the SUV lumbered eastward. Except for Silas, there was little conversation. He chatted away with the little girl.

"What's your bear's name?" he said, pointing.

"Her name's Fluffy," she said.

"Well, Fluffy sure is a lucky bear to have you for her mom." Olivia beamed, smiling for the first time since he'd met her.

"Yeah, she's new. I just found her. I can't wait to show Daddy!"

Show Daddy? I thought Daddy was dead…

Chapter 14

James could tell Silas felt terrible for the girl. She'd never get to show her father that bear. She'd never get to show him anything again.

Olivia's childish comment plagued Silas's head. *Her father was with her in the Jeep when he was killed. Why would she say she can't wait to show the bear to him?*

"Didn't your Daddy ever see Fluffy before?" Silas asked.

The girl looked confused; Maria appeared upset. "Let's not talk about her Daddy right now."

Odd response. James looked in the mirror. He could see his son was perplexed as well. He cleared his throat, drawing Silas's attention, and winked at the boy in the mirror. He watched for several more moments to ensure his son had caught the signal.

"I just thought your girl is a little mixed up, that's all. I thought it would be a good idea to give her a chance to..."

James shifted his eyes from the road to the back seat. *What is she glaring about?* He thought, checking the look on Maria's face.

"Dad, I've gotta use the restroom. Can you pull over?" Silas winked at his father.

"Sure. Sure, son. Just as soon as I can find a place to pull off the road."

"I think it's better that the boy hold it until we get a little farther," Maria snapped.

"What?"

"I...we don't want those bandits to catch up with us again," she said. "Who knows what they'd do to you for helping us."

James turned to Silas. "Can you hold it a little longer, son?"

Silas shook his head. "It's not that. It's that I feel sick to my stomach. Like maybe I'm going to throw up."

"Oh, God, not now," Lexie said. "What next?"

"Well, then," James said, "we'd better find somewhere."

"I don't think that's a good idea," Maria said.

"Look, my son feels sick. I don't think it would be a good idea for him to throw up in the car, do you?"

"Maybe some antacids or something," Lexie said, shifting Charlotte to one knee and rummaging through her bag. James could tell Maria was fuming. *But why? What's the big deal? And why the sudden change in attitude? What happened to the grieving grateful wife?*

James scoured the landscape for a place to pull off the road so that he could talk to his son, see if he was as confused as his father was. He looked in the mirror again, caught his son's eye, and motioned with his head toward the back. When Silas looked over his shoulder at the guns behind him, he knew what his Dad meant. He looked forward again before turning to Maria, staring right at him.

Lexie turned back, caught the look on Maria's face, and paused. "Si, I can't find anything in my bag. There's probably some antacid in the medical kit in the back. Can you see it?"

Silas looked over his shoulder once more.

"I don't think that will help," Maria said. "I think it might be best to pull over, give the boy some fresh air. A drink of water. Then we can be on our way again."

Lexie looked at James and shrugged. "Yes," she said, absently. "I guess maybe that would be best."

As James slowed the car down and pulled off onto the shoulder, Silas opened the door and jumped out. At the edge of the shoulder, he leaned forward, pretending to be dry heaving.

"I'd better go see that he's all right," James said. He got out of the car and joined his son.

"Pretend like I'm puking," Silas told his father.

"Did you catch that?" James asked, putting his arm around the boy's shoulders and leaning forward. "What the girl said about how she could hardly wait to show the bear to her father?"

"What d'you think it means? You think she was just screwed up? Or in denial or something?"

"She saw the man die. She said goodbye to him." He shook his head. "I don't know, I just don't get it."

"And did you see the way Maria was looking at me? If looks could kill!"

"Yeah. Yeah, I did see that in the mirror."

"So, what do we do?"

"For starters, just stay calm. We could be overreacting here, but we can't take any chances. Keep your eyes open until we know what's going on here."

"D'you think she was maybe just angry at us? You know, for not taking time to bury her husband?"

James shook his head. "I don't think that's it. I think we may be in trouble."

Suddenly he heard the car door open and looked back. "Oh-oh."

"What is it?"

"Maria. She just got out of the car. She's stretching, looking our way."

"Everything okay out here?" she asked.

"Pretend to wipe your mouth on your sleeve," he murmured. "Yes, everything's fine," James called back over his shoulder. "He just got a little car sick. He'll be all right now." He turned back to his son. "I'm going to distract her. You get back in the car and warn your mother there could be trouble."

As Silas headed back, James motioned to Maria. They met in front of the vehicle, where James put his arm around her shoulder.

"Hey," he said, bending his face nearer to hers. "Are you going to be okay? I know you're going through a lot and your daughter must feel terrible about her father."

He glanced at the car as Silas slipped in, grabbed the shotgun, and handed it to Lexie to place to the left of the driver's seat. He held up his fingers to his lips then whispered something in her ear. Lexie reached inside the console, grabbed the revolver, and nonchalantly handed it to Silas, who slipped it behind his back and into his pants.

Outside, Maria smiled at James. "I'll be fine. We both will, once we get back on the road again."

"Okay, then, let's go," James said, sensing some anxiety coming from Maria. She had stopped crying and her brow had furled as if she was deep in thought—or mired in concern. As they returned to the car, Maria got back into her seat and closed the door as James climbed in behind the wheel. He noticed the shotgun as he stepped over it, doing his best not to look down.

"Everybody ready?" He put the vehicle back in gear, and they continued down the highway.

After nearly another hour, James noticed flashing lights dead ahead. As they drew closer, he could see there were several lights and trucks blocking both directions of I-80 as they neared the Nebraska border. It was some sort of roadblock or checkpoint.

What the hell is it now?

He looked in the mirror and noticed Maria straining to see ahead of them. Her face held an unfamiliar look of calm, her lips turning up into a half smile. James slowed, continuing ahead, until he made out the green military truck that had passed them on the highway hours ago. He slowed down further. He knew there was about to be trouble.

"James," Lexie said. "That's the same truck that passed us earlier, isn't it?"

He turned off the car's lights and ground to a halt.

"Bad idea," Maria yelled. "Turn the lights back on. Right now."

James turned in time to see the woman pull a 9mm pistol from beneath her top.

Lexie was still looking toward the road block when she felt the cold metal of the handgun press against the back of her head.

"James!" she cried.

Maria leaned forward over the front seats, grabbing Lexie by the hair and pulling her head tight against the gun's muzzle.

"What are you doing?" James cried.

"Now listen up and listen well. You're all going to do exactly as I say, or I will blow your wife's brains all over the fucking windshield. Do you understand?"

Her face was red, her breath coming in short spurts. James thought about the shotgun, but knew he could never get it up and aimed before the woman pulled the trigger.

"What do you want? Whatever it is, you don't have to…"

"Quiet!" Her eyes had turned wild, the veins in her neck straining. "Trust me, I will not hesitate to pull this trigger if I see any of you make one false move!"

"We don't want any trouble!" James said. "Why don't you just take what you want and leave us alone?"

"Don't hurt our family," Lexie cried. "You just lost your husband. Why would you want to do this?"

"Ha! You're a naive fool who deserves everything you're going to get."

"What…what are you talking about?"

"That poor soul? He wasn't my husband. He was just some man that was in the wrong place at the wrong time. My husband's up ahead, there, waiting for us," she laughed.

"What do you want from us?" James asked.

"Everything! Your car, your food, your guns, your water, your medicine, and your son."

"What are you talking about? You're crazy. What do you want with my son?"

"Let's just say some of the guys have a thing for boys his age!" she said, looking at Silas with a smile.

"You can take anything you want, but if you touch one hair on that boy's head…" His voice grew low and ominous, his eyes wide.

"Please," Lexie pleaded. "Don't harm us."

"I'll take anything I want, you're right. Unfortunately, you're in no position to bargain. You are about to be greeted by my dear deceased husband and the rest of our group. Now, turn the headlights on and get moving."

Silas, panicking, remembered the gun stuffed inside his pants and slowly reached his right hand around, hoping not to alert the woman.

Maria was growing more agitated. "Come on, hurry it up, or I'll shoot your wife right now!" She yanked Lexie's head back hard.

"Oww!"

"You can't avoid what's ahead. You can't delay it. It's your fate."

James looked back at Silas. "Okay, okay, just stop hurting her."

"Then do as I say."

"So now I get it. The military truck we saw earlier was the scout looking for victims. You were the decoy."

"Smart man. But not smart enough."

"That's how you run your little operation, isn't it? It's how you live off the welfare of others." James looked into the rear-view mirror.

"Well, aren't you the little detective?"

"Doesn't take much detective work. It's pretty obvious. Now."

"Let's just say today is not your lucky day. Turn the goddamn headlights on so they know we're coming."

James did not comply. He knew the moment he did would be their last. He only hoped Silas had the revolver and was now only waiting to make his move. He was hopeful that Silas could muster up the courage once again to save their family.

"You've got one more chance to turn the damn lights on. If you don't, I will shoot you in the head and drive on myself."

James looked down at the console.

"Oh, yes. You're right. You can open up that console and give me the handgun in the armrest. No sudden moves."

As she held out her hand, James watched Silas lean forward. Shaking, he pulled out the gun and fired aimlessly toward Maria. The first shot missed her, taking out one of the side windows. The second hit her near her left side.

"You little fucker!" she cried. She fired her gun, pointed toward James, and a bullet struck him between his chest and shoulder. He screamed out and slunk down in his seat.

"James! Are you okay?" Lexie cried.

From the rear of the SUV came one more loud shot. Silas had fired, the slug hitting Maria directly in her head and splattering the window with blood and brains.

With her eyes wide open, Maria fell back and slumped over the broken passenger-side window. Olivia looked up in horror and screamed as she stared at her mother.

"Dad," Silas cried. "You're shot!"

"I'll be okay. Get me some towels or something to compress the wound."

Silas fished around in the SUV and found an old shirt to give to his father. Lexie set Charlotte down on her seat, reclined James's seat, and hovered over him. Olivia was screaming and crying, with her head buried in her dead mother's lap. Lexie ripped off James's shirt to expose the wound.

Oh, shit. It's not good.

The bullet had torn a large hole in his body. As the blood spurted out, James winced in pain. Lexie ripped the shirt into strips and packed them against the wound.

"Stay with me here, James. I'm going to get the bleeding stopped."

She told him to bite down on a bed sheet that Silas had found. James worried that Maria's group might have heard the gunshot, heard his screaming. And figured out the worst. While Olivia huddled against her mother's body, crying, screaming, Lexie finished patching the wound and made a combination compress and sling with a full bed sheet. At least for the moment, James was safe.

She motioned for him to crawl over to the passenger seat as she exited the SUV. She gently handed Charlotte to Silas who robotically reached his arms out to grab her. Before climbing in behind the wheel, Lexie went to the back, opened the door nearest Maria, and pulled her out of the car by her hair. Her body made a dull thumping sound as it hit the ground. Silas sat calmly in his seat with a vacant stare on his face.

"Silas, you okay?" she asked. "You did good, son. You did what you had to do! You did real good!"

Stunned, he gave no response.

Lexie positioned herself in the driver's seat and slipped the SUV into gear. "We obviously can't drive on. They're waiting for us. We'll have to turn around and find another way out. We'll have to hide for the night. We can't drive very far with the lights out."

"There was an exit a few miles back," James muttered, clutching his shoulder. "Go back and we'll find a place to sleep for the night."

"What about Olivia?" Lexie asked.

"We'll have to keep her with us for now. I guess we'll figure that out later," he said, coughing.

Lexie reached back and took the revolver from Silas, handing him the shotgun up and over the seat back. He took it without saying a word.

Chapter 15

As the car sped along the darkened road, Lexie looked in the rear-view mirror.

"No one in sight," she said softly.

She looked at Silas, sitting upright in the back seat, and Charlotte, cuddled safely in his arms. Olivia snuggled up against Brownie, who was fast asleep.

Suddenly, Silas called out. "Mom! There's the exit!"

"Oh, shit!" she said, yanking sharply on the wheel. The car hopped the shoulder, skidded through the grass, and lurched to a stop at the edge of the exit lane.

"Yeow!" James yelped. "Oww, what's happening?"

"I'm sorry, honey. The exit snuck up on me. Are you doing okay?"

He grunted and let out a burst of air.

"It won't be long. We'll find someplace to hold up for the night. So long as we don't turn on the headlights, the bandits won't be able to find us."

I wouldn't bet on it, James thought. *They must have figured out by now that Maria and Olivia are MIA. If they spread out to search the area, they probably already found Maria. Dead.*

"Where are we?" he asked.

"Looks like some deserted town named Pine Bluff. We're still in Wyoming, I'm pretty sure."

James squinted into the night. "Sure looks deserted." There were no cars, no signs of people, no hotels, and certainly no safe haven. The dark of night made the abandoned town even more eerie, and Lexie had to move slowly down the unlighted roads, despite the brightness of the moon.

"What's that?" James asked. "Off in the distance there."

Lexie looked off to where he was pointing. "Looks like the moonlight is reflecting off a statue of some sort. Maybe we'll be safe there."

"Yeah, sure. Maybe." He paused. "Why not?"

Approaching the statue, Lexie saw an adjacent parking area, but it had long ago been overtaken by piles of sand and sagebrush, so she pulled the SUV to a stop directly behind the statue. Looking up at the work of art—30 to 40 feet high, by her reckoning—she thought it had to be one of the largest statues of the Virgin Mary in the world. There was an elegant kind of beauty in its simplicity. Mary had her arms open as if to say,

"Welcome." Several other smaller statues next to it had been completely covered over by sand.

"Are you okay?" she asked, turning to her husband. He was soaked in sweat and, at the same time, shivering. *Lord, he's in bad shape.* She pulled him upright in the seat and leaned across to open the passenger door.

"Just a minute, Mom, and I'll help." Silas set Charlotte on the seat and slipped out of the vehicle. As his mother took hold of James's torso, Silas grabbed his feet and, working together, they pulled him free of the vehicle. He had lost quite a bit of blood and was drifting in and out of consciousness.

"What's Dad mumbling?"

Lexie shook her head. "I can't make it out."

They laid him down on an area of old asphalt that, for whatever reason, had not been covered in the blowing sand. Silas gently placed some blankets under his head as Lexie began to assess his wounds.

"How is he? Is it serious?"

"Gunshot wounds are always serious," she said, soberly. Lifting his shirt, she saw where the bullet had entered the rear of his shoulder and exited through his lower right. "Good sign, though. The bullet passed clear through."

She had, for the most part, reduced the bleeding to a slow steady ooze and didn't want to tempt fate by changing the bandages before absolutely necessary. She told Silas to dampen a rag, which she used to clean his arm as best she could. If the bleeding started again, he would surely die.

"Here. Here, honey," she said, lifting a plastic cup of water to James's parched lips. "Drink this. It will be good for you."

He tried pushing her away—clearly he wanted her to conserve all the water she could—but she insisted.

"He doesn't look all that good," Silas said.

"I think he's still in shock."

Silas took a deep breath and leaned in for a closer look. "That's not good. Is it?"

"No," she said absently. "It's not." James's face had turned white, and he wasn't speaking. Olivia—still in the car—began to whimper. That caused Charlotte to awaken and she, too, began to fuss. As the baby's crying grew louder, Silas went to her side. Scooping her up, he cradled her, rocking her in an effort to calm her down. She had been spattered with blood from the gunshots, and Silas tried to wipe her clean with his shirt.

"Charlotte must be hungry," Lexie called out over her shoulder. "Find her a bottle in my bag, some pre-mixed formula. Feed it to her while you rock her. Maybe she'll fall asleep again. We have to keep quiet."

Rummaging through his mother's bag, he located a bottle and got it ready for his sister then noticed Olivia, still spattered with her mother's blood.

"Here," he told her, holding out a blood-stained rag. "See if you can wipe your hands and face, okay?"

The girl hesitated before taking the rag and clutching it tightly.

"It's going to be okay. Everything's going to work out fine," he told her.

"I want my Daddy," she said, fighting back more tears. "I wanna be with my Daddy."

"Well, we'll find your Daddy as soon as it gets light—in the morning. Okay? We'll try to find him then. You'll see. Everything will work out."

As Lexie cradled her husband, James began to stir. He looked up. "We can't stay here," he mumbled. "We're not safe here." He tried to sit up, but failed. "They'll be here any moment looking for us. This is too wide open. There's no cover."

"You're in no shape to move, James," she whispered. "Besides, we can't go anywhere tonight. Not without our headlights. We just can't risk turning them on with them nearby."

"I saw a mobile home somewhere as we drove into town. It had a garage. Let's get back in the car and hide the SUV in it until morning. We'll have a better chance that way," he said.

Lexie knew he was right. Sitting out in the open the way they were made them vulnerable. She looked up at the statue and noticed the illumination from some car lights shining off its arms. She looked up and back along the highway from where they'd just come. Sure enough, several vehicles were creeping slowly ahead, searching for some sign of them.

"You're right," she said. "Are you up to being moved again?"

Before he could respond, she called out.

"Silas!"

"Yeah?"

"Shhh." She motioned with her finger to her lips. "Come on over here and help me get your father back in the car."

"Are we leaving?"

"We have to hide the car," she said, motioning toward the highway.

"Who is it? The bandits?"

She put her hands beneath James's back and began to lift. "I think so." She took a deep breath. "Got his legs?"

"Got 'em."

"Okay. Lift!"

99

They struggled with him back to the front seat of their vehicle. "Can you get your legs in?" Lexie asked. He lifted first one and then the other, and settled against the seat back.

Silas looked his father in the eye. "When we get through all this," the boy said, "I think one of us will need to go on a diet!"

James smiled up at him and reached out his hand. "It's a deal," he said. "Have anyone in particular in mind?"

Once back in the vehicle, Lexie started the ignition and slowly crept back onto the street, back to that part of town where James had spotted the mobile home. She slowed to a halt and Silas jumped out and opened the door to the free-standing garage. Lifting the overhead door, he stepped aside as his mother pulled the SUV in. As everyone got out of the car, the intense moonlight was streaming through the windows in the rear. Silas helped James out before handing him over to Lexie.

"Close the overhead, will you, son? And then bring Charlotte inside. And the diaper bag." She paused. "Oh, and the camping light. Can you do that?"

She heard him grumble something before wiping the sweat from her eyes as she helped her husband hobble into the home. The place appeared empty—a field of wheat after the locusts had swarmed through. There wasn't a single piece of furniture. The green carpet that covered the floor was so badly stained, it crunched as they walked across it. The walls were peppered with holes and the placed smelled of cigarette-smoke scented filth.

"This is it?" James said. "This is what I married you for?"

"Oh, shoosh. You're alive, aren't you?"

She settled him down against the corner of what was once the dining nook, propping him against the wall.

"Not much of a hideout, is it?"

Lexie looked around. "Not much," she sighed.

Suddenly, James craned his head toward the lights flashing through the window.

"What is it?" Lexie asked.

"Crap. That's what I was afraid of."

Silas appeared in the doorway, carrying Charlotte and the diaper bag. He turned on the lantern and shone it on his parents.

"Turn that off!" James called. The boy dropped the bag and handed Charlotte to Lexie.

"What is it?" Silas asked, switching off the light.

"They're coming." He pulled himself up to the window sill and stared out at a vehicle that had just turned off the highway, heading in their direction. "If they stop here, they'll find us for sure. We're like sitting ducks."

"Where's Olivia?" Lexie asked.

"I left her in the car. She's sound asleep," Silas said.

"You'd better go get her."

"Why? What's up?"

"Hurry," she urged. Silas ran back to the garage and pulled Olivia from the seat. He tugged her by the arm, back toward the house.

Lexie looked out the window. In the moonlight, she spied two glistening streams stretching on for miles.

"A train," she said to James. "Look. It's an old abandoned freight train not a hundred feet away."

"Of course!" James said. "We can leave the car in the garage and sneak out the back door. We'll hide in one of the empty boxcars. They'll never think of looking for us there. And I doubt anyone will check the garage once they see the trailer is empty."

Lexie tucked the revolver into her pants, picked up Charlotte, and grabbed Olivia by the hand, pulling her out the back door toward the train. Silas grabbed the two long guns and put his arm around his father.

"Are you okay?" Lexie asked over her shoulder.

"Honey," James said, grimacing. "You just go on ahead and pick us out a nice one." He motioned with his palms. "Give me the baby."

She paused. "Are you sure?"

"I'm not dead," he said. "I'm pretty sure I can hold our daughter."

She handed Charlotte over to him, patted Olivia on the head, and hurried on ahead to find an open car. By the time James had crossed the yard, Lexie jumped down from one of the cars.

"Here!" she called softly, motioning with her hand. James hobbled beside his son as the lights from the approaching truck appeared down the road.

"Hurry. Can you climb aboard?"

He grabbed hold of a ladder attached to the side of the car and, turning his head, muttered, "Give me a push. I'll make it."

Once he was on board, Lexie handed Charlotte to him and helped Olivia climb in, with Silas close behind. As Lexie joined them, she heard the growl of a distant diesel engine grow steadily louder. Brownie let out a soft growl.

"No!" Silas said, holding his finger to his lips. "Be quiet, boy." The dog looked around before settling down next to Olivia.

"Do you hear?" Lexie asked.

James nodded. "Yeah. It's that military truck again. Getting closer."

"Can we close the door?"

James shook his head. "We don't want to make any noise. They don't know we're here. Let's not tip them off."

Oliva began to whimper, and Silas reached down to comfort her.

Suddenly, they heard the engine go quiet as two doors opened and slammed shut again. Through the slats in the car, James made out two men beneath the silvery glow of the moon. He held up his hand for everyone to be quiet.

"They were here, goddamnit!" one man barked. "No doubt. Look at the tire tracks over here. And the footprints in the sand."

"Sure enough," said another man. His voice was deeper, gruffer, as if he'd smoked two packs of cigarettes daily all his life. "And the tire tracks lead right across the street to that there trailer over there."

The first man lowered his voice. "Okay, let's see if the car is in the garage. If it is, we've got 'em."

"Shit," James cursed softly.

"The motherfucker that killed my wife is gonna pay! I'm gonna cut off his balls and feed them to him one at a time."

"Shh. Keep it down," the gravel voice said. "First things first, let's get the kid out before we start shooting anyone."

"All right, but as soon as I get Olivia, I'm going to go outlaw on them."

James watched as the men drew their pistols and crept toward the trailer home. He heard the garage door open and one of the men saying something unintelligible. After several more moments, he saw the men reappear at the rear of the house.

Lorenzo—Maria's husband—yelled out. "We know you're in there. Throw your weapons out and come out with your hands up!"

When there was no response, the other man shouted. "Last chance! Put your hands up and step out of the trailer!"

Suddenly, the men rushed the door, kicking it open. Guns at the ready, they stormed inside. Someone lit a flashlight, and Lorenzo's voice called out for his daughter.

"Olivia! Olivia, are you here?"

James looked over at the girl, who appeared not to recognize the voice. The men came out of the house several moments later as two others, similarly dressed in dirty fatigues, joined them.

"What's up?"

Lorenzo shone the light on the ground. "They're not in there. You and Hank go on around the front. They left their SUV in the garage. It's loaded with supplies."

"Well, wasn't that considerate of them?" he smirked.

Lorenzo paused. "Look it over. See if there's any food or guns, anything we can use tonight."

"Will do."

"And grab the keys from the ignition, just in case they have any plans to return tonight."

"Hey!" the gravel voice called. "Here's some tracks. Several different people. They lead away from the house..." He paused. "They're headed for the train."

"Let's go!"

James pulled himself up against the siding, his shotgun loaded and ready. His pulse pounded, his heart raced as he watched the men come steadily closer. They paused at the first car they came to, and Lorenzo tugged on the latch.

"Locked," he said.

"Next one's open," gravel voice said, pointing. "Let's check it out."

"Wait a minute. The footprints have stopped."

The second man looked down. "They either took off down the tracks or they're holed up in one of these cars."

Lexie stepped to within inches of her husband and whispered, "What are we going to do? They know we're here."

He shook his head, his eyes glued on the two figures drifting closer to them. "Silas, take Charlotte and Brownie over to the corner and scrunch down. It's dark there. Maybe they won't see you."

"What about Olivia?"

"Olivia, honey," Lexie whispered. "Go over there with Silas and Brownie. They'll watch over you."

James, clutching the shotgun, backed into the far corner with his family. Charlotte, increasingly uncomfortable in the stifling heat, began to whimper. James's eyes popped open. "Shoosh her up!"

Before the boy could respond, Lorenzo stopped. "What was that?"

"Came from up there. That black car. They're in that train car!" gravel voice said, motioning.

Suddenly, Olivia jumped up. "Daddy! Daddy!"

Oh, great, James thought. *What next?*

"Help me, Daddy! I'm over here."

"Olivia!" her father called.

"James, they're coming!"

James's mind raced. "Don't come any closer!" he yelled. "We are armed and we have your daughter. If you try anything, she's dead."

"Dad, what are you saying?"

He threw the boy a worried glance.

"You hurt Olivia, and I'll make damn sure you don't walk out of here alive. You or anyone else in there with you!"

James thought for several more moments. "Well, it appears we have quite the predicament then! We have four people in here with guns, and you have four people with guns. Except that you can't use your guns because we have your daughter in here. So I think I'm the one controlling this situation."

"Daddy!" Olivia called again. Lexie went to grab her, but James motioned her away.

"And I won't hesitate to shoot your girl if you try anything. Anything at all, you understand?"

"Well, ain't you the wise-ass. You gonna sit in there all night and into tomorrow's heat? You'll die in a matter of hours. So you ain't controlling jack shit," Lorenzo yelled. "So, why don't you just send Olivia out and we'll go on our merry way?"

"We're not stupid," James yelled, aware suddenly how hard his heart was beating.

It's a stalemate. At least for now…

Chapter 16

"Daddy! Come and get me, Daddy!"

James, shaking from weakness and loss of blood, had to support himself against his wife. If he sat down, he wasn't sure he'd be strong enough to get back up. Lexie looked into his eyes and took the gun from his hands.

"Look," she called, "nobody can win this fight. We don't want to hurt your little girl and I'm sure you don't want to hurt our boy and baby. Let's just end this and come to a resolution!"

"You killed my wife!" Lorenzo yelled.

"It wasn't by desire. She tried to rob us. She pulled a gun and threatened our lives. We had a right to protect ourselves. We only did what we had to do."

Once again there was a pause, an ethereal silence settling over the players. James heard the men whispering, but couldn't quite make out what they were saying. From beyond the tracks, he heard their truck door slam and saw two more men join them.

"What the hell you mean?" one of the men said. "We can't just blast 'em. Olivia's in there."

"I'm telling you. Open fire, cut 'em down. Storm them before they have a chance to react. I'll grab Olivia."

James motioned to Silas. "Put her down and grab that rifle. If we're going to die, we're going to die together."

"But, Dad…"

He nodded and watched as the boy did as he was told.

"I'm not risking Olivia. They'll shoot us before we can even jump onto the train."

Lexie held up her hand. "Here's what's going to happen," she called. "Follow my instructions and everyone walks out of here alive."

Lorenzo turned to the other man, motioning with his hand for him to circle around the back of the car. James's eyes lit up.

"No you don't!" he called. "You stay right where you are. Move just one muscle, and we start unloading lead."

"That's better!" Lexie shouted. "Now, one of you go back to the house and bring our SUV around. Park it right outside this car. Leave the engine running. You can also leave the keys to your truck in the SUV."

"What?"

"You heard me. Then you get out and walk back to your truck and wait. We'll get into the SUV and leave Olivia here with your keys."

Lorenzo looked at his partner, who shrugged. "How do we know you'll keep your word? How do we know you won't take Olivia with you?"

"We don't have any need for her. Besides, you can talk to her the entire time, so you know we're living up to our bargain. We'll drive away for good. You get your daughter and your keys, and nobody gets hurt. We all walk away. No child needs to be harmed."

The men huddled, whispering among themselves. James wished he could make out what they were saying. Finally, the leader emerged from the group.

"Okay, it's a deal. But if you harm one hair on that little girl's head, there'll be an all-out bloodbath."

James watched as the glow of their spotlights reflected off the car. *One last chance to catch us off guard.*

"And you can kill those lights and step back from the train."

Lorenzo motioned for their keys, handing them to the other man. "Now go drive our SUV around here!"

James stared at his wife with amazement. *We may just win this battle.*

"You think they're going to try to pull something?"

James shook his head. "I don't think they can. Not if they want to get Olivia back alive."

After huddling again, James saw Lorenzo hand the keys to his partner, who started running off toward the trailer. Moments later, he heard the SUV's engine rev up, the scrunching of the wheels against the sand and gravel signaling their approach.

"Have him park right next to the train car door," Lexie called as she spotted the lights of the vehicle approaching. "And no funny business."

"I want to hear my daughter's voice before you drive off. I swear on my life you'll regret any games!"

"We're not planning on any games," Lexie said. "We have enough mouths to feed without her tagging along. She belongs with her father. So, as long as you guys don't play any games, this should end up well for all."

"Except my wife!" the man yelled.

"We told you about that!" she shouted, irritated.

Lexie and Silas positioned themselves on each side of the sliding door, their guns cocked and ready. James lay down with Charlotte and Brownie by his side, blood trickling down his side. He had the shotgun pointed toward the door. Lexie positioned Olivia, now frozen in fear, right in front of the door, so that the man driving the SUV wouldn't get any crazy notion of spraying the car with lead. As she peeked around the corner, she could see the SUV's headlights.

"Here's your daughter!" Lexie called as the lights illuminated the car. "You can see she's safe and sound and anxious to be with her Daddy!"

"Daddy!" the girl sobbed. "Daddy, I want to go home!"

"All right. It's all right, honey. Daddy will come and get you in just a minute. Just be good and wait for me, you hear?"

Lexie turned to Silas. "If you ever prayed in your life, son, now's the time."

As the driver stepped out of the SUV, he went to close the driver's-side door.

"Leave it open!" Lexie called. "And come up slowly with your truck keys, hands up."

The man, his pistol at his side, approached the boxcar. "That's close enough!" she cried. "Now, throw your truck keys up here. Then walk slowly back to the others. After that, I want you all to cross over to the opposite side of the tracks and stay there until we've driven away. Then you can come get Olivia and your keys."

"Olivia is okay," the man yelled back to the others. "She looks fine. Unharmed."

Lorenzo called back. "All right. Give 'em the fucking keys and come on back."

The man pulled the keys out of his pocket and tossed them into the boxcar. They landed with a loud rattle, and Silas fell on them. The man slowly retreated back to the others.

Lexie gave the man a few minutes to walk back toward his group.

"He's reached the others," James said, still watching through a crack in the siding.

Lexie nodded. "Okay, get across the tracks!"

The men looked confused.

"Just cross over to the other side of the train!"

"Goddamn it, lady! We're holding up our end of the deal. Just get in your goddam car and leave!"

"We're not moving until you cross over. Your choice!" Lexie said.

Muttering under his breath, Lorenzo motioned the others to do as they were told and, when they had all but disappeared from sight, James barked out the orders.

"Lexie, you first. Si, hand your mother the baby. Make sure Brownie gets in the back."

"What about you?" Lexie asked.

"I'll keep an eye out to make sure they don't come after us, then I'll climb down and get in the car."

"Sure you'll be okay to do that?" she frowned.

"Yeah, just worry about them for the moment. I'll be fine."

As they shifted into action, James heard Lorenzo shout out. "Okay, we did just like you said. Now let's get this over with!"

Satisfied that the men were far enough away, James motioned his family to move. As they scampered down, he turned to Olivia. "Just sit still, honey. Your Daddy will be here in a minute to help you down, okay? Then he'll take you home."

Unsure of what was happening, she nodded, her eyes brimming with tears. James patted her on the head and clambered down from the boxcar, slipping into the SUV's passenger seat. "Everyone ready? Silas? Charlotte?"

Brownie let out a sharp yelp.

"Yeah, you, too," he said.

"Oh, fuck!" Silas cried.

"Silas!"

"Dad! They took some of our water. There's at least two jugs missing."

James looked around. "What? We have to go back. We have to go back to get our water, the sons of a bitch."

"Not on your life, mister. We're getting the heck out of here. Now!"

"But, Mom, we need our water. We could die without it. "

"We'll die if we go back!"

"How much is left? I see three, four jugs," James said. "No! Wait! Remember the stuff I hid?"

"You're right," Silas smiled, pulling out a gallon of water from under the seat.

"And I stashed more under the hood, remember?" James said. "I tied a couple of jugs to the wheel well."

"You're right," Silas said, exhaling softly, "You did."

"Let's get moving," Lexie said as she wheeled the car around and stepped on the accelerator. In the rear-view mirror, she saw the men scrambling for the boxcar. "We've got to make some time. They'll be on our trail before you know it!"

James let out a sigh and settled back in his seat. He looked up at her with a silly grin on his face.

"What? What is it?" Lexie asked. "What's wrong with you? They're going to be right on our tail, and you're laughing?"

James reached into his pocket and pulled out the set of keys the man had tossed into the boxcar. "Not without these, they won't." He held them up like a prize.

"Dad! Great thinking!" A huge grin lit up Silas's face. Brownie barked again.

"What about Olivia? If we leave them stranded, she could die."

"Not likely, once they figure out how to hotwire that truck. This just gives us a little extra time for our escape."

"Time to put more distance between us and them," Silas grinned.

"And to find some medical help for you somewhere," Lexie said.

James raised his brows. "Wrong!"

"What do you mean, wrong?"

"We have more important things to do—like finding some water to replace what those bastards stole from us." He turned around again. "Si, how much do we have stashed back there?"

The boy reached beneath the seat. "Looks like…four jugs of water. And the two under the seat…and the two you stowed under the hood."

"Well," he said, settling back against the seat, "at least that's something."

"It's not enough to get us where we're going though, is it?"

"No," he said. "We've got another thousand miles or more to go. We'll have to find some water somewhere along the way."

Silas hesitated, looking behind him to the back of the SUV. "Ummm, Mom, how much gas do we have?"

Lexie looked down at the gas gauge. "Three quarters of a tank. Why?"

"Um…because that's all we've got! Our gas is gone."

"Are you fucking kidding me? Goddamn it!" James hollered. "Those assholes!"

Making some calculations in his head, James figured they could travel about 600 miles with the gas remaining in the vehicle. While that would get them close, it would not get them all the way home. He knew he would need to find a way to get them more gas by any means necessary. There was nothing in James's mind that was going to prevent them from making it to his hometown. He briefly had Lexie pull the car over so he could grab the items that he had hidden in the engine. He was pleased to find them still intact, yet also very hot.

"But at least we're okay for now." Lexie said. "We've got some water and our food and supplies."

"Yeah. We're okay for now."

"Then we're home free."

He looked at her blankly. *Yeah, home free until the men back in town are able to hotwire that truck and be on our trail again. Or would they even bother?*

"Things could have been worse, James. Someone was watching over us back there."

Except that, unless we find more water, we won't last another three days. Not in this heat. And water is even scarcer than gas!

The situation was bleak at best, and anxiety hit both James and Lexie like a ton of bricks. They had been so careful with their stockpile only to now be left with a depleted supply. It was a hard pill for both of them to swallow and they worried desperately that they would not be able to find enough supplies to get them to Ohio. To make matters worse, all of the running around had them parched. Yet they were hesitant to drink due to their limited supply of water.

Privately, Lexie was concerned about James's gunshot wound. With no medications, no bandages or gauzes, how would they possibly manage? They had more questions than answers and the stress was becoming nearly too much to handle.

Chapter 17

He never thought in his wildest dreams he would see a lake. He never dreamed he'd get to jump into one. Nor see a pond—nor a river or stream or even a creek. His father had told him stories throughout his youth about such miraculous places. The elder man had grown up surrounded by water. He had fished and swum and sailed and canoed and waded until his skin turned all white and prune-like. He had told his son about the time his parents had taken him to one of the largest water parks in the world.

Now, finally, here he was, years later, lapping up the crystalline waves, laying on the sand, soaking up the sun beneath an azure blue sky.

"Another virgin piña colada, sir?" He turned, startled, to find a black-skinned tall thin man, dressed in a white shirt, black vest, and royal blue Bermuda shorts, standing by his side. Si's personal lifesaver, he had made it his duty to anticipate his customer's every desire—even before he desired it. Si turned toward his muscular friend lying, with rippled abs and chiseled chin, on the sand next to him, smiled, and held up two fingers.

"Very good, sir. I'll be back in a moment."

Si couldn't wait. He had other fish to fry, other things to experience. "I'll be back in a sec," he told his friend. "Keep my drink cool." His friend looked up, concerned, as Si wandered off toward the pool. Slipping silently into the waist-deep water, he felt his feet against the polished glass bottom, felt the cares of his life slip away, felt everything anyone could ever hope to feel.

He lay back, stretching his arms out and pumping his feet rhythmically to the cadence of a mariachi band playing in the distance. Giant magnolia blossoms, white and pink and red, floated by like a tiny armada of pleasures. Rolling over, he ducked his head beneath the water and kicked off hard, propelling himself along the bottom. Alone. In paradise.

He popped back up at the far end of the pool, just shy of a huge rock formation off which snaked a placid trickle of water, joined halfway down by two others so that, by the time the stream hit the pool, it was a roaring waterfall.

He stood up, worked his way to the edge of the pool, and looked out over the turquoise surface of the nearby sea. Sails of all sizes and shapes glided effortlessly across the surface. Wakes from motorboats pulling water-skiers cut sharp diagonals in the sea.

He selected a rubber tube from a rack at the pool's edge and slipped atop it, his feet dangling freely over the side. As the current picked up speed, the water splashing over him stung his face. Rolling across the manmade eddies, he spun around in a circle, letting out a playful yelp. Looking up, he saw his family sitting in lounge chairs—waving, laughing, his mother hoisting a pink fruity cocktail in mock toast to Si's accomplishments.

"Hey, you guys. Come on in. Charlotte, too. The water's great!" he called.

His mother and sister laughed and waved, but his father motioned for him to meet him at the top of the slide. Si looked around, not understanding. But as the tube spun around several more times, it slowed, approached an endless waterfall, and Si saw his father there waiting for him.

"Where are we going?" the boy asked. His father pointed off in the distance and down. Si let his eyes trace the route, turned, and shook his head.

"Uh-uh," he said. "Are you crazy?"

His father said not a word, laughed, and pushed himself off as Si watched. Down the slide he sped, faster and farther than Si could have imagined, through an opening to a giant glass tube that propelled him even more rapidly through an enormous fish tank. He finally emerged at the opposite end, where he was dumped into a deep pool at the end of the ride.

Si's father looked up and waved, and Si felt the fear strike his chest. He couldn't possibly follow him. He couldn't possibly take the plunge. But as the water behind him grew deeper and faster, the tube lifted up and over the edge of the slide and began its downward run.

"Whoooaaa!" he heard himself yell as he went under the water, struggling for air, gasping for breath.

Suddenly, he popped up again, spying his mother and Charlotte smiling and waving to him from down below. And when he came to the end of the pool, the tube smashed the wall hard, tossing Si up and out onto the hard earth-and-sand berm. He looked around for his parents, but no one was there. He dusted himself off, wondering where all the water went, when in the distance he heard the unmistakable sound of motorcycle engines. Approaching. Fast!

"Shit!" he yelled, not quite knowing why. He looked around, instinctively searching for someplace to hide and, by the time he turned back, one of the cyclists—a huge bear of a man on a Harley with long streaming hair and teeth of gold and silver—whirred by him, barely missing the boy with a chain he spun over his head. When Si looked up again, he saw two more bikers bearing down on him. He could see they were laughing. One had a swastika on his jacket; the other, a skull and crossbones.

Si whirled on his heels and, kicking up rocks and sand, began to run. Faster than he'd ever run before, faster than the bikes could travel but, when he was just about comfortable in thinking he had outrun them, the first biker was back, revving his engine and picking up speed, bearing straight down on him again, laughing that evil horrible growl.

Suddenly, as Si leaped off to one side, he found his feet growing heavy. He looked down.

"Quicksand!"

He lifted up first one leg, barely, and then the other. He thought he heard his family laughing and playing in the water and looked around desperately. He tried to call out for help, but only silence escaped his lips.

As he struggled to free himself, he lost his balance and tumbled over, his hands getting sucked into the thick mess, now bubbling and hissing like a cauldron of death. He tried to take a breath and call out again, but ended up choking and coughing. Finally, with one last Herculean effort, he leaped up with all his strength, and the slough spit him out like a child spits a watermelon seed.

Landing on his feet, he looked around and spied two men running toward him. Both had handguns drawn, aimed right at his head. As one of the men opened fire, Si ducked down, the bullet just grazing the side of his head. He turned to run, but stumbled once more into the quicksand and, when he looked up for help, he saw his mother, father, and baby sister standing at the pool's edge, laughing.

"No! No! No!"

Lexie whirled around, drawing the wheel sharply to the right. James, dozing in the front, popped his head up. "What is it? What's the matter?"

"Silas!" Lexie called, reaching back with one hand to shake his arm. "Silas, wake up! You're having a bad dream."

He let out a deep sigh as sweat rolled off his face. "Oh...wow."

"It's okay, honey. Only a dream. You're okay."

"Oh, my God. It was awful. You were in it, Mom. And Dad. And those guys who tried to kill us in the boxcar. And...and..."

"It's all right, honey. You're safe, now. Right, James?" She looked at her husband, who had already nodded off once more.

"Man that was intense! Really cool!"

Lexie had been driving for several hours when they crossed into Nebraska. It was the middle of the night and, once again, they needed to find a safe place to bed down. As they neared the small railroad town of North Platte, she exited the highway, looking for a safe place to camp. To her surprise, there were other people in the town. As she passed the local Holiday Inn Express, she saw two cars parked in the lot. She drove on.

A short distance down the road, she saw what appeared to be a railroad control center with a tower stretching up into the night sky. There were no cars and no signs of other people, so she pulled the SUV up to the building, coming to a stop safely out of view of the road.

"Wake up, everyone. We're done driving for the night."

Silas rubbed his eyes and stretched his arms as he picked up his sister who was still sound asleep. "Where are we? Are we getting out?"

"Nebraska," she yawned. "I just can't drive any farther tonight." She turned to her husband, who blearily opened his eyes and looked around.

"We there?"

"No," she said, "we're here. We're going to spend the night. We're in North Platte, Nebraska."

She took a cloth and dabbed at his forehead. He was sweating badly and seemed confused. She passed him a jug of water, encouraging him to drink. Shaking as he lifted it to his lips, he spilled some of it down his neck. Lexie grabbed hold of the jug to help steady it.

She placed her hand on his forehead. "We need to get you something for that infection. You're running a fever," she murmured absently. "Si, help me get your father into the building."

"What about Charlotte?"

"Just leave her on the seat for a minute until we get your father settled in. Lock the door."

Coming around to the passenger seat, Silas and Lexie helped James out of the car. "That's it," she said. "Put your arms around our shoulders."

"My legs are asleep," James mumbled.

"That's all right. Just hang onto us."

As they climbed the steps to the doors, Silas reached out for the handle.

"It's locked."

"Well…kick it in or something. Here. James, lean up against the building."

Silas took a large step back, raised his foot, and hit the door as hard as he could. The door didn't budge.

"Oww!"

"Careful, honey. Don't hurt yourself!"

"Don't hurt myself!"

"Come on. Try again. I'll help. On the count of three."

As she counted down, the two of them kicked the door in, springing the lock. The door swung wide, banging the wall as it gave way.

"Go get Charlotte, Si, while I find somewhere for your dad," Lexie said, glancing around.

"She stinks, Mom," he wrinkled his nose as he returned with the baby. He removed Charlotte's diaper and discarded it outside. "We're all out," he said. "What should I use now?"

Lexie thought for a moment and realized there was nothing they could do. "We'll search around for anything we can use. Until then, she'll just have to go naked."

"Gross."

"We'll look around the building. There's got to be something we can use until we find more."

She scoped out the dark building and found an area that was once a small gift shop for the visitors' center. While there was not any food or water, there was a plethora of T-shirts, sweatshirts, toys, and other train related items. Lexie collected all the clothing items she could find that would serve the family as new clothes, diapers, and bedding. She brought the items back into the main room and showed them to Silas, who was feeding his sister. Brownie was whimpering and staring at Silas and Lexie, panting and groaning with hunger. He was pawing at both of them in an attempt to be fed and given water. The time had come for Lexie to have the depressing conversation with Silas that she had hoped would never come about.

"Silas, you know we'll not be able to continue to give Brownie any water or food forever. We don't even have enough for us, sweetie," she said softly.

"What?" Silas said as he shot his mother a sharp look.

"Well, baby…Brownie is a dog! When it comes to feeding your sister, father, and you, or feeding a dog….well, I'm afraid there isn't much of a choice."

"You mean starve him?" Silas asked, his voice rising. "Let him die of thirst?" he yelled.

"It's our only option son," she said sadly.

"You can just forget that idea, Mother!" Silas's brow furrowed. "He's part of the family and I won't allow that to *ever* happen. Do you understand?"

Lexie opened her mouth then closed it again. Realizing she was not going to win this argument without alienating her son, she relented. "You know what, Silas?" she sighed. "You're right and I was wrong. We'll share our food with Brownie. We're in this all for one and one for all."

"You're damn right," he said, still glaring at his mother with anger.

"Sorry, honey." She shrugged apologetically. *This isn't the time or place for this conversation. If the time comes when we really have to choose, I'll have no choice but to force his hand. He'll hate me, but we have to do whatever we need to in order to survive. Now's not the time. Let's hope that time never comes…*

Chapter 18

With a very light dinner behind them and James already dozing, Lexie ripped a T-shirt and wrapped Charlotte in it. Silas had found some old packing material and had made a comfy-looking nest for his sister and himself. Lexie looked at James, a crease marking her forehead.

"We're going to have to get your father some help first thing tomorrow. He's only going to get worse," she said, turning around to find Silas sound asleep with his sister cradled against his arm. Lexie looked over at James, his mouth wide open, sweat running down his face.

She grabbed another clean shirt and ripped it into strips to apply to her husband's wound. James grunted in his sleep when she removed the old bandages. She poured some water on the wound and packed the hole with the cloth. James winced, but still didn't wake. She was grateful for that.

Before turning in, Lexie set the guns within easy reach of both Silas and herself. *How times have changed*, she thought, remembering the not-too-distant past when James was the family protector.

Lying down against a makeshift pillow, she heard Silas stir.

"Mom?" he said groggily.

"What is it, Si? I thought you were asleep."

"Is...is Dad going to be all right?"

"Your father is hurt pretty badly, son."

"How bad? What are you trying to say, Ma? Be real honest with me."

"I'm not trying to say anything, honey. I'm telling you he's hurt badly and we need to find him some help."

Lexie heard the heaviness in her son's throat. "Dad's going to...he's gonna die, isn't he?"

Lexie sat up and looked into his eyes. "We're going to do everything we can for him," she said. "That's all anyone can do. We have to find him help."

Silas turned his back to his mother without saying another word.

Although she was exhausted, Lexie couldn't get James out of her mind. *What if he does die? What if we can't get him some help in time?* They'd been a team since high school. If anything went wrong, if they couldn't get him through this, she knew she'd have to be strong for Silas and Charlotte, but she also knew she would feel dead inside.

There has to be a way. He's strong. He'll hold on a while longer.

Lexie realized she had drifted off to sleep because, when she opened her eyes, the light of morning shone through the windows and her mouth was dry as the dust on the floor. The room had already become so hot that she could hardly breathe. James was still dozing soundly. He'd sweated so badly during the night that his hair was clumped together, and a small pool of perspiration puddled around his head. She reached for the jug of water and, when she found it empty, made her way quietly to the SUV to grab another. Silas had placed the remaining supplies in the middle of the seat. Seeing that there were only two jugs of water remaining, she grabbed the one nearest to the door and made her way back inside.

"Hi, Mom," Silas said, looking down at Charlotte, who had just opened her eyes and was cooing softly. "How's Dad?"

"Morning, baby. I'm going to give your father some water and then I want you to drink some. Okay?"

"I'm not all that thirsty. I thought I'd go upstairs to the lookout tower? Maybe I can see something from up there."

Lexie nodded. "You need to drink something. You can't get dehydrated more than you already are."

"Okay, Ma! Can I go then?"

"All right. Be careful, though, and come right back."

She watched as he walked over to the steps and, grabbing the hand rail, took them two at a time. She turned her attention to James, who was still snoring. She lifted his bandage and saw the pus oozing from the wound and a new ring of dark red surrounding it.

This is bad. Between the loss of blood and the dehydration—and now this infection—we've got to get some help.

She gently lifted his head and, opening his mouth, trickled a slow stream of water inside. He swallowed instinctively and eventually opened his eyes.

"Good morning," he said gruffly.

"Good morning, sleepyhead. I was beginning to think you were never going to get up." She capped the jug and set it to one side. "How do you feel?"

"I've been better."

"I know, honey. We're going to concentrate on finding you some help today. There are people around town, and someone has to know where to get some medical help, or at least some antibiotics."

"I had a dream," he said, still groggy.

She chuckled. "I'm sure you did. You've been out like a light for more than eight hours."

"It was about you."

"It was?" She took a damp piece of cloth and dabbed at the festering wound.

"Oww!"

"Oh, I'm sorry. I know that hurts."

"No. It's all right."

"So," she said absently. "What about me?"

"I dreamed...now, don't take this wrong. But I dreamed that I was dying."

"James, don't!"

"No. It was all right. I dreamed I was dying, and I suddenly realized that there's nothing on earth I loved more than you. Nothing I've ever loved more."

"James, please..." She felt the tears welling up in her eyes, felt the sudden helplessness of their situation. The hopelessness.

"It...it...it's okay. I realized then and there just how lucky I've been to have you."

"And I love you, too, James. More than I could ever say."

"I realized, with you by my side, that I love you so much it hurts. I love Silas more than words can ever say. Charlotte is my little princess. Please never forget how much I love you and always will."

"James, stop it! You're scaring me. Please don't talk about death." She felt the tears break free, wending their way down her cheeks as she lifted the back of her hand to swipe at them. "Nobody is dying here today. Nobody is dying here ever. We're going to get you well. You'll see."

He looked up. "Oh, honey. Please don't cry. I'm not dead yet," he said with a half-cocked smile.

James rested his head back onto the cloth and closed his eyes. Lexie stared at him blankly, stroking his hair and holding his hand.

In the observation deck, Silas looked out, past the windows caked with dirt and grime, at the 360-degree view surrounding him. Railroad tracks spun out in every direction, like the strands in a spider's web. Dozens of trains, long since given up for dead, lay dormant along the tracks.

"Wow," he said, taking in the sight. He could only imagine the hustle and bustle of the freight yards before North Platte, too, had surrendered to the drought and heat. He imagined how many people there were, scurrying about the building—how many more ran in and out and between the cars down below in the yard. Like everything else he knew, the town was dead as was the earth surrounding it. There was nothing but brown for as far as the eye could see, other than the silent and still decaying trains below him.

And then he felt it. Slightly, at first, as if the tower were swaying. *Maybe it's just the wind*, he thought. But he was wrong. Suddenly, the building jarred and shook, and the floor beneath his feet rose up to meet him before falling suddenly away. He grabbed a railing in front of the glass windows, realizing suddenly that that was the last place he should be when a quake struck.

He tumbled to the ground and tried crawling toward the stairwell as the thick glass began to crack and crumble. Brownie, who had been with James and Lexie in the visitors' center, darted up the stairs and stood at the top, barking loudly. Silas made his way to a door frame. He grabbed Brownie and rolled into a ball, covering both of them as glass and plaster from the ceiling came raining down on them. He could hear Lexie calling out his name.

And then, just as at the cabin that day, it was all over. Silas slowly unfurled himself and looked around. Half of the windows had shattered, and the floor was covered in broken glass. He picked up Brownie and carried him to the staircase. He set him down, following him along the stairwell toward the ground floor.

As he reached the door, Lexie came running up to him and grabbed him. "Oh, my God, Silas, are you okay?"

"Wow. That was spooky. You should see all the glass up there. I was looking out the window…"

"You're all right, though. You're not hurt?"

"No, I'm not hurt." He paused, looking down. "We're not hurt, are we, boy?"

The dog let out a low whimper.

"Thank the Lord," she said. "Let's all just stick together from now on, okay?"

After cleaning up, packing up the SUV, and grabbing a quick bite to eat, Lexie helped James get back into the car while Silas took care of the baby. Suddenly, James began to jerk violently, bending over at the gut and heaving. Lexie did her best to dry his mouth and gave him another swig of water, but his stomach rejected it.

"Are you okay?" she frowned, once he'd settled back in the seat. He let out a pained sigh and nodded.

Yeah, she thought. *For now…*

They decided to take some time to explore what was left of the ghost town of North Platte in search of anything of use. The old downtown did not have much to offer, but there were several stores that had the glass broken out of the front window. While she knew it would be a waste of time, she pulled up to each store, jumped out of the car with the gun in hand, and did a quick search. As she suspected, there was nothing but dirt and dust in the stores. The old pharmacy was completely bare as not a single bottle of medication or drugs remained. The shelves were empty.

They continued down the main road and searched nearly every store, only to find the same results. The last place they looked was an antiquated and historic movie theater that had one of the old vertical signs one would see in an old movie.

The doors were open and Lexie and Silas ventured into the old theater that still smelled of buttered popcorn and stale candy. With few windows, it was very dark, but they did their best to search without tripping over the old furniture that still sat in the lobby. Making a quick sweep of the place, they were disappointed once again as they found almost nothing of use.

Silas had come across an old popcorn bucket and was collecting some remaining popcorn kernels from the bottom of an ancient popcorn machine. It was not much, but he was able to find enough to fill a few inches of the bucket. They would at least give him something to chew on, even if they were not his favorite snack. Realizing there was nothing of value, they made an about-face and returned to the car where James was quietly resting despite the heat. Charlotte was crying even though she had been placed comfortably on the back seat on a bed of T-shirts. She had had a bowel movement that had made a revolting mess all over herself and the seat.

"Oh, gross!" Silas groaned.

"It's okay, Charlotte! It's not your fault, baby," Lexie said as she began cleaning her with a T-shirt. She wiped her off as best as she could while also cleaning up the loose stool on the seat. It was not perfect but it would have to do.

"It stinks in here, Mom," Silas said. Lexie gave him a hopeless shrug.

They had turned the SUV around and were about to head toward the highway when Silas suggested they check some of the railcars before they left. "You never know what could be in there," he said. Despite wanting to get on the road toward a bigger city to find help for James, she knew it was a good idea and at least worth a quick look.

They pulled back to the visitors' center and train hub and made their way directly into the rail yard where hundreds of boxcars sat motionless, as if stopped in time.

"Let's be quick and safe, Silas," Lexie said as she handed him the revolver.

Most of the cars were open and completely empty, but they continued searching as the harsh and hot sun shone down on them. They were both covered from head to toe in sweat and were nearly ready to give up when Silas yelled for his Mom.

"This one's locked. There has to be something in here."

Lexie came over to his side and pulled on the door to the black boxcar with no luck. Silas found a large rock on the ground and began crushing the padlock with it, trying to force it open. It would not budge. Knowing the only chance to open it was with the gun, Lexie told Silas to step back, grabbed the revolver, and made one shot at the top of the lock. The loud bang reverberated off the metal train and hurt their ears, but the lock had broken free.

With all his might, Silas grabbed the heavy metal door and swung it open to find it completely full of boxes, their tops covered with clear plastic wrap. Through the plastic, they could see what looked like reddish brown cans sticking up.

"Oh my God, Mom, it's pop! The whole thing's *full* of Dr. Pepper!" he grinned triumphantly.

Lexie jumped into the boxcar and saw that Silas was correct; the entire place was filled with case after case of the sweet soda. To their dismay, it was not all in good shape as the heat of the boxcar had caused about half of the inventory to burst. There was a sticky brown syrup covering the floor, and Lexie's feet stuck to it as she walked. Thankfully, there was an extraordinary amount that was still good.

Together, they rushed back to the SUV and Lexie drove it over to the boxcar to load it up with as much Dr. Pepper as would fit. Sweating terribly, within ten minutes they had the entire car filled with about 30 flats of cellophane-wrapped Dr. Pepper. James was smiling at the situation, despite not being able to help, and weakly held out his hand for a can of the sweet liquid. Silas happily handed his father a hot can which he opened. The heat, the moving of the boxes, and the age caused the can to erupt when he pulled back the tab and the brown liquid sprayed everywhere. James and Silas just laughed delightedly as James placed the can to his lips and began chugging the contents. Lexie and Silas opened an exploding can each and clinked them together while Silas grinned, "Cheers!"

Regardless of the fact that the pop was hot, the liquid felt exquisite as it made its way from their mouths to their stomachs. They drank two cans each and were burping and laughing as they took in the rare moment of fun and pleasure. Everyone was smiling and even Brownie got to have a can as they poured the contents into an empty formula can and allowed him to lap it up. Silas and Lexie burst into laughter as Brownie was not quite used to the bubbles and burped too. They reveled in the rare moment of laughter and fun for a few minutes before Lexie shook her head.

"Someone could've heard the shot. We need to go," she insisted.

Killing the mood with her tone, they headed back toward I-80 East, their bellies full of soda and their minds reverting back to the dilemma before them. They had plenty of liquid to last them some time, but they still desperately needed medicine, formula, and food. Lexie got on the ramp to the highway and began driving in the bright light of the day. With still over half a tank of gas, she knew she could make it at least to Davenport, Iowa, if not all the way to Indiana. It was still early morning and, assuming they had no need to stop, it was quite possible they could make it to Gary, Indiana, by night time. There were sure to be people in the Gary area and, if not, they could make the short trek north to Chicago.

Lexie was certain that there would still be people in this area as it was flanked by Lake Michigan, one of the largest bodies of fresh water in the world. With their bounty of liquid, which was as good as gold in this world, she was confident that she could trade for medication, food, and baby formula. They just needed to find friendly people that were not hostile and would be willing to make a swap of goods.

Filled with confidence, determination, and new hope, Lexie pushed the pedal down, accelerated to a safe 60 miles per hour, and headed along the desolate highway.

Chapter 19

As Lexie drove along I-80 East, James drifted in and out of consciousness. Waking, he'd whimper softly, as if having a bad dream, before dozing off again. The farther they drove, the more cars they passed along the side of the road. *Like dead horses in a farmer's field*, she thought. Lexie looked over at James, who has having a coughing fit, his hands sprayed with blood. *Hold on, honey. Just hang in there a little while more...*

For several hours, Lexie drove down the interstate while the remainder of the family napped and relaxed. The hours sloughed past and the boredom of the drive was really becoming annoying for Silas. The further they drove, the more cars that began to appear on the sides of the road, and Silas made it a game, trying to name the make and model of each one. When his father was awake, he would correct him when he was wrong, "Nope. That's a 2010 Corvette, but you were close," he would say.

On one occasion, James was helping Silas to name a small compact hybrid car when he began to cough violently. Lexie turned her head to ensure he was okay and was alarmed to see his hands were covered with blood he had just coughed up. She worried that, not only did he have an infection, but that he also had internal bleeding.

She was certain she had been driving for at least four hours and the signs for Omaha, Nebraska, were becoming more and more frequent. As she continued on, not only were the abandoned cars becoming more frequent, but she was now also seeing other drivers on the highway. At first, the family was alarmed to see more vehicles on the road and they were quick to assume that each one was hostile.

As time passed and they saw more people driving without paying their SUV any attention, their fears and suspicions decreased. They were by no means going to stop anyone to make conversation, but they felt comfortable in the fact that no one had made any attempt to harass or interact with them. For the family, it was refreshing to see other human beings alive and well. Nearly all of the traffic was moving east, so they assumed there to be a mass exodus from the parched lands of the western United States. Given all the traffic heading east, Lexie was feeling optimistic that they would not only find medical help for James, but that they would find a consistent source of fresh water.

At an exit sign for Omaha, Lexie veered up the ramp into what appeared to be the downtown area. She passed over a bridge with a sign marked MISSOURI RIVER, the only indication that water had ever been there.

As she drove along the concrete canyons of what had once been a prosperous Midwestern town, she saw a handful of people milling around. Like every other town they'd come across, the storefronts, boarded and weathered, had all been looted.

"Honey," she said to Silas, "keep your eyes open for anyplace that looks like we might find help."

After turning right at an intersection, he called out. "There! It looks like a medical building or clinic or something."

Please let it be!

Turning off the street into the lot, she pulled to a stop and looked around. "You stay here and watch your father and Charlotte. I'll go check it out. D'you have the gun?"

"Right here."

"Good. Keep it ready, just in case. I'll be back as soon as I can."

Silas checked on his father. His health was deteriorating fast. From the corner of his eye, he saw a pair of figures working their way slowly toward the car. Clutching the gun in his lap, he watched them approach and peer inside. One of the men tapped on the glass.

Tightening his grip on the revolver, his heart beating fast, he rolled down the window. As he did, he looked out on two grimy men. One wore a baseball cap, had a light beard, and appeared to limp. The other was tall, thin, and dressed in old and torn clothing. James opened his eyes at the sound of voices.

"Yes?" Silas said.

"We saw you drive in. Thought maybe you needed some help. He looks to be in bad shape," the man in the cap said, motioning to James. "Your father?"

Silas nodded. "Yeah. My mom went into the building to see if she could find some help." He shifted the gun in his lap to be sure the men knew he had it.

The second man nodded toward the building. "In there? Shee-it. Ain't gonna find nothing in there but more dust and dry. Ain't gonna find nothing of use for him."

"Well, then, we'll be leaving soon. Soon as my Mom gets back."

"Leavin'? You just got here. What's your hurry?" the man in the cap said as he surveyed the inside of the SUV. "There ain't no need for that there gun, boy. We're friendly," he smirked, nonchalantly pulling back his shirt to reveal a .45 pistol inside his pants.

James, drawing on every ounce of strength he could muster, raised the shotgun from his side. "So are we, mister," he coughed out the words.

"And just to prove it…" He turned to Silas. "Give them each a can of pop. Then they'll be leaving."

"A can of pop?" the man grinned. "How about the whole pack, you really wanna be friendly?"

Silas quickly handed two cans of Dr. Pepper through the window, just as Lexie came out of the clinic.

"I said *all* of it, boy."

Coming up behind them, Lexie pressed the barrel of the rifle against the back of the man in the cap. "Now, you two gentlemen are apparently unaware of just how much damage this can do at point-blank range."

The man raised his hands. "Easy, lady. We didn't mean no harm."

"We wuz just having a little fun," the other man stammered.

She waved them off with her head. "Have it somewhere else."

Silas let out a sigh as the two men slowly backed away in the direction from which they'd come. Once Lexie was sure they were gone, she got back inside the car.

"No luck?" James asked.

She could see the disappointment on his face. "I looked everywhere," she shrugged. "There's just nothing there. We'll need to go find some people we can trade with." She turned back to James. "What do we have the most of that we can live without?"

"Si, can you take a look in the back, son? See what we can trade."

Silas, still trembling at the close encounter, rolled up the window and set the gun on the seat beside him. "That's easy. Pop. We've got Dr. Pepper coming out of our ears!"

"Okay," Lexie said, putting the key in the ignition and starting the car. "Pop it is, then. We need to find some medical supplies—antibiotics and maybe some real bandages, gauze, tape, whatever—and some fresh water, and hopefully some diapers and formula for Charlotte."

"Brownie could use a few doggie treats," he said. "He loves those Beggin' Strips® ."

She grinned. "Let's not push our luck."

Driving the SUV around town, whenever she spotted people congregating, she slowed down. When they reached an apartment building where several cars were parked and people were lounging in the shade, she ground to a halt. Rolling down the window, she pointed to several gallon containers of water sitting out on the steps.

"Hey," she said, "Excuse me, but can you tell me where you got that fresh water?"

"Just missed the Red Cross truck," a young woman wearing only a pair of minuscule shorts and a black bra said. "Pulled away five minutes ago. You can probably catch it at the next stop if you head in that direction," she pointed west.

"Great," Lexie smiled. "Thanks. In the meantime, I don't suppose anyone has anything to sell or trade? We're looking for food and antibiotics."

A scraggy and dirty woman—who was probably in her 30s but looked like she was 50—approached, dressed in tight shorts and only a bra for a top. She had the look of someone on meth, with sores covering her face, missing teeth, and very fidgety. "I'm Roxy," she stuck her trembling hand out to Lexie who shook it and introduced herself. "I have some stuff I can trade, but what you got?" the woman asked.

"We have soda pop," Silas called from the back.

"Enough to wet your whistle," Lexie added. "And the sugar will give you energy."

"Yeah, I ain't had a pop in forever. I have some jerky I can trade, but I can't help with any medicine. I haven't seen any around here for a dog's age."

A young man with long wavy hair woven into dreadlocks came up behind her. "I've got some granola bars I can trade for some of that pop," he said, in the gravelly voice of a marijuana user. He pointed toward the stoop at a box filled with individually wrapped bars.

"Perfect!" Lexie agreed. "Four boxes of granola bars for a six-pack of Dr. Pepper. Fair enough? And ten of those Slim Jims for a six-pack of soda for you," she said to Roxy. "Okay?"

"D'you know anywhere I can get medicine for my husband?" Lexie asked, after making the exchange.

"No one I know got anything like that," the man told her. "But there's a bus leaving this evening for Chicago. They can probably squeeze you onboard. I don't know about the dog, though."

"What's in Chicago?"

"Well, folks says they still got water there. Pretty much everyone is trying to get there."

"Well, thanks for that information. I think we'll try to catch up with that water truck and keep heading east. Thanks for the trade and good luck to you!"

Lexie was about to pull away when the man motioned that he had something else to say.

"Yes?"

"Just thought of something. There's a zoo down the street. What used to be a zoo. They got some veterinary buildings there. It might be worth a try," he said. "It's down that way just a bit," he pointed up the street. "Could have some medicines he could use."

Lexie thanked the man and set out for the Omaha Zoo. She headed down the street before coming across a sign reading HENRY DOORLY ZOO and following the arrow to the parking lot. Finding an employee-only access road leading off behind a cluster of buildings, she drove past some empty cages and parked in the shade of one of the buildings.

It was just after noon, with the temperature already soaring. Lexie rolled down the windows and turned off the ignition. James looked up at her. "Where are we?"

"We'll be right back, honey. Just hold the fort," she smiled. "We're going to try to find some medicine for you." She took Charlotte from Silas and placed her on James's lap. "Don't drop her!"

He nodded. "Good luck."

She set the rifle next to her husband and grabbed the shotgun. "Ready?" she asked Silas.

"Let's hit it," he said, exiting the car and closing the door. "Stay!" he told Brownie.

"Be safe," James said.

Silas looked around. "Which way?"

Lexie pointed to a sprawling pedestrian bridge that stood guard over the dust, dirt, and rocks below. "Let's check out that building over there."

"Wow. What is it?"

"You mean, what was it?" The area that had once housed several gorillas was now little more than a primate graveyard. The skeletons of the primates were scattered about the habitat, eerie reminders of its past— toys, tire swings, big red balls, and other props to keep their former occupants amused. In the chimpanzee area, dried blood smears stained the glass—streaks from the animals' bloody fingers where they'd been pawing to get out. Their skeletons lay below.

Lexie led the way toward the back of the building.

"Mom, what happens when animals die? Do they go to heaven?"

"That's a tough question, son. I'd like to think so."

"I hope they do."

So do I, she thought.

As they approached the building, Silas noticed a door marked EMPLOYEES ONLY.

"Probably leads to the veterinary area," Lexie said. "This is what we're looking for."

"It's locked."

Lexie took several steps off to one side and told Silas to pull out his gun. Standing at a 45 degree angle to the lock, he leveled the pistol, aimed, and squeezed. The door popped open.

Hurrying inside, Lexie told him to round up any medical supplies he could find and set them on the table in the middle of the room. Then she began rifling through the cabinets.

Medical tape, bandages, scissors. Here's some hydrogen peroxide. Some gauze. Oh, and a bottle of antibacterial spray.

"Check around for more," she said. "Let's not miss anything!"

They found a cabinet filled with vitamins, food additives, creams, and several types of ointment. Lexie identified some anti-diarrheal medication, anti-fungal creams, pills for parasites and worms, and even fertility medications designed for gorillas. "I think we'll pass on that," she mumbled. As she tore through the supplies, she grew increasingly frustrated.

"There's got to be something more useful than this junk. Keep searching."

Silas opened a small drawer on a stainless steel operating table and found several bottles of prescription medication. He pulled one of them out.

"Is this any good? It's called Cef…Cef…Cef something."

Lexie grabbed the bottle. "It's Ceftriaxone. It's an antibiotic! Great job, Silas. Your Dad can use this."

Although expired for several years, she knew it was likely still good.

"There's an empty duffle bag over here we can use to load up the supplies."

"Good idea."

After dumping her supplies into the bag, Lexie looked around for some syringes, finding a bag of them on a nearby medical cart. "Here, these, too. We'll need them to inject your father with the antibiotics."

On the way back to the car, Lexie ran ahead of Silas but, when they reached it, she stopped short. James's head was slumped forward while Charlotte cried and wriggled around his lap. *How can he sleep through that?*

Suddenly, the terrible truth struck her. She grabbed the baby and handed her to Silas, who had just come up behind her.

"James! James!" she screamed to no avail. He was sweating, breathing heavily, his head on his chest. "Silas, set Charlotte in the driver's seat. We're going to have to move your father to the back seat and lay him down."

"Is he going to be okay?"

"I…I…he needs to rest while we get the antibiotics in him," her voice quivered. "Rest and liquids. Come on, help me. Now. We'll have to move some things around in the back."

Silas stashed the remaining cases of pop in the back, along with their other supplies, leaving just enough space for Brownie to lie. The two of them picked James up and carried him around to the rear door, urine streaming from his soiled pants. Lexie turned her attention to her husband, cleaning him off with the pillowcases and stripping him of all his clothes. She wrapped the only remaining clean blanket around him and attempted to get him to drink.

Turning to Silas, she saw him fighting back the tears. "Baby, I know this is hard, but I need you to be strong for Dad's sake. Okay? We're going to get him through this."

"But he looks like he's dying."

"Silas, you have to believe that everything happens for a reason. We'll do everything we can for your Dad. If we're going to save him, we need to be strong. I'm going to need your help!"

"You know I'll help, Ma. But…I'm scared!"

"I'm scared too!" she snapped, taking a deep breath. "We all are. But we're still all together, and that's what matters."

Lexie made her husband comfortable, covering his genitals with the blanket. As she began dressing his wound, the sweat beaded on her forehead and dripped down onto James's face. She poured some of the hydrogen peroxide over the open wound, the liquid foaming up and bubbling. Still unconscious, James abruptly turned his head and winced. Lexie repeated the process twice more before spraying some antibacterial liquid over the area. Silas ripped open some fresh packages of gauze, which she applied as a compress to stop the bleeding. Finally, she taped the wound closed to prevent an additional infection from setting in.

"Hand me a syringe and the Ceftriaxone." *That'll be the only real crap shoot, administering the antibiotics without knowing the proper dose.* She knew that, in James's weakened condition, she was playing with her husband's life. She also knew that, unless she acted fast, he would be dead by evening. She loaded the syringe and shot the medicine into the arm closest to the wound.

"Is that close enough to the wound?" Silas asked.

"It's systemic. It will pass through his entire body. The infection has spread. It's everywhere. Hopefully, this will attack and destroy it without…" She cut herself short. Removing the needle from James's arm, she pressed a sterile pad against the spot for several seconds before removing it.

"There," she said. "Done. If we do that once again this evening and then once a day for the next four or five days, that should do the trick." She hugged Silas. "Thanks, son."

He clung to her. "Should I get Charlotte some food?"

She smiled. "I don't think she'd object to that. Why don't you grab a bottle and sit up front next to me? Let's leave your Dad stretched out back here."

Lexie knew that every moment counted where her husband's health was concerned. Once she'd finished dressing him, she got back behind the wheel and began wending her way out of the parking lot.

"If we can just make it to Gary by the end of the day," she told her son, "we'll be only a day's drive away from Lorain and that much closer to our goal."

"You really think we'll find water in Lake Erie?"

"We will if they're sending busloads of people to Chicago for the water in Lake Michigan. One Great Lake should be as good as another."

Finally, she thought, *things are starting to go our way. We're only two days from home, we have plenty to drink, enough to eat, and we've got sufficient baby formula to last us. And now, those critical medical supplies for James!*

With James resting comfortably in the back, Lexie looked down at the gas gauge. She knew they couldn't make it to Lorain on the amount that was left. She gazed out toward an abandoned shed. Several zoo vehicles sat dormant out front. *There has to be some gas left in some of these cars.*

"What are you doing?" Silas asked as she pulled over to the shed.

"You stay here with Charlotte and your Dad. I'm going to check out these cars, see if there's any gas left in them."

"And then what? Are we going to change cars?"

"Then I'll get the gas from them and put it in our tank."

"How are you going to do that?"

She sighed. "I'm going to need some tubing or something, a piece of hose, something I can use to siphon the gas out of the tanks and into a can. Leave your dad and Charlotte and see if you can find something. Quick!"

They got out of the SUV and began searching the area for anything that could work as a suction device. Silas was digging through an old blue dumpster while Lexie was looking through the mechanics' area. To Silas's dismay, the dumpster proved to be nothing more than old vegetables and food that had decomposed to a dust-like substance. He moved on and started looking through the zoo cars and trucks, hoping to find something of use. The afternoon heat was so bad they were both getting the usual dehydration headache which was never a good sign. Silas ran back to the SUV and got two cans of soda to ensure they did not pass out or become ill.

For a brief moment, Lexie was thrilled as she found a plastic siphon with a ball at the end to use for pumping gasoline. Quickly her hopes faded as both the tube and the ball had large tears in the plastic, rendering them useless. The only tape they had was medical tape which was breathable and would not be air tight. She and Silas kept looking.

Silas swiftly walked behind the gorilla habitat to a nearby area with a weathered sign indicating SIMMONS AVIARY that had what looked to be a former manmade lake or pond. It was dried to the bone, showing only cracks in the earth and various bird skeletons. Pink feathers were still

132

present under a layer of dust from what must have been a pond for flamingos. He milled around the area, looking for anything of use, and stepped on what appeared to be black rubber tubing that crisscrossed the former lake.

He knelt down to take a closer look. The tubing looked like it had been used to irrigate, filter, or add water to the area. It was nearly glued into the dry ground, and Silas struggled to pull out a usable piece without it breaking or tearing from the tugging. Every time he tried, the old rubber tubing would crack. Frustrated that he was this close to a solution, he poured his can of Dr. Pepper around an area of the hose that was sticking up and not completely buried. The soda slightly softened the area around the tube, allowing him to begin to free one end of the hose. Slowly and carefully, he pulled it close to the base as he moved forward with it. To his surprise, it did not break or crack and, before he knew it, he had a five foot piece of usable black hosing to bring to his mother.

Thrilled at his accomplishment, he ran full speed toward Lexie, waving the hose in the air. "Look what I got, Mom! Look, look, look," he shouted with excitement.

"Oh my goodness, Silas! You're amazing!" she grinned, giving him a sweaty bear hug. He was brimming with pride and smiling ear to ear.

"It was nothing, Mom," he beamed.

As Lexie headed for the vehicle closest to them—an old Land Rover painted government brown—Silas set Charlotte on the seat and got out to help.

"Look," she said, "I'm going to stick this down here and, if it comes up wet, we know there's gas left in the tank. Why don't you try to find some empty cans in case we need them? I saw some in the mechanics' area. Grab as many as you can carry and bring them back with you."

As Silas followed his mother's orders, Lexie struggled to remove the gas cap and thread the hose down into the tank. She pulled it up again and grinned.

"Yes!" she called, punching the air with her fist.

Silas came back with half a dozen cans and, as he held one still, she sucked on the hose to get the gas flowing. The hose was thin, so the job was laborious, but they couldn't help but grin at one another as they watched the amber gold liquid slowly transfer from the tank into each of the cans. Standing still made the heat all the more abusive and sweat poured down from their foreheads. The heat, combined with the gas fumes, was making her dizzy, but she continued to press on.

Suddenly, Lexie heard noises from the car. "James? Are you okay?" she called out. "Silas, go check on your dad. Quickly," she frowned, when there was no response.

"Mom!" he called back to her. "Dad's throwing up. He's shaking something awful. I'm not sure what's wrong."

Oh, Christ! Pulling the tube out of the last can, she screwed the cap on and ran over to the car to check. James was on his back, choking. She grabbed him and turned him on his side to clear his air passage. "Pull his arms up over his head to help him breathe!"

As Lexie wiped up the mess, she noticed a rash on James's face and up and down his torso. His face appeared swollen.

"What's wrong with him, Mom? Help!" Silas screamed, struggling to hold his father's arms out as James instinctively sought to pull them back in.

She thought for several seconds, felt his forehead—*He's burning up!*—and continued mopping up the mess.

"I don't know, son," she said helplessly. "I just don't know."

Just as James seemed to stop, he had an explosive loose bowel movement all over the seat on which he was lying.

Chapter 20

Lexie stood frozen to the spot as James began thrashing around. His body was twisting, turning, contorting, flopping over the rear seat as if with a mind all its own.

"What's happening, Mom? He looks like he's dying."

Charlotte, awake in the front seat, began to cry. Brownie, assuming someone was yelling at him, dug his way beneath some clothes in the rear of the SUV.

"Come around this side," Lexie urged Silas. "He's choking on his tongue."

They quickly traded places and, as Lexie lifted James's head, she snaked her index finger down his throat and pulled as hard as she could. His eyes rolled back in his head before locking onto hers, staring back blankly.

"Hold his feet down."

"I'm trying!" Silas threw both arms around his father's legs and clamped down on them. "What's going on?"

"I think he's having a seizure."

Shit. We're going to lose him!

Her eyes welled with tears as she forced James's head forward. Slowly, the choking noises subsided and the seizure stopped.

"Silas, run back to the building and grab all the towels you can find—and any cleaning solution. Even rubbing alcohol will work."

Silas ran off while Lexie stood above her ailing husband. His eyes flickered and then opened as he tried to speak. A small gurgling noise came out.

"Don't talk, sweetheart. Just rest. Silas is getting some towels and we'll get you all cleaned up."

James's lips curled down and tears flowed down his cheeks. Lexie understood how sad he felt, how he hated putting them through this.

"Listen. You're sick, and we're going to get you well. That's the same thing you'd do for us, isn't it? So, don't you give up on me! Do you hear? You have more fight in you than any ten men I've ever known. So, just keep fighting. We're going to find you the help you need."

James's eyes rolled to one side as he nodded.

Just as quickly as he had left, Silas returned with a supply of towels, some professional spray cleaner, and a large bottle of medical-grade alcohol. He and Lexie pulled James up into a sitting position, and Lexie cleaned up the mess, discarding the towels to the wind. Pouring the alcohol on the seat and carpet, she did her best to sanitize them.

Finally, they managed to coax James back down against the seat where Lexie continued cleaning him. She was used to changing Charlotte, but she had never envisioned the day when she would be forced to clean up after her husband. Nonetheless, she would do anything for him, as would he for her.

When she had finally finished, Silas said, "Mom, does he need more medicine? Maybe you didn't give him enough."

"That's what I ws thinking, Si. I just don't know how much to give. I'm not a damn doctor. I just wish I knew!"

She grabbed the bottle of antibiotics and filled yet another syringe with the cloudy yellow liquid. This time, she decided she would give him a two gram dose and in his buttocks. She had Silas gently roll him over as she carefully injected James with the crucial medication. Silas carefully allowed his father to roll back over and wept as he talked to him.

"Dad, I know you're sick, but I know you can get better. I love you, Dad. I don't know what I'd do without you. I can't go on without you!" He was now hovering over his father as the tears fell onto James's face. "Please get better, Dad. Please!"

Lexie knew that, for James, time was running out. Her only option was to drive back into Omaha and try to find help. She gave Silas a warm hug, helped him to the passenger seat, and placed Charlotte on his lap.

"Be strong, son. Be strong," she said, starting the SUV and heading off toward the city center.

"It's so hard! I don't like seeing him like this."

As they drove on, Silas pointed toward an old Catholic church. "Look. Over there. Those people. They've set up some tents or something. What d'you think?"

"It's worth a try. Hang on!"

She rounded the corner and came to a stop right outside the church. Jumping out of the car, she called out, "Is anyone here a doctor?" She looked around at a dozen confused faces. "We need help! Does anyone know where we can find a doctor?" The people stared at her as if she were from another planet. "Look, my husband is badly hurt. We need a doctor. Please!"

Finally, an anorexic elderly African-American woman came up to her. Covered in wrinkles, her gray Afro sprouting in all directions, she held out her hand to Lexie as if she wanted to embrace.

"There are no doctors, miss. There are no doctors here."

"Do you know anywhere I could find one?"

"No, miss. There's only a veterinarian who I haven't seen in days."

"Do you know where we might find him?"

"I'm not sure, but you might try looking at the art museum. If you find her, please tell her that Mama is looking for her. My daughter's name is Shelia."

"Your daughter? She's the vet?"

The warmth of her voice stood out in sharp contrast to the cool Lexie had received from the others. "My daughter, Shelia, yes."

"Oh, thank you. Thank you so much. Can you point us in that direction?"

"Just keep going straight until you reach Dodge Street in the Old Market. You can't miss it."

"Thank you again!" Lexie cried as she rushed back to the SUV and jumped into the seat.

"God bless and good luck," the woman waved.

Lexie floored the accelerator, the tires spinning as the SUV raced off down the street. She looked into the rear-view mirror. James had slipped back into unconsciousness.

"Where did she say her daughter is?" Silas asked.

"She said at the art museum on Dodge Street. She said we'd run right into it."

"There's Dodge, Mom."

Lexie took a sharp right and, sure enough, several blocks down stood the Art Deco structure bearing the name, Joslyn Art Museum. The building was enormous, with a set of wide stone stairs leading up to massive stone pillars. *How on earth will I locate the woman's daughter in such a huge space?*

Coming to a stop, Lexie told Silas to stay in the car and guard the family as she got out and raced up the steps and into the building. Inside the cavernous lobby, she noticed the temperature was so much cooler than outside. *Must be why Shelia lives in here.*

"Shelia!" she called out. "Is anyone here named Shelia?"

Hearing voices off to one side, she raced down a corridor to the Western Americana Gallery where she found a small city of people huddled around a makeshift tent city. They looked at her blankly.

"Does anyone know where I can find Shelia? She's a vet. I need medical help."

Several people looked down. One stone-faced older man looked up at her. "'Most everyone needs medical help, miss."

"Yes, sir, I realize that. But would you possibly know where I can find her? Or if she's here?"

"You'll most likely find her in the Arts of Asia Gallery. If she's here. That's where she usually sleeps," he said listlessly.

Lexie thanked him and headed off in the direction he had pointed. There, lining the walls of Asian art, were more than 3,500 years of history. Off in one corner, a family of four was sleeping. A single female sat beneath a painting Lexie recognized from her studies.

"Excuse me," she said, going up to the woman. "Is your name Shelia?"

The young black woman glared at her. "Who wants to know?"

"I met your mother over...at the Catholic church. She told me I might find you here. My husband has been shot and I was hoping you could help us."

The woman's eyes lit up.

"You saw Mama?"

"Yes, I did. A few minutes ago. Can you please help me?"

"Where's your husband?"

"He's in the car, with the rest of my family. Right outside. He's very sick."

"I...I'm only a veterinarian, you understand, and I don't have any supplies. None whatsoever. But if you bring him in here, I will take a look."

"We've got supplies. Some. In the car. My son is watching our infant daughter. I know it's a lot to ask of you, but could you possibly come down with me to help? My son and I couldn't possibly carry my husband all the way up those steps by ourselves. He's unconscious. And the baby..."

The woman sighed, looked down, and held out her hand.

"Oh, thank you," Lexie said, helping her up. "Thank you, thank you so much!"

Back down at the car, Silas passed Charlotte to Shelia, who seemed delighted to see a healthy baby girl. When Brownie crawled out to sniff her, Shelia set Charlotte down in the seat and patted the dog's head, scratching him around the ears.

"Okay," she said, looking in on James. "We'd better try to carry him, two people on his torso and one on his legs." After positioning themselves, they slowly managed to pull him out of the back and began carrying him, staggering like drunken sailors, up the steps and back into the building.

"Let's get him to my room and lay him flat on the ground. We can roll up a blanket like a pillow to support his head."

As they laid him out in Shelia's office, Lexie gazed down at him, realizing just how bad the situation was. James's skin was pale gray, his body was covered in a rash, and his face and limbs were swollen. He was dehydrated. She was shocked at just how quickly he had deteriorated.

It must have been all that blood he lost.

Lexie sent Silas back to the car to fetch Charlotte and the medical bag. When he returned, Shelia took a quick inventory of what they had. She set all of the items out on the floor, then picked up the vial of Ceftriaxone. After swirling it around, she held it up to the light from a nearby window. She sniffed it and turned to Lexie.

"Did you give him any of this?"

"Yes, two injections—one gram earlier today and two grams an hour or so ago."

Shelia turned her attention to James. She examined the rash and the swelling, looked in his mouth, felt his head, and gently probed at the gunshot wound. She removed the old bandages, cleaned the area again, and patched him back up. After taking his pulse, she lay her head against his chest to listen to his heart and lungs, and then began examining his lower body. From the look on her face, Lexie knew it wasn't going to be good news.

"Can you tell what's wrong with him?"

"Miss, I really don't know how to tell you this," Shelia hesitated, looking down upon her patient.

"What? Please. What is it? We have to know."

"Why don't you have your son step out into the hall for a moment?"

"No," Silas cried. "Whatever you have to say, I want to hear it, too."

Sheila looked to Lexie, who nodded.

"Well, this Ceftriaxone that you gave your husband, it looks to me to be bad. It turned quite a long time ago."

"What do you mean, bad? What does that mean?"

"Well, not only was the medicine likely bad, but also he's having a severe reaction to it. He's lost a lot of blood and he's extremely dehydrated. The wound must have been exposed to some bacteria, because it's badly infected. He has a lot of serious problems going on right now."

"What can be done?"

Shelia paused, looked down at him, then straightened up. "If I had the proper equipment, I could get him on an IV and some strong antibiotics. He also needs a blood transfusion. But I don't have any of that."

"Well, what can we do without it?"

"You can make him comfortable. That's all. I'm afraid he is too far gone for anything more."

Lexie had known the words were coming; she'd seen James's condition grow worse by the hour. Still, she was stunned. "You mean, that's it? There's nothing that can be done?"

"Nothing. Unless you could find a hospital, and that's quite impossible. In his condition, it's only a matter of time. Two days. Maybe more." She paused. "Maybe less."

Silas dropped to his knees, leaned down, and took his father's hand. Lexie knelt down next to him. Tears ran down her face, down his. Even Charlotte began to cry. Shelia picked her up and walked her around to calm her.

"I'm going to step out into the hall and leave you alone with James."

"Why?" Silas cried, turning to his mother. "You said he'd be okay. You said to have faith and he'd be okay. You lied! Why is he dying?"

Lexie shrugged helplessly. "I don't know the answer to that. I never lied to you. I thought he would be okay. I never expected this to happen."

"We're like...helpless. It's like we have to watch him die, Mom. I can't go on without him," he said as he broke down into a hysterical cry.

"Oh, baby, please don't say that. I know you don't mean it. I know you're upset. We all are. But we all have to die at some point in time. This is just your father's time, that's all. We'll all be together again one day in heaven. You must believe that." *I have to be brave for Si. I can't break down or I'll never be able to stop.*

Silas rubbed his eyes in his sleeve and turned to her. "I wish I could believe that. But I can't."

Suddenly, an idea struck her. She didn't know why; it didn't make any sense. But it seemed their only option. "Silas, Dad isn't gone yet. Let's get him home. Let's get him to where we're headed."

"Why? What's the use? He's going to die anyway, no matter where we are."

"Okay, Silas, I need for you to be a man right now. For me, for your sister, and for Dad. Let's get him to the car so that we can get moving. We're not that far away now."

"And what if we get there? We're not going to find anything there. You know we're not. Do you think there's gonna be supermarkets, hospitals, malls, water? Mom! There's nothing left in this world. Nothing. We're just...completely screwed!"

"You don't know that. We have to try. Now let's get Dad out of here and get back to the SUV before someone steals it. You just never know, baby...Dad could make a miraculous recovery. Miracles happen every day."

"So you think it's still possible? I mean, for him to get better?"

"Anything's possible, Si."

She and Silas picked James up and, crossing his arms on their shoulders, carried him toward the door.

"Let me help you," Shelia said.

Lexie tried to smile. "If you could bring Charlotte down...and maybe get the medical bag..." She and Silas carried James toward the lobby. As they approached the SUV, they noticed several people milling around, peering through the windows. When Shelia came down the steps, she stopped.

"You! Get out of there. Get away from that car!" she yelled. "Get away immediately!"

The people, like deer caught in the headlights, leaped back.

As Lexie and Silas got James situated in the rear, Shelia handed Silas his sister.

"Silas," she said, patting the baby's head, tears running down her own face. "I know this isn't easy or even understandable for you, but have faith. It will all work out, son."

As Lexie thanked her and put the key in the ignition, Shelia waved and called out, "Good luck!"

Still in shock, Lexie and Silas waved goodbye as they pulled away from the museum, thankful they had met such a caring individual. She did not have to go out of her way to help a family she did not know, but had done so without any hesitation. Given their ordeal, it was wonderful to know that good people still did exist on the harsh and dead planet. They did not talk for several minutes, but both worried about the negative turn of events with James.

Not only was it difficult to process, but they silently feared for their safety and future with him in such a grave state. Silas had been strong, but he was still just a young boy and could only help so much. Moving forward, Lexie knew she would need to be the leader, the strong one, and the person that would do anything to save her family. She hoped that Silas was wrong about Lorain, but she knew it was quite possible he was correct. They had not seen fresh water their entire trip and what reason would she have to actually believe there would be a utopia in Ohio?

Compounding her stress was the extreme guilt she was feeling as a result of giving James the bad medication. *What the hell was I thinking?* She secretly blamed herself for his current condition. While she knew that she was only doing her best to attempt to help her very ill husband, she also realized she should never have tried to do anything medically that she was unsure of. Giving James old antibiotics with no idea of the dosage was just stupid. It was hard for her to accept the fact that, after all she did to try and save her husband, she would ultimately be the one that caused his death. It was yet another brutal reminder to her of their everyday struggle to survive in the harsh conditions.

They found their way back to I-80 and set their sights on Ohio. Lexie was not willing to put her family at risk, so she knew that she could only drive so far before she needed to rest. Silas was far too young to drive and had absolutely no experience, so she quickly ruled that option out. Her plan was to drive as far as she could with the time remaining in the day until she was feeling too tired to go on. Then they would find a safe place to sleep and could make it to Ohio the next day. She had no plan and she could not save her husband, but she felt the pressing need to bring him home. *That is what he wanted and that is where he would want to take his last breath.*

She was hoping that he could hold on until they made the roughly 800 mile trek.

Chapter 21

It was late in the evening. The closer they came to Chicago, the more traffic they encountered. It amazed Lexie that so many people were able to salvage older cars and find gas to run them. Even with the world coming to an end, humanity continued to display its adaptability.

As Silas slept up front, James lay unconscious in the rear, moaning periodically. Every time he did, it tore out a piece of Lexie's heart. Brownie had curled into a ball, his head on James's lap. *Man's best friend,* Lexie thought, *to the end.*

As she approached the Great Lakes, she realized she'd have to decide if she wanted to veer north into the Windy City or bear south toward Gary and eventually Lorain.

She was seriously leaning toward Chicago. The words of the man in Omaha kept replaying in her head: *Well, folks says they still got water there. Pretty much everyone is trying to get there.* If people were flocking to Chicago in busloads, she theorized, there had to be water and a better way of life there. But if they were wrong, she and Silas would be heading right into yet one more community of lawless ruthless people.

Besides, James's wish was to see his home town once more. She wanted him to spend his last days in a place that brought him emotional comfort. There would also be fewer people in Lorain than there would in Chicago, which meant less competition for whatever resources were left.

She decided to keep on course for Ohio. Instead of stopping for the night in Gary—another city notorious for its crime—she made the decision to overnight in Joliet, just south of Chicago. At the very least, she reasoned, it would be safer than Gary.

While all the other cars on the road passed the Joliet exit sign—headed for the big city not far to the north—she turned the car off the highway and onto the ramp.

"Where are we?" Silas asked, awakened by the rough road. "Why'd we get off the Interstate?"

"We have to stop for the night. I'm getting too tired to keep driving. I'm going to find us a safe place to park."

Silas looked back toward his father and cringed when he saw that he was no better. In his dream, he had seen his father have a miraculous recovery and they were all in Lorain. His grandparents were by his side and they were drinking iced tea on an old wooden deck that overlooked the blue waters of Lake Erie. Everyone was happy. He was brought back to reality as the strong odor of the car filled his nose, his father's moans began to become more frequent, and Silas's stomach growled for food. It was a demoralizing moment after having found some temporary peace and joy in his slumber. Charlotte woke up suddenly and was crying.

"She needs a bottle, Mom."

"In the back."

Silas reached behind the seat to get a can of formula which he mixed into a bottle. As he fed it to her, she looked up at him, soft gurgling sounds rising from her mouth.

At first, Lexie was going to try and find a parking spot at a downtown casino that looked to be the perfect place to park. That idea was quickly put to rest when they drove by and saw several men fighting in the front. From a distance, it looked like many homeless people had made the former hotel and casino their new home. It did not look safe and she was did not want to interact with any people at this time of night. The streets were very dark and she was having a difficult time navigating the downtown area, but had some assistance from the bright stars and moon. Silas noticed a sign with an arrow pointing to the right for a stadium of some sort on a road called Mayor Art Schultz Drive.

"Looks like a baseball stadium over there," he said. "Probably nothing more now than one great big parking lot."

"You may be right," Lexie sighed.

Following a service road off to one side and around to the rear of the stadium, she turned the vehicle up the gravel path, through an opening in the stadium walls, and stopped safely inside.

Once parked in the stadium, they turned their attention to having some protein and nourishment. Lexie was exhausted, but knew she needed to care for the family before she got any rest. Her first priority was to try and get some fluids into James who was still unconscious in the backseat. With Silas's help, she pried his mouth open and slowly trickled some water down James's throat. Miraculously, it was working and they found that, the slower they trickled the water, the more he would actually swallow. They did this for over fifteen minutes and were ecstatic to see he was able to consume a reasonable quantity of liquid. This was the first piece of good fortune that they had had in days. James even opened his eyes for a brief moment and stared at Lexie and Silas while also squeezing Lexie's hand. He immediately closed his eyes again.

"Mom, let's eat! I'm starving."

"Me too, baby. Can you grab whatever we have left?"

Silas grabbed a few Slim Jims, two granola bars, and one MRE from one of the boxes in the rear. She allowed Silas to eat the MRE, which consisted of chicken cordon bleu with rice, while she had two Slim Jims and a granola bar. They both had a small amount of water and a can each of the soda. Silas was still holding Charlotte and suddenly screamed out, "Oh gross! She just pooped on me!" He held her away from his body. "We need diapers!"

"We don't have any way to get diapers. We're going to have to start rinsing out the T-shirts so that we don't completely run out."

"With what? It's not like we have some Tide and a washing machine."

"We have enough Dr. Pepper to last a long time. Using one can to wash out the shirts is no biggie."

Lexie opened the door and took the soiled T-shirt and began slowly pouring the soda onto it, rubbing it together vigorously with her hands. She grabbed a clean shirt and had Silas wrap it around Charlotte while she placed the slightly clean shirt that she had just washed on the top of the car to dry in the arid nighttime air. Silas looked at it skeptically. "That's seriously gross Mom."

"It's the best we can do for now, honey. We'll find some diapers in Ohio."

When morning came and the dark night was behind them, Silas snuck out of the SUV to get a view of Silver Cross Field while his mother still slept. He had always wanted to see a major league stadium and wished he could see a baseball game more than anything in the world. He knew that dream would never come true, but he used to enjoy watching old recorded games of his father's favorite team, The Cleveland Indians. His father still proudly wore a Cleveland Indians Championship hat and shirt that he had received many years ago when they won the World Series against the Chicago Cubs.

Silas looked around at the magnificent baseball stadium and imagined what it must have been like in the olden days when the grass was green and the stands were full of excited cheering fans. As it stood now, it was still wonderful to see, but the former green grass was now nothing but dirt and sand. The stands of green stadium seats were now sun-faded and covered in oxidation.

He found a set of stairs in the concourse that led to the press box. Ascending them, despite the annoying heat, he found his way to the door that led into the main press box. He was amazed at the view and was envisioning what it would have been like to see actual players during a real game. He had seen enough about it on television to know everything about America's sport and was thrilled to be looking down on the former field. Like most thirteen year olds, he still had a vivid imagination and suddenly found himself holding the broken microphone, pretending he was the announcer.

He could hear the funny organ music playing in his ears while he began calling the game. "Well, Ladies and Gentlemen...this is what you have all been waiting for. It's the bottom of the ninth inning, there are two outs, and the Tribe is down one run with a runner on first. Here comes the first pitch which is right down the middle. Strike one looking. The pitcher gets set, and throws the next pitch—high and outside!"

The organ music became louder and the crowd was cheering so loudly that Silas could barely hear himself talk. "He's set, and here's the pitch. It's a looong drive, deep right center....it may have enough distance. Going, going, gone! The Indians win the World Series again!" The crowd went crazy in his ears. He could envision his father and himself jumping around, high fiving and celebrating.

His fun was short lived as he knew he had to get back to the car to wake his mother and get on the road. He was concerned she may have already woken and be wondering where he had gone. He frankly did not know exactly how long he had been away and did not want to scare her. He walked down the steps, past the old concession stands and swore he could smell the hotdogs, mustard, nachos, and burgers. His stomach growled at the thought of the food he would probably never have again.

His thoughts shifted toward his father and the depressing realization hit him that they would never have any more memories made together. The memories he currently had were all that he would ever have. With his father unconscious and unlikely to wake up, he wondered if he would even see his father's eyes again. The idea was terrifying, sad and, naively, nothing he had ever expected to happen in his lifetime. He opened the door to the SUV, which woke his mother.

"What's going on?" Lexie mumbled, rolling over on her blanket. "What time is it?"

"I don't know. It's morning. Early. Go back to sleep."

"Early is already too late. Come on," she said. "Up and at 'em. Get Charlotte ready. Let's move. I want to get home. We need to get home."

"It's so hot already. I can't stand it."

"It's going to be a scorcher today. That's for sure."

She handed Charlotte to Silas who fixed another bottle and began feeding his now fully awake sister. She always woke up extremely happy and she was smiling, laughing, gurgling, and blowing raspberries. She was so clueless to the world around her and she could live her short life happy, which was a blessing in itself.

Lexie started the SUV, turned around on the brown turf, and made her way back out of the service entrance and onto the road. The car was quiet as she drove, Charlotte ate, and James slept, and it was easy to hear the loud sound of oncoming motorcycles. At first, the noise did not really alarm her and she assumed they were just riding around town but, as she peered into her rear-view mirror, she noticed them quickly approaching from behind. They were still too far away to see clearly, so she sped up in order to reach the highway and gain some ground in case they were hostile.

"Silas, don't be scared, but it looks like we may have some company. Make sure we have the guns ready."

"What? What's going on?"

"Just stay calm. There're some motorcycles approaching behind us. Let's just hope they aren't looking for trouble."

Silas grabbed the revolver and ensured it was loaded, locked, and ready. He got the shotgun loaded too, made certain it was ready to fire, and set the safety. He passed it to his mother with the barrel facing away from everyone.

Lexie made the turn onto the highway ramp and floored the gas until she was speeding at 85 miles per hour on I-80. She was driving in the middle of the highway without regard for the faintly marked lanes so she could avoid the many potholes that lined the areas closest to the middle and shoulder. She knew hitting a bad pothole or part of the road that had warped could be devastating to the car, so she was driving extra carefully. She checked the rear-view mirror and the pack of motorcycles had once again appeared, gaining ground on her. She could count at least five bikes and faintly make out the images of the men riding them. Silas turned around and saw the motorcycles, driven by a band of men that looked terrifying.

"Oh shit, Ma. This doesn't look good."

"Let's just stay calm."

The bikers were all wearing white sleeveless undershirts, shorts, and had thick and heavy beards. They all had the same red bandanas on their heads, but the more scary part was that they were wearing some sort of mask. It was difficult to determine what kind they were, but the bikers were clearly covering their faces with something and it was not a good sign.

The sound of the bikes was now impossible to ignore as they continued to gain ground on Lexie, who was now speeding at almost 90 miles per hour. The men had to be going well over 100 and she knew they must have some sort of agenda. Within a minute, they were right behind the SUV and all were brandishing firearms. Some had rifles on their shoulders, some were carrying handguns, but all had the exact same disturbing mask on. They were a silver metallic color with a skull-like nose, white bones around the eyes, bones around the top of the head, and long scary white teeth. Silas and Lexie knew by their appearance alone that these men were not coming in peace.

147

She was traveling now as fast as the SUV would go, yet the motorcycles were pulling past her on both sides. The men were waving their guns and motioning them to pull over to the side of the road. There were two bikes on each side and one that had pulled ahead of her, trying to pump his brakes to force her to slow down. Lexie had a decision to make and she did not have much time.

The men were getting impatient and signaling intently for them to pull the SUV over. She knew if she did they would be robbed, their supplies would be taken, and they would all be in danger. The men could kill them and take everything. She was not going to take that chance. *They can't be thinking clearly. We have a massive and heavy SUV and they're on two wheel motorcycles with no helmets.*

"Silas, I want you to duck. Crouch down in the seat and cover Charlotte with your body."

"Hell, no, Ma. I want to help!"

"You can help by doing what I say and don't argue," she said firmly.

Pouting, Silas obeyed his mother and crawled down into a ball-like shape with Charlotte pinned beneath him crying. It was then that Lexie made her move. She smiled at the men, waved to them to indicate she was pulling over, and then turned her right signal on and began to merge right. The men got her nonverbal signal and began to move with her, but were still so close to the SUV that she could see their eyes.

Swiftly, she turned the car sharply to the left, hitting the motorcycle closest to the car. The collision made a load scraping sound and thump as the man driving the cycle lost control, veered into the cycle to his left, and both went into a roll. She looked in the rear-view mirror and could see the motorcycles tumbling and rolling as the men were thrown from both bikes and likely killed instantly. The man in front of the SUV saw what had happened and hurriedly pulled further to the left to avoid the same demise.

Startled by what happened to their friends, the men on the right side of the SUV pulled out their weapons and began firing aimlessly at them. Lexie could hear the bullets penetrating the metal of the vehicle and one made it through a window in the very back, showering Brownie with broken glass. The men were clearly not very intelligent as they were still very close to the SUV and Lexie knew what she had to do.

"Hold on, Silas!"

She turned the car sharply to the right and struck both motorcycles at once, sending the men spinning off the road and off their bikes which then sped forward and crashed into the desert. Once again, she looked in the rear-view mirror and this time saw the men's bodies lying on the road, motionless. The lone man remaining clearly now feared for his life as he slowed down to allow the SUV to pass. When they did, he began firing at it with a small pistol. His shots were not aimed well and hit the lower side of the car as he was trying to concentrate on the road.

"Give me the revolver!" Lexie said to Silas. He handed her the gun and resumed his balled-up position.

Lexie unrolled her window, steered the car with her knees, and began to open fire on the lone driver of the motorcycle. While she missed, it was clear to her that the man did not expect them to be armed, so he appeared shocked at the return fire. In what appeared to be a complete retreat, he brought his bike to a stop, turned it around, and drove back to check on his friends. Sweating profusely from the stress and heat, Lexie wiped her forehead with her hand and then continued down the highway, never looking back.

"It's over, baby. You can get up. We're safe."

"Wow, Mom! You really kicked ass back there. Holy cow!"

Lexie did not respond. She was not feeling good inside about having to turn to violence yet again. She was worn down both emotionally and physically. *Honestly, what more can possibly happen to us? Can we please just catch a break?*

Chapter 22

They had been driving for a little over two hours when they found themselves approaching Granger, just north of South Bend, about four hours from their destination. They had enough gas, relatively full bellies, and a shred of optimism. Lexie just knew a body of water the size of Lake Erie couldn't evaporate. *Not overnight. Maybe in decades, but not before. Never!*

As their journey neared its end, she couldn't wait to reach their destination—just like when, as a child, she sensed the family wagon growing closer to their favorite vacation spot, Cedar Point.

Suddenly, James started wheezing.

"Si, check on your father, will you? Make sure his throat is clear."

Before he could respond, James spit up the morning's water and erupted into a massive seizure. His body was twisting, turning, and flopping as his head smacked against the car door. Moaning, he made a hollow haunting ghostlike sound.

Silas set Charlotte down on the floor, hopped over the seat, and lifted his father's head, trying to prevent him from swallowing his tongue. By the time Lexie had found a place to pull over, the seizure had stopped.

"Is he okay? Is he breathing?"

"Yeah. He's okay. He's breathing."

Lexie jumped out of the car and came around to the rear. James had opened his eyes once again. This time, he seemed much more alert, even aware of his surroundings. They looked down at him, Lexie clasping one of his hands.

"Where are we?" James muttered.

Lexie's eyes lit up. "We're just north of Fort Wayne, babe. We're almost home!" She gave his hand a squeeze.

James sighed, forcing his eyes to focus. "There's something I need to tell you. Both of you."

"Sure, honey. Anything."

James cleared his throat and pointed to the jug of water sitting nearest to Silas. After taking a sip, he closed his eyes for several seconds, tightening his grip on their hands.

"It's real," James said. "It is all real. There's something beyond death."

"What's real, James? What are you talking about?"

151

"I was there! I saw something that I can't explain. Something peaceful. Something beyond words. It's….it's just too hard to explain."

"Dad, you were dreaming."

James cleared his throat again, struggling to maintain enough energy to speak. "No, Si, it was no dream. It was real. Vivid. It was amazing. I was there. I was in the ultimate peace."

"What did you see, James?"

"I can't describe it. It's too incredible. It's not what we ever thought it was. It's everything we thought it would be, but nothing like we thought it was." He paused a moment to gather his strength.

"I don't understand, honey."

"We're all correct. Everybody. No religion is right and no religion is wrong. It's just the ultimate peace. Serenity. Everyone is right and no one is wrong. I know there is something beyond death. We'll all be together!" He smiled.

"What exactly did you see, baby?"

James was rapidly growing weaker.

"Dad?"

James blinked and cleared his throat. "It isn't about religion or what we believe. It's something beyond that. It's something incredible." He paused, blinking his eyes. "It's warm. It's quiet. It's peaceful. You see…well, it's..." And, with that, he slipped off once more into unconsciousness.

"James?"

"Dad!"

Lexie studied him. "It's no use, Si. He's sleeping peacefully."

Silas turned to her, his eyes wide. "What do you think, Mom? Do you think he really saw something?"

She touched her palm to his forehead, running it down his cheek. "Let me ask you something, son? Do you think he saw something?"

After all, she thought, *it's possible that what James said was actually the truth. That all religions are the same in the end. From the ancient Druids to the Native Americans. From the Muslims and the Hindus to the Buddhists and the Sikhs. Who's to say one is right and the others are wrong?*

In an odd way, it suddenly all made sense to her. It was hard to comprehend, but it made her rethink everything.

"But," Silas said, "If Dad was right, then everything we know about religion is wrong."

"I don't think that's what your Dad was trying to tell us, Si. I think what he was trying to say is that what he saw incorporates all religious beliefs. Maybe it's something we just can't understand until our time comes."

He thought for several seconds before adding, "Maybe." He paused. "Just maybe."

Lexie and Silas drove on for the next three hours down I-80, across the Ohio border, and onto the old Ohio Turnpike. It astonished her to see just how dead and brown everything was. Nothing but a diseased and wasted desert for thousands of miles.

The traffic had dwindled to nearly nothing, and even the abandoned cars were so few that, when they spied one, they gawked at it. The turnpike was in bad shape, the potholes and buckles in the pavement looming ever more ominous the farther they drove.

Tempted to exit the turnpike to take a different road—one that ran parallel to Lake Erie—she kept to their plan and continued onward. As they neared Sandusky, only 45 minutes from Lorain, she knew they'd learn the fate of the lake and their own home town soon.

From the back, James continued to cough, choking and moaning, goading her on to reach their destination as quickly as possible.

It was mid-afternoon when Lexie spotted the sign for Baumhart Road. *Yes!* She thought, a surge of adrenalin racing through her veins. The exit took her past the old abandoned toll booths, north toward Lorain and Lake Erie. *I can't believe we actually made it!*

She looked out over the barren horizon. *Well,* she thought, *nearly.*

"Si, are you up? Only a few minutes more and we'll get our first look at Lake Erie."

Strange, though. No sign of human life, no cars, and a dust-covered road—like driving in dry brown snow.

Ahead, Lexie saw the end of Baumhart Road where it came to a "T" at West Erie Avenue. She recalled how, while driving into Lorain, she used to be thrilled to see the blue waters of Lake Erie, which changed from thundering waves and whitecaps to water as flat as glass in mere minutes. She'd always hoped for calm waters, since that meant boating, fishing, or a refreshing swim just around the corner.

"Look," she told Si. "Get ready for the sight of your life!"

Silas looked out over the landscape.

"Mom, it's all dead, nothing but brown trees."

Lexie strained to see north toward the lake. As she continued forward, her joy gave way to depression. She drove on through the intersection and, when she got to the vacant lot that had once bordered the lake, she pulled in. She turned the engine off and stepped out of the SUV. Walking forward like a zombie, she saw what was once the shoreline.

There's no life here. Only death! There's no water. None!

The lake basin had turned into a sprawling brown canyon. Where the shoreline once stood, a cliff hung over the wasteland. Skeletons of boats loomed everywhere. Old tires, trash, and driftwood sprouted from a bed of dirt and sand.

Lexie glanced to her right at the piers and jetties that no longer led to water but rather to a steep drop-off into baked earth. Farther down the shore stood the historic landmark of her town, the Lorain lighthouse. Once a vibrant and crucial part of navigation, now it was a ghost. It had once protected the harbor from the rough waters and served the locals as a great place to fish. Now it was a memory.

Lexie dropped to her knees in disbelief. Silas approached her and placed his hand on her shoulder. She turned and looked at him as tears rolled down her cheeks and onto the dead earth below her.

"Honey. It's gone. Everything. The whole lake. The water. Everything. Everything is gone."

Silas could not think of anything to say.

"It's impossible. How could the entire lake just be gone?" she cried, turning away. "It doesn't make sense. It's like it just vanished into thin air."

"We don't know that it's gone, Mom. What if the shoreline just shrank back? There could still be water and life out there."

She thought for a moment about Silas's words and tried to strain her eyes to look toward the horizon.

There, out toward the center of the lake. That's Canada. The international border that divides our country from theirs. Straining her eyes, she thought she could see something many miles out, but wasn't sure what.

"Silas, can you see anything?"

He strained his eyes. "I think I do, Mom. It looks like there's something out there, but it's so far away. I think I see, like...blue water or something."

"I wonder if there's water out there in the middle. But it doesn't matter, does it? I mean, we still have to get your dad home, don't we?" *The hell with the water. The hell with everything. Except for James.*

They walked back to the SUV, where James was coughing badly and having a difficult time catching his breath. Jumping back behind the wheel, Lexie started the engine, pulling back onto West Erie Avenue heading east. They drove past the old courthouse, the iron ore loading area, and the dried-up Black River. They crossed the ancient Charles Berry Bascule drawbridge and could see the desolate abandoned Marina International—now no more than a graveyard for boats and barges that sat on the lake floor. The dried-up Black River was below them.

As they came upon the intersection near James's childhood home, she turned right onto Montana Avenue, where the large long tan brick building came into view. Despite the desolate surroundings, the home

154

itself seemed to be in good condition. She pulled into the meandering driveway adjacent to the wooden fence.

Oh, my God. We made it! It wasn't easy. And for a while, I never thought we would. But we made it!

Parking the car in the driveway, Lexie carried Charlotte into the unlocked house and placed her on the carpeted floor of the sprawling living room. "Here you go, baby. Home at last. And what a nice warm soft carpet to lie on!"

After going back outside and carrying James in, they managed to get him settled, still unconscious, in his old bedroom. It had been untouched since James had moved out years ago—the parquet floors, the same wallpaper, even his old bed. He opened his eyes, acknowledging where he was with a smile, before falling back to sleep.

Silas stepped out of the bedroom as Lexie finished tucking her husband in. The boy wandered into the kitchen, where he found a handwritten note on the table.

> My Dearest Lexie,
>
> If you and your family are reading this note, then you are still alive. We figured you would eventually try to make your way home and we hoped this would be your first stop.
>
> As I write this note, we are leaving for the Cargill Salt Mines in downtown Cleveland. If you don't already know, there is water in Lake Erie but it is several miles north and the journey there is very dangerous. There is one road, but it is rocky and very difficult driving. Once you get there, there is a tent city along the shores. Nearly everyone in the area has gone there. It is not safe. Stay clear of it!
>
> Instead, please come join us at the mines. It is much safer. The mines are thousands of feet underground and the temperature remains steady and comfortable. Not many know about it, so it is not yet overrun with people and they are still letting families in. There is food, water, solar electricity, and security. Take I-90 East to exit 170A. Turn left on W25, left on Mulberry, and right on River Road. You will see the entrance there. Tell the guards that you want to speak with Bill Nyberg. He knows to allow you in.
>
> We are both fine and in good health. We are sad to tell you that James's mother passed away several months ago.

Please give him our condolences. And do come to the mines where it is safe just as soon as you can.

We love you all more than words can say. We can't wait to see you! Be safe, travel safe, and we hope to see you soon. Give James, Silas, and Baby Charlotte a kiss from both of us.

Love,

Mom and Dad. Grammy and Poppy

Even after reading the letter several times, Silas could not believe his eyes. Not only were his Grammy and Poppy alive, but they were nearby and in a safe place with food, shelter, and water. All this, and they had given them the instructions on how to get there! He bolted for his father's room.

"Mom, Mom, look here! Look at what I have!" He held the letter out to her.

Taking hold of it, Lexie stopped to read it, her eyes filling with tears.

"Oh, my Lord, thank you! I can't believe it, Silas. My parents are alive. They're actually alive! Mom and Dad are alive!"

"I know. I had to read it three times before it sank in. Are we gonna go?"

"Yes." She stopped at the sound of the word. "I mean, no. No, net yet. Let's hang tight for a while and rest. We need to keep your dad comfortable. For tonight. And then…we'll see."

"I know, but we'll go eventually, right?"

"Yes. We'll go. We need to find Grammy and Poppy."

As night gave way to the silver caste of the moon and stars, James rested comfortably. Silas had found, and consumed, some canned beans hidden in Grammy's cabinet. With their supply of baby formula getting low, Lexie searched the house for the stash her mother-in-law once kept on hand for unexpected visits and found a can of Gerber's.

Before long, the family, exhausted from their travels, retreated for the night to the master bedroom, but the body odor emanating from them all was so strong that Lexie had to open the window just to breathe. Once Silas had climbed into bed, she settled Charlotte in beside him with Brownie dozing at the foot, before creeping into James's room to lie on the floor beside his bed.

Within a matter of seconds, the trauma of the day and the pleasures of the night and other nights still to come claimed their dreams. Even the sickening heat in the house could not hinder their need for rest.

Chapter 23

Lexie opened her eyes suddenly and looked toward the window. The glow of the sun was just faint enough that she knew dawn was only minutes away. She had woken up as she had a terrible nightmare along with a sinking feeling in her stomach that something was wrong. It was then that she heard a very weak James quietly calling for her. Her heart started thumping as she sat up abruptly.

"What is it? James?" She quickly pulled herself up. "What is it? Is something wrong?"

He looked confused. "Where am I?

"You're home, baby…in your old room."

"Oh. Oh, I thought it looked familiar." He stopped, swept his eyes quickly around the room, and centered back on his wife. "It's so good to see your face. And it's so comforting to be home. Is there water here?"

For a brief moment, she considered telling him a lie.

"No, James. I'm afraid not. It's dry."

"Shit. I was afraid of that."

"I know. But we'll find some. There has to be some nearby." She touched his head, "How do you feel?"

James closed his eyes as if he was straining or in pain. He paused for a few seconds before he could muster the strength to speak.

"It's almost time. But I have some things I need to tell you first."

"James, I wish you wouldn't…"

He held up his finger to her lips. "Please, Lex. Please don't say anything. I need you to listen. Okay?" She hesitated and finally nodded. "From the very moment I laid eyes on you, I knew I had found my soulmate. Lexie, I love you now just as I've always loved you. You are and always will be my one and only true love."

Fighting the tears back from her eyes, she mumbled, "Oh, James. I love you, too, and I always will. You're my world, and I don't know what I'll do without you. I loved you even before I knew what love was."

His voice was weak and raspy. He began to cough and wheeze. "I promise you that we will see each other again in the most magnificent place you could ever imagine. I want you to promise me you will keep on fighting. Keep fighting for the sake of Silas and Charlotte. Keep fighting for the slim chance that there can be happiness again on this planet. Will you do that for me?"

She felt a tear slip down one cheek. "Yes, James. I will."

"There's one last thing. Remember this, so that when Charlotte is old enough to understand, you can tell her. Tell her that her Daddy loved her and always will. Tell her that I'm looking down on her and watching her grow up. Please tell her that I'm sorry I missed so much of her life. Tell her all of that for me, will you, Lex, when she's old enough to understand?"

Unable to hold back the tears, Lexie nodded.

"Good girl. See why I love you so?"

She threw her arms around him, felt how emaciated he was, how weak, how close to the end. James's eyes began to get heavy and he would close them briefly, drift out of consciousness for a few seconds, and then come back. He was becoming almost too weak to breathe. Each breath had become a painful and labored process.

"I don't have much time. Please, now, go get Si," he whispered, coughing. He held his hand out toward his wife, and she clasped it tightly. She bent down and they embraced in a gentle kiss she knew would be their last. With their lips pressed together, the couple held the moment for several seconds before James turned his head.

"Remember, Lexie, I will always love you!" He let out a long and drawn-out wheeze.

As she stepped back, the tears still flowing, she managed a weak smile, mouthing the words, "I love you," as she stepped away, blew a kiss at him, and left the room.

She met Silas in the hallway.

"I heard something. What is it?" he asked. "Is it…is it…Dad?"

She nodded. "He wants to see you. Be strong for him. Tell him…" She struggled with the words, "Tell him whatever it is you want to say. This may be your last chance."

"What? No, it can't be. Please don't say that, Mom."

Fearing the unknown, Silas summoned up his courage and passed the rest of the way down the hall to his father's room. James looked up, stifled a cough, and motioned for him to come close.

"Son…" He broke off, holding up his index finger as Silas grabbed hold of his father's arm. "Just a moment," he whispered, wheezing.

"Are you okay, Dad? Can I get you something?"

James tried to force a smile. He had heard that people near death often feel a sense of peace and tranquility before passing, as if one door to the universe is closing just as another is swinging open. His entire body had become engulfed in an overwhelming sense of peace.

"I'll be okay, Si."

The boy looked at him, at how pale and weak he appeared to be, at how thin—withered almost, like a living skeleton. It was difficult for him to see his father like this, thinking back over all the years to when he had been robust, focused, strong, resilient. The boy realized finally that those days were gone forever.

James clasped both hands around his son's arm.

"Si, I just wanted to tell you how special you are to me. Your mother and me. How we couldn't have asked for or—" He paused to clear his throat. "—or gotten a better son."

Silas lowered his head, the tears he knew should be falling failing to materialize. Raising his chin, he pulled one hand free and stroked his father's arm. "Thanks, Dad. But it's all because of you. You're the best Dad, always there for me, for Mom, for Charlotte."

"I want you to know how proud I am of you, son. And here you are, growing into such a wonderful young man. I had always dreamed of having a son, and you've surpassed all my hopes and desires." He coughed again. "I want you to know that I love you dearly, as I have since the moment you were born. I'll always love you and I'll always be a part of you, even after I'm gone."

His voice began to crackle, and tears streamed down his face. "I'm just sorry that I'm going to miss your teenage years. I'm sorry I won't be there to help guide you on your journey. I hope someday things will be better here on Earth. I do so want you to be happy. And to remember that a true father gives his all for his family, just as I hope you'll have the chance to do one day for a family of your own. To meet someone, fall in love, and be the strong loving center of the universe you'll need to be."

Silas took one arm and brushed the tears from first his left eye and then his right.

"I'll do the best I can, Dad. I'll remember everything you taught me."

"And I know you'll be a terrific big brother to Charlotte. And a supportive rock for your mother. After all, you're going to be the man of the house now."

"I...I'll do my best. But...but...I won't be able to go on without you."

James smiled. "Do you remember our talk before?" He grabbed Silas's fist and put it up to his heart. "I'll be with you, son. Every minute of every day. Please talk to me as often as you want. I'll be listening."

"I know, Dad, but it's...it's not the same. I...I need you."

"And I need you, Silas. Be strong for your mother and your sister. And we'll all be reunited again one day. I've never been more certain of anything in my life. We'll be together again one day, and it will be awesome."

"But, Dad...do you really have to go? I don't want you to leave me."

"I'll never leave you son...never."

Silas bent down, hugging his father before resting his open palm on his chest. As he pondered what else to say, James slipped off again into unconsciousness—his breathing strained, his wheezing louder. Fluids were filling his lungs, Silas could tell. But he was going to stay with his Dad until he took his very last breath, and if that meant sitting with him forever, so be it.

Lexie brought Charlotte into the room and slowly lowered her face to that of her father. And as she imagined the infant kissing him, she began to weep.

"It's okay, Mom. Dad understands. And we'll see him again someday. He told me we would."

"I know, baby." She said very softly.

She sat down on the edge of the bed, allowing Charlotte to nestle up against James's side as the orange glow of the sun began peeking through the blinds. For several hours they sat together, as a family, while the hot sun of the day continued to rise. She rubbed her husband's back, she held his hand, and she gave him several kisses on the forehead. Silas sat mostly in silence, staring out the window and weeping softly. At one point, she heard Silas snore lightly and realized he must have drifted off. Brownie sat with his head on James's rear and occasionally let out a half-bark.

Around what had to be approaching noon, Silas woke. At the same time, James's breathing suddenly intensified before becoming very slow and labored. As he began struggling for each breath, his eyes opened briefly and met Lexie's. He made a final glance at Silas. A single tear rolled down his cheek before he closed his eyes. He let out a slight gurgling sound, gave one final gasp for air, and then went silent. Lexie held his hand and then gently kissed him on the lips. The love of her life had passed. Silas sat up, but found himself nearly paralyzed with fear and sadness.

"Oh, baby," Lexie said gently. "Daddy's gone. He just went peacefully. He's in a better place now. We can be certain of that."

Silas looked at his dad closely. He didn't look dead. He didn't look any differently than he had only a few hours earlier. But there was no movement of his chest, no sounds coming from his mouth.

At first he felt like lashing out, and then screaming. And, finally, once he'd given the words a chance to sink in, he simply sighed. "That's all we can ask for, isn't it, Mom? I mean, that he went peacefully. That's something good, right?"

Lexie forced a smile. "Yes. That's something good, baby."

"Mom?" Silas asked.

"Yes, baby."

"Can I have a hug?" he said, choking back tears.

Lexie did not need to respond. She lunged for her son and they met in a bear-hug like embrace. The months of stress, trauma, and hardship had finally caught up with both of them. They became dead weight and fell into each other's arms. They cried, moaned, and even screamed as the

160

pain of James's death became more real. The noise woke Charlotte who began to cry along with them. Brownie joined in with a sad and deep howl.

When the tears stopped falling, they stayed lying on the bed. Silas was in the fetal position and he stared blankly at the wall. Lexie cuddled him from behind and did her best to comfort him by rubbing his back. They stayed still, on the bed, for several hours until the heat became too much to stand.

Lexie finally forced herself to sit up and Silas soon followed. Wiping his eyes, he looked over at his lifeless father on the bed. Suddenly, Silas's brain kicked in to the reality of their situation. "Mom! What'll we do with him? I mean, we can't just leave him here. And there's not exactly any funeral homes nearby."

Lexie thought for a moment and decided they should bury him in the backyard. The temperatures were nearly intolerable, so they could dig a hole, taking turns manning the shovel.

"It's probably what Dad would have wanted anyway," Silas said, as if trying to convince himself that they were about to do the right thing. "I mean, to be buried where he had grown up. He always loved this place so much."

With Lexie in the lead, they went out to the garage to find a shovel. But the garage, like almost everything else, had been stripped bare. Digging a hole was not an option. Putting their heads together for an alternative solution, Lexie suddenly remembered the crawl space in the basement that tunneled around the perimeter of the home. They decided to wrap James's body in a sheet and tuck him into the hole, where he would lie in peace, as if in a mausoleum. It wasn't ideal, but it was the best they could think to do.

Dusk crept in upon them. They had earlier wrapped a sheet around James, opened the door to the crawl space, and carried him downstairs. He had lost so much weight that moving him had seemed effortless. Laying him into the hole, they bowed their heads and had a brief moment of silence before climbing back out and latching the door.

Looking around, Lexie turned to her son. "We have to be strong. For the time being, it's just you, me, and Charlotte now, Si. Be strong. We'll all be together again someday."

"And Brownie."

She smiled. "And Brownie."

The boy came up and gave his mother a hug. "Are you all right, Mom?"

She ran her hand through his hair. "Are you?"

"It's a good place for him. Better than outside. It's where he grew up, in this very house. I'm glad you thought of it."

"Come on," she said. "We'd better get going. Even though we won't have your father with us anymore, his spirit won't be far away."

Silas smiled sadly, and began gathering up their things. Lexie wondered how on earth she would be able to go on without the love of her life at her side.

Chapter 24

Lexie felt sick with grief and her stomach was in knots. Despite the fact that they did not feel like eating, they knew they would need nourishment and were not sure when they would have their next meal. They raided the remaining cans in the pantry and sat down for a quick meal before they left the home forever. Lexie scraped just enough formula from the bottom of the can to make one last bottle, Silas had chicken noodle soup, Brownie had a can of beef chili, and Lexie ate a can of beef and barley soup.

They rounded up clean linens to use as diapers, and took the few remaining canned food items and a bottle of wine which was covered in dust. Lexie found a clean outfit in one of the closets and it felt wonderful to her to wear clothing that was not rags. Silas tried to do the same, but all the clothes were too big with the exception of a Cleveland Browns shirt that he found tucked away in a drawer. While it, too, was not quite his size, it was still better than the stinking rags he had on previously. They took one last pass through the home to find anything of use, and then headed out to the driveway and loaded the SUV with their few possessions.

It was not easy saying goodbye to James, to the home where he had grown up, to the place where Lexie used to hang out as a teenager. As they backed the SUV out of the driveway, Silas looked forlornly at the house, while Lexie fought off yet more tears.

The quicker we get away from here and focus on our survival, the better off we'll be. Especially now that we have to face the rest of our journey...alone.

She knew they'd have to fend for themselves from that point on. She knew that the tent cities that had sprouted up around the perimeter of the lake were both dangerous and lawless, while the salt mines—easier to defend—were still a safe haven. She yearned to see her family again, and so did Silas.

"Well," she said, "I guess the best thing to do is to head down East Erie Avenue to I-90 East."

"Sounds like a plan," Si sighed.

Lexie forced a smile. "Well, then, what are we waiting for? Let's go find Grammy and Poppy!"

Neither Lexie nor Silas was in any mood to talk as the thought of James weighed heavily on their minds. No matter how hard Lexie tried, memories of James danced through her head. Good memories. Bad memories. She couldn't get the images of the final minutes with him out of her racing mind.

As they drove through town, death and decay closed in on them. The street that had once been the domain of the wealthy, where the most gorgeous homes once stood with their bright green lawns and sprawling decks overlooking the crystalline waters of Lake Erie, now held dilapidated buildings overlooking an endless desert canyon. Lexie gazed off toward what once had been the lake.

Holy shit. Where did all the water go? The shoreline—it looks like a crater on the moon or Mars. The land dropped off sharply into a parched barren bowl. With its craters, cliffs, boulders, and the trashed remains of expensive boats that had once pulled perch and walleye from the waters, the scene looked as if it were from another planet.

When they finally reached the highway, Silas was musing about the salt mines. "Mom, have you been there before? To the mines, I mean?"

Lexie shook her head. "No, Si. To tell you the truth, I'd never even heard of them until I read that letter."

"What do you think they look like? I mean, are they really, like, made of salt?"

"I imagine so."

"That doesn't sound very nice! Living like a bunch of moles in tunnels lined with salt!"

Lexie chuckled. "I don't think they're all that bad. After all, if Grandma and Grandpa could put up with it, they must have some redeeming virtues. And, even more importantly, they're safe."

As they drove on, they passed signs announcing the distance to the city of Cleveland. Finally, as the buildings came into view, Lexie marveled at the ghost town radiating out from the city center—the concrete canyons, the towering temples, few cars, no people, and no signs of life anywhere.

"Where do you think everyone went?" Silas asked.

"They've probably set off to follow the water. Whether in the tent cities or the mines, I don't know. Maybe both."

She followed the directions her parents had left for them and, before long, they had pulled to a stop on a wide gravel road outside the sprawling Cargill Salt Mining Company.

"Is this it?" Silas asked.

"I'd say so." It was an impressive sight. Towering mountains of salt that had been brought to the surface on miles of conveyer belts, standing guard over a crusted dry river and the great Lake Erie Canyon beyond.

"This looks like the Antarctic or somewhere. It looks like we're surrounded by giant glaciers."

"It does, doesn't it? So white and pristine. It's hard to imagine this was all once underground."

Lexie veered off to the right.

"Where are you going?"

She nodded off in the distance. "I think I see someone, some guards. Let's ask them if we're in the right place."

"There's the gate, with a lock on it."

"And a uniformed guard. Could be the entry to the mines."

She pulled the SUV to a halt and rolled down her window. "Hello," she called, waving her hand to show they came in peace. She slowly opened the door and stepped out.

"Mom, look over there," Silas said, pointing. "Look at that pile there. It must be 30 feet tall."

Lexie smiled as the guard approached.

"Can I help you?" the guard asked, his hand on the butt of his holstered pistol. He was tall, thin, and cleanly shaved; dressed in a neatly pressed uniform.

"Yes, are these the mines where the people are being sheltered? My mother and father are here."

He looked her over, up and down, peered through the window at Silas, and told her to wait where she was.

No doubt about it. This guy is serious. Dead serious!

She watched as the guard walked back to the gate and took the rifle from the second guard who, hand on pistol butt, approached. Lexie stood silently, smiling. Sweating.

The second guard, also tall and thin, and sporting a thick red beard, had a stern demeanor.

"State your business here, please."

She motioned with her head and pulled the letter out of her pocket and handed it to him. An I.D. badge on his shirt said Frank.

"We were told to come here by my parents. They left us directions back in Lorain. We're supposed to ask for a man by the name of Bill Nyberg."

The guard read the letter and handed it to his partner, who had sneaked up behind him. After huddling together for several seconds, the bearded guard turned to her.

"Wait here, please. I'll see if Bill is available."

"Thank you!" Lexie cried, realizing at last that the adrenalin was racing through her body. "Thank you," she said again, more sedately. "Sorry. It's been a long trip, and my parents…"

"I understand," the first guard—his name was Al—said. "Just a few minutes. Please."

Lexie watched as the bearded guard stepped into an elevator cage, pressed a button, and pulled a lever. He began his descent into the bowels of the cavern. As she looked around, she noticed that most of the equipment surrounding them was run down; the rest, destroyed. She had the distinct impression that the mine must have once consisted of far more than the rickety elevator framework and the small hut still standing next to it.

"So, what exactly's down there anyway?" she asked.

"Sorry, Ma'am, but I'm not at liberty to say."

What? She looked at him, her eyebrows raised. "Really? Why's that?"

"I'm sorry, Ma'am, but I'm not at liberty to say that, either."

"I mean, there are people there, right? This is like a safe house, right?"

He flicked his head to one side.

"I know, I know," she said. "You're not at liberty to say." She shrugged. "Well, what are you at liberty to say?"

A sardonic smile tried to blossom across his face. "Nice weather we're having. Only going to be 120 or so today."

She grinned. "Oh, come on. You can do better than that. We're not spies, for heaven's sake. My parents are staying here."

"Sorry, Ma'am," he said, the smile disappearing. "I'll ask for your patience. You can direct any questions you have to Mr. Nyberg."

"Okay. I'm going to wait in the SUV, out of the heat." The guard nodded and, as Lexie returned to the car, she filled Silas in on what was happening. Finally, after several more minutes, they heard the sound of the elevator clunking to life and, when the cage reappeared, the steel-mesh door opened and the guard emerged. He motioned for Lexie to join them.

"You'll need to leave your car keys with us. We'll tag them and park your vehicle in a secure lot. Absolutely no firearms of any kind are permitted inside these gates so, if you have any in the vehicle, you'll need to check them here with us. Do not leave anything of value in your car, or we can't guarantee you'll get it back when you return. Anything you want taken down, point to it and I'll tag it."

She motioned for Silas to join her and, when he got out, she instructed him to round up all their weapons and valuables and deliver them to the guard house.

"About the only thing of value we have is the soda," she said, turning to Al. "We can't carry it all down there. Can someone watch over it for us?"

"Soda?" The guard looked perplexed. When he walked up to the vehicle and looked inside, he winced. "Wow. Whoa. What did you do, knock over a Dr. Pepper factory or something?"

"I wish it had been that easy," she said. "Of course, we'd be happy to share with the others."

The guard nodded. "That's really nice of you, Ma'am. We'll take care of it for you. This is a real luxury, let me tell you. This will put a smile on a lot of faces tonight. A real treat. We'll make sure it gets down to the colony safe and sound."

"You guys take a couple cans for yourselves, too, okay?"

Al looked at Frank who was staring at the pop and making soft purring sounds. He shrugged. "Thanks," he said, his demeanor softer than it had been earlier.

Lexie turned to help Silas stuff their few personal possessions into a couple of well-worn duffle bags. Lexie grabbed the last can of baby formula they had left and told Silas to take his baby sister and let Brownie out of the back.

"Make sure to put him on his leash," she said.

Finally, with all the transfers made, Frank took one last look at the pop and instructed them to follow him down into the mine. "It's a long ride—about five minutes. We'll be traveling some 1,800 feet underground. The only light until we reach the bottom will be the small light on my headlamp, so please stay close and keep your hands inside the cage."

As they followed the guard, Silas turned and looked around.

"Sir, what's down there?" he asked Frank.

"Mr. Nyberg will explain all that to you when you see him," he said.

"Is there electricity?" Silas asked.

"Yes, we have acres of heat-resistant solar panels on the canyon floor, and we draw water from the deepest part of the lake and pump it through pipes back here into the shaft."

As they slipped deeper down into the cavern, Lexie felt her ears begin to clog. She swallowed. "Si," she said, noticing he, too, was having problems. "Just hold your breath and swallow."

As they continued deeper into the guts of the shaft, she noticed a strange smell in the air—earthy, damp. Neither she nor Silas could put their fingers on it.

"Yuck!" the boy called suddenly. "It's salt. I can taste it!"

The guard grinned. "You'll get used to it, son. Just think of it as the 'new normal.'"

Finally, five minutes into their journey, the elevator slowed to a crawl, eventually jarring to a stop far beneath the Earth's surface. They couldn't believe how refreshing the much cooler temperatures felt to them. Off in the distance, Lexie heard men talking. The guard pulled on the cage door and slid it open. There was nothing to greet them but a large grayish-white room with high ceilings, sprawling archways, and walls that seemed

167

to stretch into infinity. The room was illuminated by several overhead bulbs hanging from the ceiling. Beyond the wall lay what looked like an oversized garage door. The guard stepped out of the elevator and walked up to it, pausing to press a button. The door slowly raised, and more light shone through.

"I wish we could skip all this and just see Grammy and Poppy," Silas whispered.

The door opened wide and a series of tunnels stretched out in several different directions. Huge towering arches and rooms glowing a familiar translucent gray greeted them.

"Are these walls really made of…salt?"

"These are the salt tunnels, yes, Ma'am," the guard replied.

"They look so smooth and clean."

"Yes, Ma'am."

At the far end of the main hall, half a dozen armed men stood at attention, apparently guarding what lay just beyond. Lexie glanced at Silas, his eyes as large as saucers, as the boy took in the scene. Out of the darkness, just beyond the opening to one of the tunnels, a silhouette appeared. Walking slowly, it grew larger, gradually lightening in color. By the time it had halved the distance between them, Lexie made out a good-looking middle-aged man with neatly combed graying hair. He was wearing jeans and a freshly laundered polo shirt.

"Hi," the man said as he reached them. He stretched out his palm. "Welcome to the Cargill Salt Mines. I'm Bill Nyberg."

Lexie introduced herself and Silas and, when Bill saw the dog, he bent down to pet him. "And who is this?"

"That's Brownie!" Silas said.

"Well, welcome, Brownie." The dog wagged his tail. "Welcome one and all to what we here like to think of as Utopia. Or, more accurately, Saltopia." He let out a little chuckle before adding, "And James? Your husband? Where is he?"

Once again, Lexie was overcome with emotion. The mere mention of James caused her eyes to well up, her stomach to churn, and her heart to ache. She did her best to keep her composure.

"I'm afraid we…we lost him just a short while ago, back in Lorain," she said.

"Oh, I'm sorry. You must be devastated."

Lexie began to go into the circumstances of what had happened before stopping short. Having to relive the story broke her heart, but she knew she needed to tell it. Every sentence of the story was painful. She tried to keep it short and simple, but she knew she was rambling on. The only thing she really wanted was James by her side. She wanted to hold his hand, embrace him, kiss him.

"I'm sure it has been extremely difficult," Bill said. "For the entire family." He looked at Charlotte, craning her head as if to better understand what was happening. "But I want you to know that you're safe here, all of you. And, best of all, there are two very special people who have been waiting to see you for quite some time now."

"Grammy and Poppy," Silas squealed.

"Oh, God, we can't wait!"

"But first, we have a long ride ahead of us, so let's get going. I'll explain whatever it is you want to know on the way to reception."

They climbed aboard an electric vehicle and started off on their journey deep below the middle of the former Great Lake.

After some time, Silas turned to Bill. "What's up with all the guys with guns?"

"Well, this is a peaceful place where people are sheltered from the outside world. We protect our safety at all costs. Every person over the age of eighteen has a job here, and many of them are guards. Particularly those who have had law-enforcement training and are skilled in using firearms. The job of our guards is to watch over the internal entrance and prevent any outsiders from penetrating any farther into the cavern than the elevator shaft."

"Has that ever happened?" Lexie asked.

"It hasn't yet. Nothing serious, at least. The people outside know we're pretty well protected in here. They'd have to be crazy to try to force their way in. Most don't even know the mines exist."

"I'm good with guns! I wanna be a guard!" Silas said.

"Silas! That's not going to happen."

"How long before we get there?" Silas asked, his anxiety getting the better of him.

"Oh, probably fifteen minutes or so. I'll try to explain some things as we go along. If you have any questions, don't hesitate to interrupt and I'll answer them the best I can."

Cargill Mines, Bill explained, had been in business for decades. Few people knew about the place, even among the locals. The mines had closed down many years ago, when the need for salt to melt the snow and ice along the streets of Cleveland had dried up along with just about everything else above ground. So the mines sat empty, but remained virtually fully intact.

"Here," he continued, the car wending its way deeper into the structure, "we're entering what's known as the Great Eastern Salt Basin. When things started going to hell—excuse my French—several former miners and mining engineers began working on building this place. They recognized that the temperatures down here remained a constant 80 degrees, despite what was going on 1,800 feet above us. So they recruited a group of reliable people to help them build what you are about to see.

"For years, they hauled lumber and steel and all kinds of other material down here so that the place could be made livable. They installed hardwood and laminate floors, carpeting, ceramic tile, and studs to frame out each of the units and the commercial venues. They finished off most of them with drywall for the ceilings and walls. They brought in electricians to wire the individual rooms and solar engineers to establish the solar fields directly above us. They used the most creative and skilled plumbers to run water lines directly from the bottom of the lake, where there's still plenty of water, thank God, and run them directly here to us."

"That's amazing," Lexie said. "But what about food?"

"Well, at present, we have approximately 200 people living here, including several doctors and dentists. There are so many rooms—we call them condos—so we still have plenty of space for new folks, but we limit admissions to the immediate family of those already here. Sadly, that means we're occasionally forced to turn people away, but for good reason. There are only so many resources here. Food, as you've already hinted at, is our biggest challenge, and we fight that battle daily. We have a group of volunteers who go out every day and risk their lives to search the various neighborhoods and stores for whatever remaining food items they can find. Thankfully, they continue to be successful.

"We've found many homes that had been abandoned, some with huge underground bunkers of stored food. We have several FEMA people here who were able to get trucks of shelf-stable food delivered to us. It's always a work in progress but, so far, we're able to maintain at least two months' supply of rations, and often more."

"That's incredible," Lexie said, "considering what's going on outside."

"Not only that," he added, grinning, "but, with our strict allotments and rationing, we've solved the growing nationwide obesity problem. You won't find any fat people down here!"

Lexie laughed.

"Are you the leader?" Silas asked.

"The...Oh, no, son. Thank God! No one is the leader here. We all work together, and there's a group of people who've been elected to represent everyone's interests. We call them the Saltopia City Council. That's what we actually consider ourselves here. A little city within or, more precisely, below, a city.

"To help lift spirits, we even have a small gym, a basketball court, a small meditation room, and a restaurant we call Morton's. And, yes, that pun is intended. We have working landline phones that, of course, only work down here. We have very good radio communication in several rooms throughout the mines. We're able to not only keep in contact with FEMA and the Canadians, but also we can hear some of the 'chatter' from some of the Warlords. The engineers placed an antennae outside the mines so that we can have radio communication down here. The Canadians have been very helpful in regards to intelligence as the RCMP is still partially intact. Despite being 1,800 feet below surface, we have some amazing technology."

"RCMP?" Silas asked.

"That would be the Royal Canadian Mounted Police," he said. "They've sorta morphed into the only functioning protection that still exists. At least in this area," he added.

Lexie peered ahead at the endless tunnel. "So, what should we expect when we arrive?"

"Well, you'll find our residents, including your parents, waiting to greet you. We don't get newcomers here very often, so I'm sure there'll be quite a turnout. We have a room already assigned for your family. You'll be able to bathe, get into some clean clothing, and have a bite to eat while you catch up on the news with your mother and father. Tomorrow, you'll be given several options for jobs. We have a list printed out, so you can look it over and think about what it is you'd like to do while you're here. We presently have a need for cooks, cleaners, carpenters, electricians, food procurers, runners, and a number of other gigs." He paused before turning to Silas. "And you, son, will start school once you get settled in."

"School? Are you serious?"

"Yes, we have two classrooms—one for the younger children and the other for those over thirteen. We're very fortunate to have some of the best teachers in the country here with us."

"I think I'd rather just take one of the jobs," Silas said.

Lexie tousled his hair. "No, I think you'd rather just go back to school, where you belong!"

Bill laughed. "Ahh, the world may have gone to hell, but some things never change."

After several more minutes of questions and answers, the car slowed to a halt. An oversized door loomed before them. Bill got out and, grabbing hold of the handle, turned back toward his guests. "Are you ready for the treat of your lives?"

Lexie breathed in and exhaled, nodding. "We're ready!"

Pulling up on the door, he raised it to reveal a small sea of strange faces, all waiting to greet them. And two who weren't that strange—Lexie's parents, Artie and Bea.

"Lexie! Oh, my God," Bea called, rushing forward with out-flung arms. "Let me hug you. Oh, my God, honey, it's been so long! Let me get a good look."

"Oh, my. You guys look great!" Lexie said, the tears and emotions from the past several weeks finally washing over her. "It's so good to be home." She brushed the hair from her face as Silas handed her a handkerchief. She laughed. "Even if home is 1,800 feet below the Earth's surface!"

Artie came forward. "And who's this big strapping young man?"

Silas grinned. "It's me, Poppy. Don't you remember?"

"Why, I'll never forget!" He turned to his wife. "Will you look at this, Bea, how big Silas has grown?" And, as Bea and Artie traded places, the others crowded in to get a look at their newest arrivals. Lexie's parents then turned their attention to Charlotte whom they had never met. Bea gently took her from Lexie's arms and cradled her. Artie leaned over, stroked her hair, and kissed her on the forehead.

"She's absolutely beautiful," he said with pride.

"She's a doll," Bea said.

"There's so much to tell you, so much to say." Lexie dabbed at her eyes as Artie hugged her all the tighter.

"I've got my own gun, Poppy!"

Lexie looked at her son. "He was such a big help on our journey out here. You wouldn't believe it. We never would have made it without him."

Silas grinned.

"It must have been a harrowing journey," Bea said, clutching Lexie's arm and rubbing it.

"You wouldn't believe it," she said. "We'll tell you everything."

"Where's James? Is he gathering your things?" Artie asked.

Lexie hesitated before her eyes welled up with tears. The reality of James's death along with their harrowing journey suddenly hit her like a ton of bricks and she fell to her knees. Bea and Artie knew immediately from the look on her face that James was not with them. Bea handed Charlotte to Bill. As Lexie began to retell the story in tears, her parents held her in their arms. Silas joined them for the first family hug in a long time. But a family without James.

Chapter 25

After introducing them to their neighbors, Bill led the family down one of the corridors to see their new home. It was an open room with wooden floors, yellow painted walls, several bunk beds, a small bassinet, numerous chairs, and plastic storage containers for their belongings. There was even a comfortable looking reclining chair. As was the case nearly everywhere, there was a single light bulb hanging from the ceiling.

"Wow, this isn't so bad," Silas said.

"They are pretty amazing," Bill said, looking around as they walked. He turned to Lexie. "I'm afraid you'll have to share your quarters with two other people." He motioned behind them to Grammy and Poppy. "I hope you don't mind."

Lexie laughed. "Are you kidding? This is a dream come true! Oh, my, we're so glad to be with them both again." Lexie took the baby from Silas's arms. "Aren't we, honey?" She nuzzled her nose into Charlotte's tummy. "To share a place with Grandma and Grandpa."

"I thought you'd like that," Bill said, pausing before their front door. "I'll give you some time to get acquainted and be back to check up on you later. See if there's anything you need."

Lexie paused to speak, but nothing came out. Finally, the tears began rolling down her cheeks again. "I...I don't know what's the matter with me today. I'm just blubbering like a little child." Her mother came up and hugged her, and Bill smiled. "I guess it's everything we went through to get here, everything we endured just to survive. And somehow we did it."

"I know exactly what you're talking about," Bill said. "I went through the exact same thing myself to get here from Dubuque. And I kissed the ground we stand on once I finally arrived." He squeezed her arm. "I know just how you feel. All of you."

After getting them something to eat and drink, Bea showed Silas to the showers and laid out some clean clothes. He immediately went to the men's room where he took the most amazing shower of his life. He watched as layers and layers of brown dirt rolled off his thin body and into the drain. Just when he thought he was done scrubbing off the dirt, he would find more areas of grime.

Meanwhile, Lexie was catching up with her mother.

"How long have you been expecting us?" Lexie asked.

Bea laughed. "Since the day we arrived here ourselves, practically. We knew it would only be a matter of time before you made it home. Didn't we, Art?"

"Yep, yep. Every morning when we got up, I'd roll over in bed and turn to your mother and ask her if she thought that was our lucky day. And every morning she answered, 'I hope so.'"

This is so great, Lexie thought. *Being reunited with Mom and Dad.* But then the reality of the situation hit her. James was not with them to share in the joy. She knew that all he ever wanted was to find safety and supplies for the family. It devastated her to know he was not with them to share in the happy moment. She felt her eyes welling up with tears. She looked at Charlotte, bouncing on Poppy's knew. Why couldn't James be here to share this special family moment?

Silas, wearing clean shorts, a brand new T-shirt, and neatly combed hair walked back into the room, looking completely refreshed.

"Wow, Mom, I can't believe how great this place is!"

Lexie nodded. "You're not kidding, Silas. And everything looks so neat and clean. It's just perfect."

Grammy smiled. "Well, we have the scavengers to thank for that. Fortunately for us, there's no shortage of brand new furnishings and appliances and everything else you see around you. You might say we have the best of both worlds—the one we left behind, and the one we forged for ourselves down here."

"This recliner chair is great." Silas said. "Does it have a vibrator?"

"You don't need a vibrating chair!" Lexie said. "Why don't you go with Poppy and take a look around. I'm sure he wouldn't mind giving you a tour of the place, would you, Dad?"

"Oh, cool," Silas said, turning to his grandfather. "Is there a gym here? And tennis courts? How about a pool?"

Lexie shook her head. "He's pulling your leg, Dad. Don't let him get away with it."

"Actually, we do have a little gym here and a small basic basketball court."

"Wow!"

She smiled. "I think I know where you're going to be spending all of your free time."

"I'm afraid we don't have a pool, though. Sorry. Using water recreationally that way just seemed to rub people the wrong way."

"Can you show me around?"

"Sure can." He turned to his daughter. "You want to come along, Lex? Momma can watch the baby."

She smiled. "No, you two go ahead. I'll stay here with Mom and catch up on the latest news." She turned to her mother. "Speaking of which,

174

how's Karen doing? We've lost touch with her since the grid went down. Have you heard from her lately? Is she here yet?"

Her mother's eyes glanced at Artie, sticking there for several moments. He looked back at his wife before, finally, she shifted uncomfortably on her feet and motioned toward the sofa.

"Sit down, honey." She nodded toward Silas. "You, too, Si."

Lexie knew in a heartbeat she'd asked the wrong question. Or, more likely, the right question that had the wrong answer.

"What is it? Something's wrong."

Artie stepped forward, put his arm around his wife's shoulders, and patted her hand. "Lex, you know how determined Karen is! She went to visit the tent cities to see if there was any way she could help you and your family make it back home. And to make sure FEMA was there with whatever aid you might require. We begged her not to go, but you know how your sister is."

"And? What happened? Where is she?"

Her mother interrupted. "She's not come back, Lexie. She said she would be back in three days, and it's been eight weeks now. We haven't heard a word from her since. Not a single word."

"Reports from security are that people up above are being abducted—sold into slavery or prostitution or even worse," Artie said. "Given what we've heard from the security team here, we think that may be true. We also think Karen is still alive. But we're pretty sure that, if she is, she's in the hands of the Warlords."

Lexie had to take a moment to absorb what she had just heard. *This can't possibly be happening,* she thought. *First I lose the love of my life and now my sister.* She wanted to cry, but she gathered her strength and carried on.

"Warlords? Who in hell are the Warlords? You mean that biker gang in California?"

"Worse, I'm afraid," he sighed. "We told you in the letter that the tent cities were bad. Lots of bad things happening up there. They're run by militias and gangs of thugs, none of which is good. They're basically the new U.S. government, and they're preparing to wage war on the Canadians for their water. I've heard they believe that, by gaining control of it, they'll be the most powerful political force on Earth."

"I don't understand. What does kidnapping Karen have to do with waging war on Canada?"

"Well, one of the reasons they kidnap people is to force them to join their gangs—to fight for them."

"Honey," Bea said, taking a deep breath. "Karen is…well, we're not sure where she is. But we're almost positive she's been taken captive."

"But why? Karen's not a fighter! She's a Natural Disaster Coordinator, for heaven's sake! She wouldn't know a gun from an I.V. drip!"

Bea wiped a tear from her eye. "The gangs out here, like the Warlords—the really bad ones—they don't prey on people's good, like in the past. They're not looking only for food and water and gasoline. They're looking for…other people."

"What do you mean? Why? To fight with them against Canada?"

"Sometimes." Grammy sighed. "Sometimes for other reasons."

"So, what are they asking for her release? Have they given a ransom request? We could maybe…"

"Honey," Artie said. "They're not holding her for a ransom. They're holding her for…"

He stopped suddenly, dropped his head, tears falling from his eyes. His shoulders heaved, his knees slumped down. Lexie looked at Silas, who looked back, confused.

"Lexie, sweetheart, I'm afraid your sister is being held for the…" She paused, unsure of just how much to say in front of the boy. "To sell into slavery."

The word struck at her like a stiletto. "Slavery!"

She stood up, looked around the room, the shock of the word finally sinking in. Like an animal locked behind steel bars, she took several paces forward, turned, and took several back. She crossed her arms across her chest, dropped them to her sides, and waved them furiously above her head. "They can't sell my sister into slavery! No way! They just can't!" She glanced at Silas.

Easy, Lex. Get control of yourself. For Silas's sake. Easy.

"Honey," Artie said. "Remember. That's just one of the rumors."

She looked from Grammy to Poppy and back again.

"But if it's true…are you saying slavery…like…real slavery?"

Artie shrugged. Bea nodded.

"You mean like for the sex trade?"

At the words, Bea broke down, sobbing, and Artie took her in his arms to comfort her. "Momma. It's all right. We don't know for sure. We just don't know. The things we hear down here, some turn out to be true. Most not." He pulled a handkerchief from his back pocket and gave it to his wife. He turned to Lexie. "We're just hoping for the best, honey. Hoping to hear some good news any day now. Hoping we're wrong."

"So what's being done to save her? What's being done to find her?"

"Well, there's only so much that *can* be done, honey. We have our normal security team looking for her, but they'll only go so far. It's not like we have a military or anything to help. We have to hope and pray she makes it out on her own," Artie said.

176

Bea nodded, the tears falling faster. And the faster they fell, the more he tried to comfort her. But there was no comfort left in his arms that evening. No comfort in Lexie's heart. No comfort anywhere.

Karen was gone.

Chapter 26

Lexie summoned Bill to their apartment, and he told her it was true. At least, to the best of his knowledge. The slave-trade gangs had learned long ago that, while water and food and other tangible goods were in short supply, there was no shortage of attractive vulnerable females. They preyed on them all. If a young girl had shown any signs of blossoming into adulthood, she was a target. If an older woman had any life left in her at all, she was a target. The only difference was that the young girls would be used, abused, and traded to other gangs time and again—sometimes fifteen, twenty times during their lives. The older women would be used and abused once or twice and then killed. Why spend resources feeding and housing someone who had no intrinsic value in the marketplace? Unless, that is, they could be used for slave labor. In that case, they were kept alive.

"But how do you know Karen isn't just...missing?" Lexie asked.

"We have our sources," Bill said. "We have people on the outside who communicate with us on a regular basis. Spies, I guess you'd call them. Moles. We have one woman on the inside now who used to be a sex-slave victim herself. She managed to escape from the Warlords and make her way back here to the mines. And when we asked her who else in particular was still being held in captivity and showed her some relatives' photographs, she picked out Karen right off."

"Well...where is she, this woman? Who is she? Does she know if Karen's okay? Is she healthy? Is Karen...is she still..."

Lexie didn't know how to end the question. Sexually abused, a concubine, mutilated? What? Alive? Dead? Dying? She had seen the worst of humanity on their escape from California to the Midwest. She couldn't imagine the depths of depravity to which a gang like the Warlords could sink. A gang that survived by kidnapping women and selling them into slavery. She couldn't bear to think about it.

Bill reached out and patted her arm. "Her name is Doris. She's still here. I'm sure she'd be willing to talk to you, to tell you everything you want to know. If you're prepared to hear it, I can arrange for you to meet her if you'd like?"

Lexie did not have to think twice about the offer and quickly accepted. Bill agreed to arrange the meeting immediately.

Doris sat on the sofa across from her. She appeared to Lexie to be stoic, calm, relaxed, and comfortable. And that didn't sit right for someone who, only weeks ago, had been a sex slave for the Warlords.

But nothing seems right anymore, she thought. *Not after all we've been through. If only James was here to help us through this. He was my rock. God, do I miss him.*

"Hello, Doris. I'm Lexie. Karen's sister."

"Pleasure to meet you."

"Where was she when you saw her last?" Lexie asked.

"The last time? About twenty kilometers from here, north of the city. In a tented community the Warlords have set up there. Maybe you've heard of it. They call it CanAm?"

Lexie shook her head. "I don't think so."

Lexie looked down at the woman's feet—petite, dainty, recently pedicured. At the age of 30, she was demure, short, clear complexioned with dark straight hair and unusually large brown eyes, almost as large as her earrings. Her lips were full and plump and, when she talked, the right side of her mouth turned up more than the left.

A result of her trauma? Lexie thought. *Or perhaps a childhood malady?*

"How do you know she's being kept a prisoner?"

Doris looked taken aback. "Well...I know because she was always under the watchful eye of the gang's enforcer, some guy they called Rafael. Wherever she went, he wasn't far behind. Even when she turned in to sleep in the evenings, he remained right outside her tent."

"So she was alone in the evenings? I mean, she wasn't..."

Doris looked Lexie in the eyes. "Raped?"

Lexie let out a deep sigh. "Yes."

"Not in the evenings, no."

Another sigh.

"But in the mornings, it was another matter. The leader of the community, a man named Singo, he came by every morning just after breakfast, went into her tent, and posted two armed guards outside."

"Singo?"

"And after half an hour or so, he came back out, and she didn't show herself until later in the day. Much later."

Lexie felt her stomach turn, her hands twitch, her heart thud.

"Who else... I mean, was anybody else..."

Doris looked down contemptuously and spat on the floor. "No. Only him. Only that pig—Singo."

Lexie paused, her mind racing. "And he's... I mean, they're still..." She stopped to take a breath. "Are they still there? Where you last saw them? Do you know?"

"I cannot say for sure, because I managed to escape their evil clutches weeks ago. But from the size and the logistics of the camp, I would say they are still there, even today. And they will be there tomorrow. Moving an operation that size takes time and resources and effort. And why? Why move? What have they to fear by staying exactly where they are?"

I have one pretty good idea, Lexie thought, wondering how difficult it would be to retrieve her guns and car from the guards at the front gate.

Lexie poured a glass of water and a second for the woman and held it out for her. Taking it, she drank gingerly, as though out of politeness more than thirst.

"What are your best thoughts about Karen's current health?"

Doris looked at her, squinting. "You mean physically?"

Lexie nodded.

Doris shrugged. "Physically, she didn't seem to be any the worse for wear. Physically. As for emotionally, who can say?"

"How about her location? I mean, if you were to venture a guess, would Karen...still be at the same camp?"

She paused. "Yes." She sipped from the glass before setting it down. "Unless Singo has grown tired of her."

"Tired? And then what? What would he do with her then?"

"I don't think you want to know."

Lexie set her glass down, glared through widened eyes, and held back as long as she could before exploding. "I have to know, do you understand?" She pounded her thigh with her fist. "It's not a question of wanting or wishing or desiring. I have to know!"

Doris looked sheepish, a child caught with her hand in the cookie jar. Her game had just taken a turn for the worse. Her team had just lost. She had no other choice.

"I imagine, then..." She paused again. "That he would turn her over to the camp for them to have their way with her. And once they were satiated, they would sell her to a rival gang. To start the cycle all over again."

After thanking Doris, Lexie, pale and shaken, stumbled back to her parents to tell them what she had learned. And to tell Silas, too. Torn at first, she realized he had a right to know. He was in this situation himself; he was part of the New World that threatened to destroy everything they believed in.

"What are we going to do, Mom?" he asked. "We have to do something. We can't just leave her there, with them."

"I don't know," she said. "I'm not sure. All I know is that I don't trust that woman."

"Who? Doris? Why? Why not? She told you everything she knew, didn't she? She told you the names of her captors and what they..." He paused. "And all the other stuff."

"Really, Lexie," Artie said, "I don't think we have any alternative other than to believe her. Which must have been difficult for her...having just gone through what she has."

"Besides, honey, why would she lie?" Bea said. "What would she have to gain from lying about Karen's situation?"

Lexie shook her head. "I don't know." Her eyes wandered across the room, sweeping first across Silas, and then Artie, and finally Bea. "Where's Charlotte?"

"Sound asleep," Bea said. "She has a full belly and plenty of water, clean diapers, and a safe place to rest. Thank God."

"Yeah," Lexie nodded absently. "Thank God."

Rolling over in bed later that evening, Lexie's eyes scanned the room. Only the phosphorescent glow of a night light plugged into the wall across from the sleeper betrayed her locale. No windows. No moon. No stars. But still, she was with her family. And they were safe.

"Mom?"

She craned her head. "Si? What is it, son? I thought you were asleep."

"I think I was, but I woke up."

"Well, go back to sleep. Tomorrow will come soon enough. We'll have a full day ahead of us, getting settled in, making plans...thinking."

"Were you asleep?"

She paused. "No."

"Why not? Aren't you tired?"

Surprisingly, she wasn't. She didn't know why not, after all they been through the last few weeks. But she wasn't.

"I'm going to get some sleep soon. You, too, now. Go ahead."

"Are you worried?"

"About what, son? We're safe. Finally safe."

"No, I mean are you worried about your sister? Are you worried about Aunt Karen and about what that lady told you, that Doris?"

Yeah, she thought. *Yeah, yes, I am.*

She cleared her throat. "I wouldn't say worried. Not so much as...concerned. I'm wondering about Karen, whether or not she's...actually a captive. Or maybe just hiding out somewhere, waiting for the right chance to break away and get back home here to us."

She listened for a reply and, hearing none, assumed her son was nodding off. Several minutes passed.

"So you don't believe what Doris told you? About Aunt Karen, I mean?"

"I'm not sure what to believe, Si. I suppose it could be true. Or maybe she's just…wrong."

"She said she was there. She said she was a captive and that, when she escaped, Aunt Karen was still being held hostage."

She did, didn't she? Why would she…

"I know, son. I know what she said. But she could have been wrong. She could have mistaken anyone for Karen. It's not as if they'd been lifelong friends. Somebody gave her Karen's photo to identify and, based upon that, she said she saw her being held hostage. But who knows?"

Silas hesitated before responding. "You're thinking about going after her. Going after Aunt Karen, aren't you?"

"Son, why don't you just forget about this for tonight and go back to sleep. Everything will look brighter tomorrow. You'll see. The day always seems darkest before the dawn."

She listened for a response and, when she heard Silas rustling beneath the covers, knew he'd decided to take her advice and go back to sleep. She rolled over, too, away from him, but suddenly heard his voice in the dark.

"Yeah, but, down here, how will we know when it's dawn?"

The ringing of the phone startled her. She reached out, blindly searching, until the light suddenly went on. Bea was sitting up in her bed, Artie softly snoring away beside her. Bea picked up the receiver.

"Hello?"

She paused, listening.

"Hello," the voice on the other end said. "Is this Bea?"

"Yes. Who's this?"

"This is Doris, Bea. I know it's late, but I was wondering if Lexie is still up. I was wondering if I could have a word with her before she turns in."

"Just a minute," Bea said, covering the mouthpiece of the phone and turning toward her daughter. "It's Doris. She wants to know if she can talk to you."

Lexie crawled out of bed and skittered across the room, taking the phone from her mom.

"Yes. Hi, Doris, this is Lexie."

"Lexie, I hope I didn't disturb you."

She looked around the room, saw Silas and Artie sleeping soundly, with Charlotte and the dog over in the corner, and covered the receiver. "It's okay, mom. I'll talk to her. You just turn off the light and get back to bed. I'll hang up when I'm through."

Her mother looked at her, her brows creased, and did what her daughter had said. She reached out for the lamp and clicked it off, bathing the room in emptiness. Lexie felt her way across the room back to her bed and settled in.

"No. No problem. What is it, Doris?"

"I was just feeling…kind of bad…the way I sprang all that on you earlier today. About your sister, I mean. And then just got up and left. I mean, what you must have been going through, after what I'd told you."

What on earth is she saying?

"Yes?"

"Well, I mean, your parents are such wonderful people and all, and they've treated me so well, like a member of their own family, really. And you seem like such a warm, genuine person. And Silas, your son, too. I can't imagine what the two of you—what all of you—must be going through, thinking the very worst."

"Thank you. I appreciate that. It *has* been difficult."

"Well, I just wanted to call and let you know that I've given it a lot of thought and have come to realize that I'm the only one who can help. And that it's my obligation as a good citizen and a concerned member of the community to do so."

Lexie paused. "To help with what?"

"Why, to help with freeing your sister."

Lexie leaped upright in her bed. "What?"

"Everything okay, Lex?" Bea asked.

"Yeah, Mom. Everything is fine. Don't worry. Just go back to sleep." She partially muffled the receiver and spoke more softly. "Did I just hear you right?" she said into the phone.

"I said, since I'm the only one who knows where she is and since I've been intimately acquainted with her captors, and with their camp, it only seems logical that I be the one to take you to her, to help you help her escape."

"You can do that? I mean, you would do that?"

"I don't know if I could live with myself if I didn't. I don't think I could look myself in the eye in the mirror."

"But, I mean…how would we do it? How would we go about it? They're…they're a gang. There's, what? Fifty? A hundred of them? We're only two. Unless you know of someone else who…"

"No. I'm afraid you're right there. It would be just the two of us. You and me against the world. With an operation as clandestine as this, I wouldn't even trust my own baby brother. A slip of the lip, you know…"

"Well, then, how would we…how would we possibly pull it off? Freeing Karen and getting her back here to safety?"

She hesitated, and Lexie thought she heard the sound of someone drawing on a cigarette, followed by a weak cough. *Doris? The sound seemed to come from farther away than her.*

"I know them. I know their schedule. Tomorrow is Wednesday. Two days later, it's Friday evening. That's when they post two guards at the camp entrance, and the rest of the gang goes into the city to look for booty—and more hostages. They usually leave around seven at night and don't get back until well after midnight. Sometimes, if they score some booze, they'll go over to another camp somewhere and drink the night away. And more. That's how I know. That's what they did to me after they found me cowering in the rest room of an old gas station. So, between the hours of seven and midnight, that's when we'd have our best chance to make contact with your sister, to free her."

"Contact with her where? Isn't she in some sort of...jail...or something? Somewhere under lock and key?"

"She's in a mobile home on the outskirts of the camp. It has a padlock on the front door and locks on all the windows. It would be simple enough to get a pair of bolt cutters from the mining crew, sneak up, and snip the lock. After that, it would be easy."

"But, why...why...why..." She stopped to catch her breath. It was too good to be true. Could this woman whose word she had doubted turn out to be her very own guardian angel? And her sister's, too? "Why would you take such a chance, just for us? For Karen?"

"I told you. My conscience is bothering me. I don't think I could live with myself if I didn't at least offer you the opportunity to save your sister."

Two days. It's only two days until Friday. Karen could be back here with us an hour or two after that. She could be back home safe and sound!

"I...I just don't know what to say. I mean, of course I'm thrilled. It's such a fantastic thing to think that a perfect stranger..."

"Hey, now, honey!" Doris said, her voice rising. "No one ever said I was perfect."

Lexie smiled. "I can't...I mean, the only thing I can say is thank you. From the bottom of my heart. And for Karen and our family, too."

"Save that for when your sister is home free," she said. "Do you have access to a gun or any kind of a weapon? A pistol maybe? And some shells?"

Lexie found herself nodding involuntarily. "Yes! We have three guns that we checked with the guards at the gate. One is a pistol. I'm sure I can get that back. And the shells."

"Good. I don't expect we'll need it, but you never know."

"Right," she said. "Absolutely."

"Unfortunately, I don't have any weapons. I've never been much of a firearms person. I don't think I could shoot a mouse if I found it eating my last crust of bread."

"I know what you're saying, but you get used to it."

Doris paused. "Could *you?*"

Could I? Could I what? Shoot a mouse? Or another person? What an odd question!

"Shoot a mouse, you mean?"

"Or anything else?"

She felt her backbone stiffen. "Just try me."

Doris muffled the phone, saying something, or perhaps clearing her throat, before returning to Lexie. "That's good. I'll feel better knowing I'm with G.I. Jane to keep me safe."

"I wouldn't go that far, but I won't hesitate to use it if I have to."

"Good." She paused. "That's good to know."

"So what do we do next?"

"Next? We get some sleep. I'll get together with you in the morning, and we'll go over our plan. I'll work up a rough map of the area we'll be going to, where your sister is being held, the layout of the trailer, and we'll iron out all the details before Friday. Fair enough?"

Fair enough? It was fairer than anything she could possibly have imagined. Fairer than anything she could possibly have dreamed. *Is this woman a godsend or what?* Yes, it was fair enough.

"Thank God," she whispered, before clicking off the phone and settling back down to bed.

And that night, Lexie thought, she would sleep the sleep of the angels. Sleep with all her might, comforted by the thought that, in less than 48 hours, she would be united with her sister. Once and for all. And she would have her entire family around her for good.

But, like before, James entered her mind and her heart sank. She would not, in fact, have her entire family around her. James was not coming back and *he* was her family. She would never have her family whole again. She tried with all her might to fight back tears, but failed. She crawled back into bed and cried into her pillow.

Chapter 27

The following morning came upon them all too soon. When Charlotte began fussing for her feeding, Lexie stuffed her own head beneath the pillow. After several more minutes, she rolled over and, checking her watch, groaned. Instinctively, she went to reach for James only to find the empty space. Reality hit her once again.

Seven o'clock. It's morning already!

Hoping for another five minutes before getting up to greet the first day of her new life, she glanced toward the kitchen, where Bea had already taken the child, prepared her formula, and was getting ready to feed her.

Five more minutes. Just five more.

What seemed like only moments later, Lexie looked at the wall clock and leaped up from bed. "Nine fifteen!"

"Good morning!"

"Morning, Lex."

"Mom! Dad!"

"It's all right. I fed the baby, and Art is going to give her a sponge bath. We found a cute little jump suit at the commissary for her to wear. So, you just relax."

She breathed out deeply and looked over at Silas, still sound asleep. "Nine fifteen. I can't believe it. Why didn't you…"

"You were so tired, honey, overtired. I could see it in you yesterday. With all you've been through the last several weeks, it's no wonder. And Doris calling in the middle of the night didn't help any."

Doris. Oh, my God, yes! She shook the webs out of her head. "Oh, that's okay. I slept like a baby, anyway."

"Art!" Bea called toward the bathroom.

"Yeah?"

"Do you have the baby shampoo?"

"Got it," he said.

"Well, don't forget to use it!"

"Abuse what?" he called.

"I said… Oh, never mind. Jesus, that man's deaf!"

"Yes, everything's fine. We'll be out in a few minutes."

Silas rolled over, opened his eyes, and looked around the room. A jack-o-lantern smile spread across his face. "Wow," he said, stretching. "I can't believe how well I slept!"

Lexie pointed at him. "And snored!"

"I did not!"

She stared at him.

He frowned, his frown turning into an impish grin. "Well, maybe just a little."

"Uh-huh."

He paused before blurting out, "But you did, too!"

Artie came into the room, carrying the baby belly down on his forearm—clean, scrubbed, smiling, happy. And, most of all, safe.

"Should we grab a cup of coffee and get ready for some breakfast?"

"Sounds like a plan," Lexie said. "But don't go to any trouble. We're not used to real meals yet. Whatever we have will be closer to normal food than we've eaten in ages."

"Well, in honor of the special occasion, your first morning here with us, Art and I thought we'd treat you to breakfast out."

"What?" Silas said, jumping up from bed.

"What do you mean, out?" Lexie asked.

Artie took off his glasses, blew on the lenses, and wiped them in his polo shirt. "We have a really good restaurant in Saltopia—Morton's. Serves the best breakfasts and the tastiest damned bear claws you ever had in your life."

"Bear claws? Down here?"

He looked at her. "Hey, just because we're half a mile underground doesn't mean we have to rough it."

"You two get ready," Bea said, "and we'll treat you to the finest meal this side of the Mississippi."

Lexie looked at Silas who grinned from ear to ear before he jumped up, grabbed some clothes, and hurried off to the bathroom.

"Any other surprises you haven't told us about?" Lexie asked.

Artie shrugged. "Oh, I don't know. One or two maybe." He motioned to her duffle bag. "You'd better hurry. That son of yours looks hungry enough to eat a bear."

"Or a bear claw," she grinned.

"I have some clean clothes that should fit you if you want," Bea said. "We can stop by the commissary after breakfast so you and Si can pick out some new duds." She set Charlotte down on a blanket she'd arranged on the sofa. "After all, it wouldn't do to have the neighbors think we're beneath them."

Seated at the table, Lexie was amazed at how much like a real restaurant Morton's actually was. From the wooden floor and the painted walls to the antique tin-panel ceiling and overhead lighted fans, if she hadn't known they were half a mile below the surface, she would never have guessed.

After finishing their meals, Silas and Artie went off to the commissary to see what they could find, and Lexie turned to Bea. "How do we pay for this?" She looked around, as if for some sign explaining the new monetary system. "I mean, with what?"

Bea smiled and patted her daughter's arm. "It's already been paid for. By the community. They provide the owners with the location and the food and other supplies and, in exchange, the owners provide the labor."

As Lexie and her mom made their way back to their room, Bea opened the door and hurried to pick up the phone.

"Hello?" She paused, listening. "Oh, yes, Doris. Fine, just fine. And you?"

Lexie looked at her mother closely for the first time in years. *She's aged, no doubt about it.* She watched the animated twinkle in the older woman's eye as she chatted with her neighbor. *But she hasn't lost the family charm! Or is it blarney?*

"Yes," Bea said. "She's right here. I'll put her on."

Lexie took the receiver. Doris was calling to ask if she wanted to meet her at the gym.

"What time?"

"No time like the present," the voice on the other end said, "if that works for you."

"Let me find some shorts, and I'll meet you there in a few minutes. It's right down the hall from the restaurant, right?"

"Three doors down on your right. You can't miss it."

"See you then."

The moment Lexie walked through the door, she paused, stunned. *My God, this is pretty darn nice!* Her eyes scanned the small room from one end to the other. The grayish walls of salt seemed to disappear behind the façade of the makeshift gym.

Rows of machines lined one wall, leading to a series of closed doors at the far end of a narrow hall where there was a changing room. The doors were all stained hardwood—oak or pine, she couldn't tell. The walls were painted a bright green. The only sign that she was standing in an old salt mine over 2,000 feet below the Earth's surface was the glistening salt dome twenty feet over her head.

"Hey!" Doris called. "Glad you could make it." The woman stood in front of her, hands on hips, and motioned with her head. "Well, what do you think? Will it do?"

"Do?" She let out a low whistle. "It's absolutely amazing, considering where we are. This is incredible. Everything looks so...new. So...nice."

"Nothing but the best. Not when you're in the position we're in." She laughed. "Besides, most of the older folks avoid this place like the plague. They'd rather play shuffle board or cards or Bingo. Less strenuous things like that. Hardly anyone but we younger gals use it. And a few of the boys."

Lexie looked at several framed windows on the walls. "What are those?"

"What?" Doris looked in the direction of Lexie's finger. "Oh, our 'windows?' The designers read somewhere that plants and greenery and outdoor spaces help boost people's morale and can actually help them remain healthy. So they had the carpenters recreate some faux glass windows with some photographs in them to simulate the scenic views of downtown Cleveland—some parks, green spaces, the old lakefront, the band shell. Just taking it all in makes it easier to forget where we really are, and how far distant those photographs are from reality."

"That's fantastic. And I see what you mean. This room seems so much warmer and more inviting than most of the sterile gyms and even some of the spas I've been to in the past."

Doris draped a towel over the bars of the closest Nordic Trak® Incline and climbed aboard. "So," she said, "have you given it any more thought?" She set the simulator for the Cleveland lakefront. "Tomorrow's Friday. We'll have to finalize our plans and be ready to go shortly after dark so we can reach your sister and get back home by midnight."

"By midnight. You make it sound so simple. Like going to the store to buy a quart of milk."

"I'd like to know where you've been shopping lately!"

Lexie laughed. "Well, maybe not anymore." She climbed aboard a treadmill next to Doris and set the controls. "But, yes, I did manage to talk to Bill earlier today, and I told him what we were planning to do. He said he'd have the guards waiting with my pistol and some shells at the front gate."

Doris nodded. "Good. We're going to have to take your car, too, so be sure to have them bring that around front, probably sometime around eight."

"My car?"

"Yeah. I don't have one anymore. The bastards took it and traded it for supplies while I was being held captive. I don't know where it ended up."

Lexie paused. *What if something goes wrong? What if someone identifies the vehicle as the one Si and I drove to the mines the other day? What if someone we'd stopped to talk to identified us? If we were to lose our SUV, the way Doris had lost her car...*

"Anything wrong with that?" Doris asked.

Lexie shook her head. "No, of course not. I'll give Bill another call."

Doris slowed her pace to a crawl as the machine wound down. She let out a deep breath. "Wow. I'm out of shape."

"*You're* out of shape? I feel like I just ran the marathon." Lexie paused, breathless. "Twice!"

"I was thinking," the woman said, grabbing a towel and blotting her face and arms. She threw her head back, her glistening mane dancing in the overhead spots. "Might not be a bad idea to bring your son along, too."

"What? No!"

"You know, to act as a lookout for when we're in the trailer, freeing your sister. If he sees anything suspicious, he can lean on the horn to tip us off."

"Oh, no. Nooo. No. Not Silas. I don't like the idea of that at all."

Doris looked surprised. She handed her towel to Lexie, who took it, gingerly dabbing at her neck. "There's nothing that can go wrong," the woman said. "I mean, it's just as a precaution. Besides, it might look better in case someone sees us driving around town late at night. You know, to have a male in the car. It'd be less likely anyone would get any ideas and try to force us off the road or something. Before we got to the Warlords' camp, I mean."

Lexie thought for several seconds. *This is not what I bargained for. I never intended to get Si mixed up in this. Plus Si is just a boy...far from a protective man.*

"Come on," Doris said. "Let's get a drink and wind down. We can relax in the sauna."

Lexie followed her, watching her behind sway rhythmically in her leotards. *No wonder the Warlords grabbed her. I just can't believe they let her get away. If I were a slave trader, I would have kept closer watch over...*

She broke off her thoughts when she realized how attractive her own sister was—how tight and firm her body, how classically chiseled her features. The thought made her shiver. She took a bottle of water and, unscrewing the top, guzzled half of it down before following Doris through a cedar-lined doorway with a thick glass window in the center of the door.

"Holy crap," Lexie said.

"What? Hot enough for you?" Doris chuckled.

"It's grueling. How can you stand it?"

"Think of it this way. Once we get out, everything else will seem like it's air conditioned by comparison."

191

Just what I need in this horrible land we're stuck with. Like an Eskimo going to the North Pole on vacation!

Doris sat down and motioned for Lexie to take a seat opposite her. "Just five minutes or so," she said. "Just to open the pores and clean out the toxins."

Lexie sat down, the steam already working its magic. As she felt the perspiration form on her brow—a good perspiration, from a wet heat for a change—she closed her eyes. "Feels good," she said.

Doris ignored the comment. "I'm thinking if we leave here by eight, we'll get there around eight forty-five. We'll take a look around the camp's perimeter, just to make sure the gang has gone for the night. We'll park your car somewhere it will be safe, and you and I will take it from there."

"How will we be able to get into the trailer? You said the doors and windows were all locked."

"No problem. I have a key. One of the morons who was guarding me dropped it one day, and I picked it up. I heard him tell someone else that he thought he'd lost it, and the other guy gave him his, saying all the locks were keyed alike anyway."

Lexie opened her eyes, looked across the cubicle to Doris, her head laid back, her eyes open, staring at her.

"There's no chance anything could go wrong? I mean, I'm not going to expose Si to anything if there's a chance anything could happen."

"Honey, I swear. Everything will go exactly as planned. I've been thinking about this for a long, long time, about the best way to go about it."

"You have?"

Doris glanced toward the door, as if half expecting someone else to enter, before instinctively reestablishing eye contact with Lexie. "Yeah, absolutely. I mean, your parents told me about your sister going missing, and I figured that, sooner or later, someone would ask me to intervene. You know, considering my history with the gang and all."

"But, they knew she was missing. They didn't know she was being held hostage."

"Hey," Doris said, obviously anxious to steer the conversation in another direction. "What's the difference who knew what, when? Someone told me your sister was missing, and they described her to me, and I remembered seeing her being held hostage while I was there." She draped her towel around her neck and nodded toward the door. "Had enough?"

Yeah. More than enough! Lexie smiled. "Sorry. I didn't mean to sound like a detective. Or a D.A."

Doris waved her off. "Don't think twice about it." She got up and opened the door. "So, we're on for tomorrow night at eight. You'll arrange with Bill for the car and you'll have your guns and some ammo. And Silas will be our setup man."

"Our what?"

She smiled sheepishly. "I mean our lookout. Sound good?"

Lexie grinned, picked up her bag, and followed the woman out of the steam room and back out into the corridor. Several older people, dressed in tennis shorts and shoes, were walking toward them, laughing.

"I'll see you before then, most likely," Lexie said. "I'm sure."

"I'm sure, too. In fact..." Doris hesitated, her mind drifting. "Yeah, why not do dinner tonight? You and me and Silas? We can fill him in on the details. Make sure he's comfortable with the plan. And, at the same time, all three of us can get better acquainted. It's hard to believe by midnight tomorrow, we're all going to be back here, sitting around and laughing. With your sister joining right in. I can hardly wait!"

"Yeah, I know. Me, too. I'm not sure about dinner, though. I'll have to check with Mom and Dad. I don't know if they have plans for tonight, and we have to have someone watch over Charlotte."

"Oh, of course. I almost forgot."

"How about if I check with them and give you a call later this afternoon?"

"Great. I like to eat around seven. We can meet at Morton's. They have some pretty good rehydrated steaks and fish tacos."

"Rehydrated steaks?" She laughed. "Oh, yeah. This place is so much like paradise, I almost forgot!"

"Well, one good thing," Doris said, chuckling. "At least the wine isn't reconstituted!"

"Okay. Let me check with my folks, and I'll see that Si is free, and I'll let you know."

"Good," she said, and then she reached out and kissed Lexie on the cheek, taking her aback. "Talk to you soon, then."

"Yeah, talk to you, too," Lexie said, curious as to what had brought that on. A genuine show of affection? Or Judas kissing Christ before betraying Him?

Chapter 28

Dinner was an exceptional affair that neither Lexie nor Silas could have anticipated. Doris—glib, comfortable, relaxed—kept flirting with both of them. Not sexually, but playfully. At one point, after the waiter had delivered a second bottle of wine, Doris asked Silas if he had a girlfriend. The boy blushed, and his mother stepped in to help him out. "He hasn't had much time for dating, not really." *And that's the truth*, she thought.

"Well," Doris said, "that's one of the nice things about being a student. When that's your advocacy in life, you always have years left ahead of you to play out, examine, discover. Your education comes first. After that, the world is your oyster. You do like seafood, don't you?"

Silas laughed. "I like any kind of food. Just ask mom!" He caught sight of Lexie frowning at him. "Well, pretty much any kind of food. And you?" he asked. "How about you?"

"Hmm?"

"What kind of food do you like?"

She laughed, raising her glass and sipping before setting it back down. "Let's just say that, if it's bad for me, I like it."

Lexie couldn't help but grin before speaking up. "Say, I was just wondering what you do here. What's your job?" She watched the expression in the woman's eyes. "You never did say."

"Oh, I guess I do a number of things. But mostly I'm a procurer."

"A procurer? What's that?"

"You know. I'm one of the people who goes out and tries to procure food and supplies and medicine and furnishings—whatever it is that might prove useful here in Saltopia."

"Isn't that dangerous?" Lexie asked.

Doris chuckled, the way a paramour might laugh off his date's simplicity. "Not for me."

"Why not?"

"Because I grew up here, in the Cleveland greater metropolitan area. I know every nook and cranny of this city. Every inch of the neighboring terrain. I know where the bad guys are and I know where there's likely to be material goods that can come in handy for us down here."

Lexie looked at her, her glitter top, short black skirt, and white blouse and thought for a moment of Andie MacDowell in *Michael*. And then she looked closer at the large gem dangling from her neck. "That's quite beautiful," she said.

Doris instinctively reached for it, fondled it, and held it up for closer inspection. "Why, thank you. It was a gift. From my mother. When she died."

"Oh, I'm sorry to hear that," Lexie said.

"Oh, no, that's all right. She's been gone six, seven years now."

Lexie glanced at Silas, who already looked confused, before turning once more to Doris. "So, you've had it all along?"

"Hmm? Yes. Why do you ask?"

"I mean, you had it while you were in captivity? How is it the Warlords didn't grab it from you your very first day?"

She raised her brows. "Oh, the Warlords? Yes, well, I was lucky enough to have...hidden it."

Lexie squinted. *Hidden it? Are you kidding me? Where? You mean somewhere they never got around to searching you? Where would that have been...?*

"That seems incredibly...fortunate."

Doris's lips widened and her eyes turned to tiny slits. "Yes. Wasn't it, though?"

Halfway through their meal, the waiter interrupted them to inform Doris that she had an incoming radio call. Pushing her chair back, she said it was important and asked that she be excused for a few minutes. As she got up and wandered slowly toward a radio communication room, Lexie glanced at Silas, who was squinting after their host.

"Odd," she said, pushing back her own chair.

"Odd," he agreed, adding, "What are you doing?"

Lexie got up and, glancing around the room, said, "I think I'll get a little exercise. I'll be right back."

She watched Doris closely.

"Be careful!" Silas whispered.

When Doris opened the door to the communication room and disappeared inside, Lexie positioned herself next to it, the toes of one shoe pressed against the bottom of the door. She pushed ever so slightly, and the door cracked open.

She looked back at Silas, watching intently from their table, before leaning in toward the door.

"His name is Silas," she heard Doris say. "I think thirteen, fourteen, fifteen maybe. Why? Does it matter? Over." She paused, obviously listening to the voice on the other end. "Because he's one of you, that's why. Over." Another pause. "What do you mean, what do I mean? Think about it, Elton John! I mean he's one of you, and for that you should be paying me double. When you're through with him, you'll recoup your investment and then some. In the meantime, think of all the fun you'll have! Over." More dead air. "All you have to do is let us get to the trailer and free Karen. Then you pounce on us before we can get away. You get Si, Lexie, the car, and the guns all at one time. And you still have Karen. And I get the cases of bottled water, like we agreed. Over."

Lexie heard Doris's voice again. "You can slap me around a little so that, when I get back to Saltopia, I can say we ran into a patrol, and they jumped us. I managed to escape, but I wasn't sure what happened to anyone else. Over." A pause. "Yeah," she said finally. "Maybe they'll even set me up with another 'rescue party' and send us out again—and you'll have even more hostages to do with as you want! Over."

I knew it. She's been working for them the whole time. If I don't play along, pretend like everything's okay, I'll never have a chance to spring Karen. And if I do...

Lexie heard Doris finishing up her conversation and hurried back to the table.

"How'd it go?" Silas asked as she slipped quickly back into her chair. Out of the corner of her eye, she saw Doris come out of the rest room.

"Not good," she whispered. "She's in up to her eyeballs with the Warlords."

"Are you sure?" Before Lexie could respond, Doris was back.

The threesome finished their meals and Doris ordered more wine. What did she do before she had to leave home, where had she worked, how much schooling had she had? Lexie was writing all her answers into the stone tablet of her mind.

Silas asked how they were going to pay for the meal.

"We already have," Doris said.

"Who has?"

"You, me, and everyone else here. Through our work. Through *my* work, mostly, and that of the other procurers like me. We go out and secure the necessities of life and, in turn, everyone benefits. This is the ultimate utopia. The Stalag that Marx never dreamed could one day actually exist. All of us united by a common goal—avoiding capture or, worse, death by the hands of the enemy. In times of crisis, people band together."

"Oh, my..." Lexie said, holding her hands to her head.

"What is it, Mom?"

"Are you okay?" Doris asked. "Are you feeling all right?"

"Yeah," she said. "I mean, no. It's just that all that wine—well, I think it's gone a little to my head. I'm not used to this much drinking, it's been a long time."

"Of course. I should have known better. Maybe we ought to get you back home," she said.

"I can walk her back," Silas said.

"Well, let's help her up. Can you walk, Lex?"

Lexie nodded. "I think if I just get up and moving and drink some water and lie down for a while, I'll be fine."

"Are you sure?"

Lexie smiled. "I'll be fine, thanks. Si can help see me home."

As Lexie turned and made her way slowly toward the door, Doris reached out and grabbed Silas by the arm.

"Take good care of her," she told him.

"I will."

And then Doris leaned forward and whispered, "What a good son you are. And so handsome." With that, she kissed him lightly on the cheek. He looked into her Hollywood starlet eyes and smiled.

"Thanks."

On his way toward the door to catch up with his mother, he felt nothing but curiosity.

"I didn't think you were really plowed drunk," he grinned.

"Do you think Doris did?"

"I'm pretty sure."

Bea poked her head out of the bedroom. "Oh, you're home. I thought I heard voices."

"Come on in, Mom. I want to ask you something."

"The baby's sound asleep. What a little angel she is. No trouble at all."

"Mom," Lexie said, frowning. "Do you remember saying anything to Doris about Karen being missing? I mean, ever?"

The woman thought for several seconds. "No. No, I can't say that I do."

"Are you *sure?*"

She shrugged. "We really haven't been that close to her until recently. I mean, we knew her to see her, and by her reputation as a procurer. But other than that, we really didn't have much contact with her."

"Dad, too?"

"I'm sure he never said a word. Why would he? He knew less about her even than I did." She paused. "Why do you ask?"

Lexie forced a smile. "No reason. Just curious as to how much Doris might know about Karen being missing."

"Well, I don't suppose she knows all that much at all. Whatever you've told her. And maybe Bill."

"Um-hmm. I guess you're right." She smiled. "Why don't you go on back to bed, Mom. Sorry I woke you."

"There's coffee in the carafe, if you're thirsty," she said. "And, Si, there's some pop in the fridge."

The two watched as Bea turned and plodded back toward the bedroom. Finally, Silas looked at his mother and asked what was going on.

"I'm not absolutely certain," she replied. "But I think we're in for trouble with Doris."

"You mean like…"

"Uh-huh. I think she's working for the gangs. I think she just might be setting us up for something bad."

A frown crossed the boy's face. "What're we going to do? Shouldn't we tell someone?"

Lexie thought for several seconds before finally shaking her head. "No. No. I think if we tell someone, we'll miss our one and only chance at finding and freeing Karen. I think if we play this thing right, we can get Doris to help us free her and make it back home to safety."

Si stared at her blankly.

"If we play this thing right…"

Before closing her eyes, Lexie's mind drifted to James. The only thing she really wanted, other than her sister, was for James to be next to her. The longer he was gone, the more she realized just how much she loved him. Their love was as strong as any she had ever known or seen.

She wished he was here to help her on this next adventure. But, knowing he was not, she looked up to the ceiling and talked to him for the first time since his death. "Hey, honey. I really don't know how to do this praying thing too well these days. Anyways, God, how I miss you, baby. I miss your smell. I miss your touch. I miss your gentle embrace. I miss everything about you."

She paused as her emotions began to get the better of her. "I don't know if you can hear me. Or see me. But if you can, and if there was ever a time I needed help from above…it's now. Please watch over Si and me tomorrow and give us the strength we need to get through this…well…I guess we'll certainly take any help we can get. I love you, James. I always have and I always will. I'll never forget you."

Chapter 29

The next day rolled by quickly and, when evening dawned with no more ceremony than a humdrum day on the links, Doris showed up a few minutes before their scheduled departure time. As they prepared to leave, Grammy and Poppy each hugged their daughter and then Silas but, as Doris led the way out the door and down the corridor leading to the elevator, Artie stopped.

"Psst!" he said.

Silas stopped in the doorway and turned back. "What is it, Gramps?"

"Here," he said, reaching into his pocket. "I have something I want you to take with you. I know your mother wouldn't agree, but I think you should take it anyway. Just in case."

"What is it?" the boy asked.

Artie opened his palm to reveal a compact Colt .32 semi-automatic pistol.

"Wow!" Silas said, his eyes widening. "Poppy, where'd you ever get this?"

The boy took it gingerly from his grandfather, pointed it toward the floor, and fingered the cool hardened nickel case.

"Si!" Lexie called from the corridor. "Come on, son! We're in a hurry."

"I'll be right there!"

"Look here," Artie said, pointing. "This is a semi-automatic .32 caliber pistol. See?"

"A .32? Dad's gun is a .38." He eyed the weapon suspiciously. "How much good is a gun this small?"

"Well, this one? Pretty darned good!" He pulled a spare clip from his pocket and held it up to the boy. "See this shell in here? It's called a hollow point. When the slug hits its target, it enters just like any other .32-caliber shell would. But the minute it encounters any resistance, the hollow point flattens out to six times its original size. It comes out the back side like a mortar shell."

"Wow," he said. "I never heard of such a thing."

"Just understand that whatever you hit—or whoever—isn't going to get up and walk away. Clear?"

"Yeah," Silas said, taking the spare clip from his grandfather and slipping it into his pants pocket.

"Now, do you know anything about handling a semi-automatic?"

"Yeah. I did some shooting with a couple of different models at the range with Dad. A Ruger and some other German gun. Nothing like this, though."

"Well, they're all pretty much the same. Just remember that, on this gun, you have two safeties. This little lever here locks the slide so it can't chamber a shell. And this one, built into the handle, automatically locks the trigger until you squeeze the handle to fire, which unlocks the firing mechanism. And you're ready to go."

"Great. Wow."

"Just tuck it away in your pocket. It'll be safe until you need it."

"I'll bring it back to you when we return."

"No, it's yours. I want you to have it. You've earned it. Just be careful, buddy! Okay?"

"For sure!"

"Si, are you coming?" Lexie shouted impatiently.

"Coming, Mom," he said. "Jeez, thanks, Gramps," he added, throwing a quick hug around his grandfather's neck. "We'll be back soon as we can." He turned and hurried down the hall, slowing to look back over his shoulder. "And we'll have Aunt Karen with us!"

Back above ground, the sweltering air closed in on them like the sea around a drowning man. The guards handed Lexie her pistol and gave her the keys to her car, which they had already fueled for her. After jumping inside, the three took off down the road, with Lexie and Silas putting all the faith they could muster in a woman they didn't trust as far as they could throw. The mood was tense, their anxiety high. After driving in silence for several minutes, Doris pointed to a side road.

"Here. Pull off here."

"Where? Here?" It looked like little more than a hiking trail, a rough path that used to be a Great Lake. They drove slowly down the bumpy path for nearly 45 minutes, passing ghost ships, sailboats, and motorboats. The SUV slowly swayed back and forth as the tires hit large divots and craters. The moon was nearly full and provided all the light that they needed.

It was eerily quiet as they slowly approached the tented city. They could see the faint glimmer of oil lamps off in the distance along with fires burning in barrels. The entire scene reminded Lexie of the *Pirates of the Caribbean* ride at Walt Disney World. As they turned a corner, the moon's bright reflection could be seen on what were the new shores of Lake Erie. Lexie and Silas stared in amazement as they saw fresh water for the first time in so long. The rolling waves and small white caps captivated both of them. They could even smell the dead, pungent water as they approached.

"Wow," Silas said. "I can't believe my eyes. Never thought I'd see the day."

"It really is stunning, isn't it, son?" They both continued to stare on in amazement.

"Okay! Okay! Back to the mission, guys," Doris interrupted. "This will take us around to the back of the complex."

"Is it gated or anything? Will we need to climb a fence to get in?"

She shook her head. "*Nada*," she said. "It's all open." She peered out the window as Lexie inched the car forward, straining to see through the night.

Either she's the coolest son-of-a-bitch I ever saw, or I've got her pegged all wrong. But what about the radio conversation? How do you explain that?

They slowly crept down the rocky road which was once the floor of Lake Erie. As they came closer to the eerie complex that hugged the shore, they could see some faint lights and barrel fires off in the distance. To avoid being seen, Lexie killed the headlights. "There are some trailers up ahead," she said.

"It's one of them in the last row. Up there," Doris pointed. "Better stop here. Pull in behind that pile of rocks there and be very quiet."

Lexie did as she was told and, when they had parked well off the road and clear of spying eyes, she turned off the engine. Doris opened the door and got out. Leaning back in, she told Silas to get out but to stay near the vehicle. "If there's any trouble, we'll come running back—fast! So be ready to sound the horn."

"I will," he said, his right hand in his pants pocket, fingering the coolness he found there.

"Come on," she said, motioning for Lexie to follow. "Do you have your gun?"

Lexie held it up.

"Good. Hopefully, we won't need it. Let's go."

Yeah, Lexie thought. *Hopefully!*

As the two slipped through the thick night air, Lexie heard a sound and peered back over her shoulder.

"Oh-oh."

Doris stopped. "What?"

Lexie motioned down the road with her head. Off in the distance was the faint glimmer of a set of headlights snaking its way toward them.

"I don't like the look of that," Lexie said.

Doris shook her head. "Neither do I."

"Where's Karen? In which trailer?"

"I'm not sure."

Lexie whirled around. "What?"

"I mean, I have to get a closer look. I'd recognize the front porch light—if it's still there. And there was a green metal awning over the front door." They could hear the purring sound of a gas generator nearby.

Lexie looked up at another set of headlights bearing down on them, and then a third. Panicking, she whispered, "Hey, something is wrong. Definitely wrong."

"Don't worry about it," Doris replied. "Probably just a random patrol on a regular run, or some of the gang heading off into town to let off some steam. I've seen it a thousand times."

Yeah. Or a setup, Lexie thought. She pulled the pistol from her belt and slipped the safety off. *If anything goes wrong, Missy...if you're a shill working for the gang, and this is just an elaborate setup, you're the one who's going to pay the price!*

"What if that's not the case? What if they're onto us? What if they know we're here?"

"I'm telling you not to worry. I'm in complete control of the situation. They can't see the SUV from the road, and they couldn't possibly know we're here. Trust me. Now, come on. And don't do anything to raise suspicion."

They passed the first two trailers, Doris inspecting them closely before signaling Lexie to continue. Finally, at the third one, she motioned for them to stop.

"What? Is this it?" Lexie felt her heart race at the thought that her sister could be only feet away. "Is it?"

Doris nodded. "I'm almost positive. There's the porch light, with the broken glass. And the metal awning over the front door." She motioned for Lexie to stay back while she approached the trailer. Grabbing the padlock, she pulled a key from her pocket and began fumbling with the tumbler.

Lexie looked back toward the road. The three sets of eyes glowing in the night had stopped.

Oh, shit.

"I've got it!" Doris said, and Lexie watched as she opened the front door and disappeared into the darkness within.

"Mom! Mom, come quick!"

Lexie heard Silas's frantic call from several hundred feet away. Suddenly, the sound of gunfire split the evening air.

"Si!" she called out. She turned and began to run as fast as she could toward the car. Looking back at the road, she saw three military trucks parked on the shoulder, several dozen armed men jumping out, shooting wildly in their direction, many with automatic weapons.

"Hurry, Mom!" Silas called again, and Lexie ducked and weaved her way back toward the sound of her son's voice. Suddenly, she caught her foot on a steel reinforcing bar and tumbled to the ground, dropping her gun. Shaking her head, she spotted the weapon in the moonlight and scrambled to recover it but, before she could reach it, she caught sight of a burly man with tattoos covering his bare torso and a scar across his face where his left eye once lived. He stopped and pointed the muzzle of an automatic rifle directly at her head.

Oh, no. Not like this. Not with Si so near. And Karen. Please!

Suddenly, she heard the burst of machinegun fire and instinctively fell to the ground. She looked up at the man, his one good eye opened wide, blood gushing from his mouth as he fell face-forward to within inches of her.

"Oh!" She picked herself up and started to run again before stopping, going back, and grabbing the man's weapon. Taking off once more, she was within sight of the car.

Where's Si? "Si!" she cried out. "Son!"

Suddenly, another man emerged from behind a decaying brick storage shed, with a second behind him, and lifted his gun as a series of retorts rang out. Silas leaped forward from the darkness and grabbed his mother by the arm, the smoking Colt in his hand glimmering in the moonlight.

"Come on, we've gotta get the hell out of here! Come on. Come on!"

As they reached the vehicle and Lexie opened the driver's-side door, she heard a woman's voice cry out.

"Lexie! Lexie, where are you?"

Silas's eyes widened. "It's Doris!" He cupped one hand to his mouth. "Over here, Doris! Straight ahead!" he called.

Oh, my God! Lexie thought. "It's not Doris, it's Karen!" she exclaimed. "Karen, we're here," she called. "Run toward my voice. Hurry! Run as fast as you can!"

As the two scoured the darkened night, they suddenly caught sight of a solitary figure wending its way toward them.

"It's her," Lexie cried. "It's Karen!"

As the figure drew closer, a new volley of gunfire erupted from the vehicles, and a woman's voice called out in fear.

"Oh, my God!" Si cried.

"Karen! No!"

"Oh, shit, Mom. They shot her." Instinctively he raised his pistol and fired off the remaining rounds in the magazine and, when it could fire no more, he shoved his mother into the driver's seat and jumped into the back. "Let's go, Mom," he said. "She's dead. We can't help her now. We've got to get back to the mine."

Doris! Lexie thought. *It really was a setup all along!* She grabbed the key and turned on the ignition, slamming the shifter into reverse and stepping on the gas. *Why did I ever go along with her? How could I have been so fucking dumb? Why didn't I follow my gut feelings?*

"Hurry, Mom. Put it in Drive. They're running back to their trucks. Let's get the fuck outta here!"

As Lexie floored the pedal, the tires spun out, spitting up dirt and dust and gravel, and the two survivors—dazed and limp but still alive—hurried back along the road from which they'd just come. Silas breathed out, his chest heaving. He looked back over his shoulder. "Seems odd, but I don't see anyone following us," he said. "I think we made it."

"Yeah," she replied, the tears rushing down her cheeks. "We made it, but..."

Once safely back at the mine, Lexie relayed to her parents the story of what had happened and how they'd barely escaped with their lives.

"And Karen?" Artie asked, the words sticking in his throat. "Are you sure she..."

Lexie shook her head. "I'm so sorry," she said, fighting back the tears forming in her eyes. "Oh shit, I'm so sorry. We tried everything we could. We called out to her. She had almost reached us when..."

Silas put his arm around his mother, battling his own emotions. Suddenly, a knock sounded against the door. Artie got up to answer.

"Bill!"

Lexie looked up as her father ushered the man in. His eyes big and dark, his lips turned down—he made her wonder how he'd already gotten word of what had transpired.

"Thank goodness you made it back alive," Bill said to her, settling into a chair opposite the sofa, leaning forward against his knees. "I'm so sorry you weren't able to rescue her."

Lexie tried to stifle her sobs, taking a handkerchief from her mother to wipe her eyes. "Thank you," she said, finally. "But how did you..."

He sighed. "Fortunately, we have a pretty good relationship with some of the boys outside. We may not be the police or the military, but we're the closest thing this community has to a law-enforcement agency. We have to keep informed of what's going on...up there." He motioned with his head.

Lexie nodded. "I just wish I'd seen through her. I never should have trusted her. She set us up. It was a trap from the very start."

"Who did? Who set you up?"

Lexie squinted at him. "Why, Doris, of course."

"Doris? You think..."

"When we got there, she opened the lock on the trailer and went inside. That's when the shooting began. I heard Si call out, so I raced back to help him. And then we saw Karen coming after us. She'd just about

206

made it when—" She stopped, fighting back the tears. "—when they killed her. Murdered her in cold blood." She paused again. "She was nearly free!"

Bill shook his head. "I don't understand. You think the Warlords shot your sister?"

Lexie looked confused. "Why, yes, of course. We saw it happen."

"They didn't shoot your sister."

Lexie paused, looking up. "What are you talking about?"

"They shot Doris."

"Doris!"

"See, Mom," Silas cried. "I told you it was Doris!"

"Why would they shoot Doris? Why would they shoot one of their own? She was conspiring against us. I overheard her on the…"

"Doris wasn't one of their own. She was working for us, undercover. She led them to believe she was working for them, when she was really part of a sting network set up by the RCMP, from Canada."

"The Mounties?" Silas asked, his eyes widening.

"I don't understand. We saw… What about her story about having been held hostage by the Warlords? And raped. And how she had escaped from them? Why would they let her…"

He shook his head. "I'm afraid that was only a cover story for the people living here, so they'd accept her as one of our own and not give away her true identity. In reality, she used to be a City of Cleveland plain clothes detective. She'd been with the department for years. When the city broke down, she got word of the Warlords' plan to begin launching raids into Canada to widen their sphere of influence. That's when she got in touch with the RCMP and volunteered her services. When she told you she wanted to help free your sister, she was telling you the truth. She thought she could pull it off, with a little help from her friends."

"You mean Si and me?"

"Si. And you. And a couple hundred RCMP who had set up camp at Manhattan Beach. They got word from their mole that the Warlords had caught on to the fact that Doris was actually a double agent, and they made plans to grab the three of you before you could rescue your sister. The Mounties had been planning a sting operation to take the gang down for months. So, working with Doris, they moved in and caught the gang in a crossfire. Unfortunately, in the process, Doris was accidentally shot trying to make it back to your car."

"So that radio call I overheard last night was all just part of the sting?"

"Radio call?" Bill paused. "Oh, you mean the one from the restaurant to her snitch. Yes. That was to get the Warlords to circle the wagons so that the Mounties could round up the entire bunch at once—or exterminate them."

"Oh, my God," Bea cried, cupping her cheeks in her hands. "If they shot Doris, that means that Karen is still…"

Bill rolled his head to one side. "We're not sure where she is, exactly. But sources tell us that she's still alive. Yes."

"And Doris is dead," Lexie said, numbly. "Trying to help us free Karen."

Bill smiled. "Fortunately, it will take more than a bullet or two in the leg to keep Doris down. The RCMP dispersed what remained of the gang members, and Doris is recouping on the Canadian side of the border as we speak. She'll be rejoining us just as soon as she's released from the medical unit."

"And there was no sign of our daughter?" Artie asked.

Bill shook his head. "I'm afraid not. I spoke to the Deputy Commissioner in Montreal just a few minutes ago. Apparently, after Doris tipped the gang off in a telephone call last night that the three of you would be attempting a rescue, they moved Karen to another location. By the time the Mounties moved in and caught them in a crossfire, your sister had been transferred somewhere else."

"But why would they have moved her? Unless they'd been tipped off that Doris was a double agent, and the Mounties had been called in on the sting. I mean, Doris never told anyone that, and certainly none of us ever said anything. Mom and Dad never even knew the details until we returned from our mission an hour ago." She paused, turning toward her father. He looked down sheepishly. "Did you?" she asked.

He glanced up at Silas, who looked down and cleared his throat. Lexie turned to him.

"Si!"

He raised his palms out to his sides. "I…I didn't tell anyone…much."

A look of horror crossed her face as Lexie turned toward Artie. "Dad? Who did you tell about Doris working to free Karen?"

He shrugged. "I, uhh, I'm not sure. One or two people." He raised his brows. "Oh, nothing specific. I couldn't have. I didn't know any of the details. Only that you and Si were going to try to free Missy—I mean, Karen. You and Si…and Doris."

Lexie dropped her shoulders. "Oh, Dad."

He shrugged sorrowfully. "I never thought…"

Suddenly, a thought came to her, a gleam brightening her face. "But, even at that, even if everyone knew what was going to happen, even if everyone knew that Doris was working with the Mounties to bring down the gang, they couldn't have gotten information to the outside. They couldn't have alerted the Warlords," she said, turning to Bill. She hesitated, panic striking her face. "Unless…"

"Unless," he replied, "one of us in Saltopia…is a traitor."

Chapter 30

It was a modest excuse for a meditation room, but Lexie was pleased there was a place that she could find peace for a moment. With candles burning, some incense smoking, and light new age music playing, she immediately felt the stress leave her body. There were two pews, cushions on the floor, a couple of yoga mats, and a large statue of Buddha. Several artificially illuminated stained-glass windows lined the left side of the room. There were dozens of random pictures of peaceful natural settings that were hanging on the walls of the other side. Lexie looked around. No one else was there.

When she'd finished her meditation focused on being thankful—and offering up a petition for her sister's safe return—she looked over her shoulder at the sound of the heavy entrance doors swinging open. She smiled.

Si! She motioned for him to join her.

"Mom. I've been looking all over for you."

"Shh," she said, placing her finger to her lips.

"I've been looking all over for you," he whispered. "What are you doing here? What *is* this place? What's that smell?"

She looked around at the solitude, breathed in, and thought for several moments. "This is a meditation room. What you smell is incense."

He seemed confused.

"It's a place to relax. To be alone with your thoughts. It's a place to just allow your mind to drift."

He shrugged. "Okay. I'll take your word on that."

"What is it you want?" She paused, watching him look around. "You know, it wouldn't hurt you to step in here now and again."

"Yeah, I know. It just seems sort of silly…"

She smiled and squeezed his hand. "You'll understand one day. Anyway…what's up?"

"Oh, yeah. Bill called and asked if you could meet him in his office as soon as possible."

"Did he say what he wants?"

He shook his head again. "Only that it was important."

"Important? Well, well. We can't very well keep him waiting then, can we?"

Lexie got back on her feet, genuflected, and felt almost dizzy from her deep relaxation.

As they walked down the hall, they stopped before the doorway marked "Administration." Lexie hesitated, wondering what Bill could want, before knocking.

"Come in!" Bill's voice boomed out from inside the room. Lexie rated it somewhere between the voice of an excited sportscaster broadcasting the big Saturday afternoon game and a frightened police officer ordering a perpetrator to put his hands up. She wondered which was closer to the real man. She turned the handle and opened the door.

"Hi, Lexie. Glad to see you. Come on in, come on in." He saw Silas standing in the doorway behind her. "You, too, son. This concerns everyone."

"Thanks," Lexie said. She turned to take a seat where Bill had motioned, then stopped short.

Silas, turning with her, let out a cry. "Doris!"

The woman stood up, smiled, and held out her hand, taking two faltering steps forward.

"I can't believe it," Lexie said, as the woman threw her arms around her. "What are you doing here?"

Doris released her grip and turned to Silas. "And I can't believe you, young man," she said, hobbling up to him. "You don't know how grateful I am to you."

"Me? For what?"

"Well, for starters, for saving my life, that's all."

Silas blushed, his eyes glued to the floor as he pulled up a chair.

"Doris," Lexie said. "What on earth are you...I mean, how did you..."

Bill got up from behind his desk, motioning once more with his hands. "Please. Sit down. Everybody. Make yourselves comfortable. Please."

"I thought you were convalescing in Canada!" Lexie pulled up a chair and set it opposite Doris as the woman made her way back to the sofa.

Doris smiled. She motioned with her head toward a crutch leaning up against the settee. "Convalescing, yes," she said. "Canada, no."

Lexie turned to Bill. "I don't understand. I thought you said..."

"I...that is... Well..." he stammered.

"It's my fault, really," Doris said. "Bill is such a terrible liar. I just knew I'd have to help him out." She looked up at him and smiled as he shrugged. "So, we got the idea for me to radio him from RCMP Headquarters and tell him about my injury, but to say that I'd be out of commission in Ontario for a few weeks. Before returning back here to the States."

"Who is we?"

"I'm coming to that," she said.

"Jeez, Mom, don't interrupt. This is like a spy movie, except for real!"

Lexie scowled.

"More so than you know," Bill said.

"Anyway…" Doris stopped, fluffed up a pillow, and settled back farther into the soft brown leather. "We figured that, if word got around that I was holed up in Canada, sooner or later that news would snake its way out of Saltopia and over to the Warlords, and we'd hear about it. And once that word got out, it could only mean that there was a mole working here in the mines."

"A mole?"

"Mom!"

Doris laughed. "Sorry. A snitch. You know, a spy."

"Ohh."

"We figured that, once word got out, we'd be able to trace the source of the leak and narrow things down to reveal who the mole is."

"Narrow things down to whom? Do you have any idea?"

Bill stood up, pulled a pipe from a rack on his desk, and slipped it between his teeth. "Mind if I…" He stopped, catching himself. "What am I saying? I don't smoke anymore. No one smokes down here. Too dangerous. The quarters are so cramped. I just pick it up and suck on it from time to time. Helps me to relax. Force of habit."

Lexie smiled.

"Anyway," he said, talking through the pipe, "we knew you'd be pretty close-mouthed, Lex. With your entire family here, and your sister being held captive. You wouldn't do anything to jeopardize their well-being." He paused, turning to Silas. "This young man, though…well…we weren't so sure. Like all adolescents everywhere, they sometimes like to boast, exaggerate their value to society, puff themselves up with their friends and acquaintances, so to speak." He pulled the pipe from his mouth and looked at it. "No pun intended."

Silas shook his head as Lexie turned to him. "Swear to God, Mom. I never said a word! Not this time."

"That's true," Bill said. "He didn't. We checked with everyone he's come in contact with over the last few days, and no one knew that Doris was counterespionage or had been shot and sent to Canada for two weeks to recuperate."

Silas beamed. "See?"

"All right, so I believe you."

"Then we did the same with your parents. Sorry to say. Not because we anticipated their being involved in any sort of collusion, of course. Not in a million years. But older folks sometimes get a little…forgetful. A little careless. They don't always remember to keep their lips sealed when it's in their best interest to do so."

"And?"

Bill set the pipe back in its place and shook his head. "No problem whatsoever. That left only one other person in the entire community who knew about Doris going to Canada."

Lexie looked up at him, her brows rising instinctively. "You!"

"Our very own 'Comrade Bill,'" Doris said, laughing.

"Safe to say no one I spoke to knew anything about it, either. I had Doris check me out. So I wasn't the culprit who spilled the beans either. Apparently not even accidentally in my sleep!"

"Then," Silas said, "if everyone checked out, there's no mole after all. Right?"

Lexie turned to Bill.

"Oh, there's a mole, all right. You can bet your bottom dollar on that."

"But...but who?"

Doris cleared her throat. "Bill was kind enough to put through a radio call to the Deputy Commissioner stationed in Toronto when I showed up the other day. We talked for nearly half an hour. Anyway, we told him of our plans, and he told us they'd gotten word from their counter-surveillance activities that the gang had moved their operations— temporarily at least—to a campsite closer to Lorain."

Lexie's eyes perked up. "And Karen?"

The woman shook her head. "I'm afraid there was no sign of her."

The words stuck in her heart, Lexie's head slumped down to her chest as Silas reached out to comfort her.

"But it's not all bad," Doris continued.

"What's not all bad?"

"Commissioner Albrecht said his men had located a group of Warlords on the outskirts of a small town just north of here. They had set up a camp, camouflaging everything so as not to be seen from the air."

"The air?"

Bill motioned skyward. "Sat-Comm Three. One of a handful of satellites Canada and the U.S. maintain for surveillance and scientific purposes. Although the U.S. doesn't have the facilities to do much tracking these days, Canada still does."

"So how did they find them, if they're invisible to satellite imagery?" Silas asked.

"They might be invisible to satellites, but they're not invisible to prying eyes."

Doris leaned forward. "One of Bill's aides had seen me in his office the other day and listened in on my conversation with the commissioner. When she realized what was going on, she wrote a note to one of her contacts on the outside and slipped it to one of our procurers to deliver to someone she claimed was her brother. She said it was a short letter begging him to give himself up and turn himself over to the community while there was still time. The procurer, thinking she was doing the right thing, delivered the note to the camp."

Bill cleared his throat. "The crazy thing is, I looked around the room as the commissioner and Doris were talking, and I thought it strange to see a couple of dark shadows beneath the crack below my office door." He pointed toward the doorway. "As you can see, there's a rather wide space between the bottom of the door and the carpeting. To allow greater air flow, I suppose. Anyway, at the time, I never thought a thing about it. It wasn't until later, after I called my aide in to take some dictation, that I noticed a note pad on the corner of her desk." He pointed to a gray-painted steel desk off to one side of the room. "She had brought the pad in with her to use for dictation. When it was time for lunch, she went off to the commissary, and I had a closer look."

"It seems that Bill's trusted aide was anything but!" Doris said.

"That's when I got the idea."

"Idea?" Lexie asked.

"Yes."

"Actually," Doris said, smiling. "It was my idea."

"Yes, well," Bill said, clearing his throat, a glint in his eye as he backtracked diplomatically, "let's just say it was our idea."

Doris nodded.

"What was that?" Silas asked.

"Well, since it was absolutely clear that my aide couldn't be trusted with information that was—what shall we call it—potentially damaging to Saltopia, it was equally clear that she wouldn't be able to be trusted with information that is potentially damaging to the Warlords."

"Huh?"

"What do you mean?" Lexie asked.

"Bill is going to arrange another radio call between Deputy Commissioner Albrecht and myself—a call in which we'll reveal some extremely damaging and potentially lethal information relevant to our community."

"I don't understand," Lexie said. "Why would you do that?"

"She won't," Bill said. "What she means is that, instead of patching through a radio call from the commissioner, I've arranged to have one of my IT people make the call, pretending to be Commissioner Albrecht. He's going to let slip the fact that the RCMP will be launching an attack on the Warlords near Lorain, and that he's going to need all the armed help he can possibly get from us here at the mines. That means he'll be requesting our armed security guards, our gate personnel—virtually everyone who has a weapon and knows how to use it—to join in the assault. Of course, that will leave the mines relatively unsecured, at least for a couple of hours."

"During which time," Doris said, grinning, "the Warlords' special forces group stationed to the north of us will be instructed to storm the mines, overthrow and kill off the occupants, and entrench themselves in a virtually impregnable fortress for as long as they so desire."

Bill went to pick up his pipe then thought better of it. "And that, of course, would provide the gang with virtually foolproof staging grounds for their raids into Canada."

Silas turned to his mother. "I think I'm missing something."

"Not at all!" Bill said, delighted. "You've got the gist of it right on, just the way the Warlords will understand it. But the kicker is, there won't be a consolidation of forces, and the mines won't be left defenseless. When the RCMP moves down against the Warlords' main camp north of Lorain, they'll have more than enough of their own Canadian troops to overwhelm and defeat them. And when the gang's special forces unit up north moves in for the kill, a second battalion of Mounties will sweep in behind them, rescuing your sister and several other women currently being held captive there before converging upon the mines and catching the special forces in a fatal crossfire."

"At last," Doris said, "you'll be reunited with your sister, and the Ohio River Valley will be free from the most vicious gang in history."

"Mom, do you hear that?" Silas turned to Lexie, grinning from ear to ear, watching the tears flowing from her eyes. "Mom?" he asked. "What's wrong?"

"Nothing," she said, reaching over and hugging him. "Nothing at all, son. Oh, God, I'm so relieved. There's nothing more on Earth I could have possibly asked for. Nothing more I could have wanted."

Chapter 31

In the meditation room, Lexie sat with her legs crossed as she absorbed the calming music coming from the small speakers. In front of her sat a picture of James and herself. It was from their wedding day, the happiest day she could ever remember aside from the birth of her children. As she sat there, looking around, she thought back to all the days she'd spent with him. All the days that she had taken for granted.

Despite the calm setting, her mind began to race with what ifs. What if they had never stopped to help the family back on the highway? She should have listened to James. What if they had gone to Chicago instead of heading back to Ohio? Would they have found a hospital? Water? So many thoughts went through her mind until she started to think of all the happy memories they had together.

Suddenly, in her mind, she was dancing with James to their favorite song. Her head was pressed against his chest, and his arms were warmly wrapped around her body. It was pure bliss and she could almost smell his unmistakable scent. She felt warm, secure, and as happy as she had ever been. He pressed his lips softly to hers.

The sound of the door swinging open brought her back to the present.

"What are you doing, Mom?"

Lexie jumped. She let out a loud sigh. Motioning to the cushion to her right, she invited Silas into the room.

"Hi, son."

"How come you're here all alone?"

She paused, still listening to the music, taking in the peace of the room, "I thought I'd come in and reflect a bit. About Dad, about Karen…about everything."

Silas grinned, a strained smile on his face, and put his hand on his mother's shoulder. "I know. It sounds peaceful."

Lexie smiled. "Sometimes it helps to think about positive thoughts."

Silas put his hands in his lap. "Yeah…I should try that too."

Lexie crinkled her brow. "There really is a silver lining to everything…I just don't know what that is right now."

"I hear you, Ma. I wish we'd start getting some things goin' our way."

"They will, baby. It's only a matter of time. Our luck is going to start to change for the better!"

As they sat Indian style while listening to the mesmerizing meditation music along with the ambiance of the candles and magical smells, a sense of peace engulfed them both.

"You feel it, too?"

Silas, tears welling in his eyes, looked at his mother and went to speak, but nothing came out. He tried again, with no success. Finally, his lips curled up lightly, and his eyes shone bright, and he nodded. "What's going to happen, Mom?"

"Well, for now, we count our blessings that you, me, and Charlotte are alive. That Karen's alive. That Grammy and Poppy are alive. And tomorrow..." she paused.

"Yeah, Mom. Tomorrow what?"

"Tomorrow we keep fighting. For us, for the people here and, of course, for Karen. We have to believe Dad is looking down on us and watching over us."

Silas nodded.

"Do you ever...like...talk to Dad. You know...like praying?

"I talk to Dad all the time, Si. In my prayers, in my heart, and in my mind."

"I feel kinda silly doing that. But I'll try. I want Dad to hear me."

"He will, sweetie. I'm certain that he will."

"Do you think we'll find Aunt Karen?"

"You know what, son? I can't predict the future, but I just get this feeling that we will. We have to trust that Bill and Doris know what they are doing."

"Me too, Mom. Me too."

"So when do we leave?"

"There's no 'we' Silas. You'll stay here where it's safe. As for me....as soon as the group is ready, I'll be there with them."

Disappointed, but understanding at the same time, Silas nodded.

"Hey, Si. Do you remember that old song Daddy and I used to sing to you all the time?"

"You mean that corny old country song?"

Lexie rolled her eyes, "Yes. That one! Mind if I sing it to you?" She grabbed the wedding picture and centered it in front of both of them.

"Sure, Mom. Of course. It'll remind me of Dad."

And, with that, Lexie's beautiful voice began to sing...

Thank you for reading *Parched*. Amazon reviews are one of the most important ways that an author can get the word out about their book. I would be extremely appreciative if you would take a few moments to review *Parched*. Thank you kindly.

www.andrewbranham.com

Preview of Parched Part II—The Lake Erie Badlands

The road was treacherous and, with every bump, her restrained hands and feet pulsed with pain. It was pitch black as the old minivan slowly crawled down the make-shift road that was once the bottom of Lake Erie. Cigarette smoke was billowing from the front seat where her two captors sat silently as they approached their destination. They had been driving for nearly an hour, and the road conditions, along with the smoke, had made her nauseous.

As they approached, she watched closely as the men picked up their radio and announced their arrival. The sliver of the moon had provided just enough light for her to make out the silhouette of a massive ship that lay deserted on the floor of the great lake. Was it an iron ore freighter? A barge? The mere size of the vessel suggested to her that it must be the former—an abandoned iron ore ship that once hauled cargo all over the Great Lakes and Canada. Several oil-burning lamps surrounded the open cargo door.

One of the men—bearded, burly, and with crooked yellow teeth—turned to her and snarled. "Welcome to your new home, Karen," he said with a smirk.

Too frail from weeks of abuse and battery, she simply lowered her head. She had bruises covering her face, arms, and the remainder of her scantily dressed body. Covered in dirt, it was difficult to make out her previously beautiful face. What was once fair skin and golden blond hair was now scarred brown skin and hair so matted it almost looked like dreadlocks. The shorts she was wearing were far too large on her nearly skeletal frame.

"Aww, not to worry, bitch! We'll keep you plenty busy."

The driver clearly found the remark humorous as he let out an annoying laugh. "That's right, you stupid whore. There's fixin' to be plenty of men on board that are gonna want that ass."

"Good one, Mutt." The burly man looked over at his partner and laughed. "Now, if you know what's good for ya, ho, you'll keep that stupid pie-hole shut. We don't need any commotion as we get ya settled."

"Hey!" Mutt yelled, "He was talkin' to you, bitch. Speak when you're spoken to."

"I understand," she said weakly and without emotion. "I'll do as you say. Like always."

"That's right, ho. That's what's up."

The minivan slowly approached the large cargo door that had a ramp lowered down to allow vehicles to enter. Several armed guards stood on both sides, waving them in. There did not appear to be any electricity on board the freighter as oil lamps lined the entrance. Burning lamps could be seen off in the distance and inside the guts of the ship.

Once inside, several guards approached the van.

"Good job, boys," one of them nodded to the men. "We'll take her from here and put her with the rest of the girls."

As the two men walked off, one of the guards abruptly opened the sliding door of the van. As Karen looked up, he grabbed her by the hair and yanked her harshly from the vehicle. She caught a glimpse of his hairy face, greasy hair, and rotting teeth. She could even smell his rancid breath.

"Get the fuck out of the van, bitch." She fell to the ground and curled up in a fetal position. "Get your lazy ass off that ground and stand up!"

She mustered enough strength to bring herself to her knees. As soon as she did, the guard wound up his leg and kicked her as hard as he could in the stomach. With a scream, she collapsed back to the ground.

"Do you have a hearing problem? What the fuck did I just tell you? Get the fuck up. NOW!"

Too tired to fight him, Karen used all her energy to stand up. Every muscle and bone in her body cried out in agony.

"That's right! Now let's go. Follow me."

The inside of the dimly lit ship had a smell she couldn't quite place but seemed strangely familiar to her. Despite it being night, it was stiflingly hot; she could smell a mixture of oil, tar, and a metallic tin. The man led her up a steep, rickety wooden staircase that brought them to what appeared to be the main level of the ship. They continued forward until he reached an immense metal door with a padlock on it the size of a grapefruit. He unlocked it to reveal a large metal room as big as a ballroom. Small iron ore pellets still covered the floor.

Immediately, Karen could hear the sounds of other people. Other women! Their voices—or rather screams—were echoing off metal sheeting. The smell in the room was nearly intolerable—feces, urine, rotting food, and unclean bodies. A few oil lamps provided a small amount of light.

As she walked in, the guard followed closely behind and then gave her a swift kick in her buttocks.

"Ouch! Christ!" she said, gathering some courage.

"Shut your mouth before I beat the shit out of you!"

As her eyes adjusted, she could see the dismal position she was now in. Every few feet lay a beaten and battered woman, chained to the floor. Most had skin so dirty that it was black. Some were dressed in rags.

Others were nude. A few looked as though they had arrived recently as their clothing was not completely stained orange from the iron ore pellets.

The guard kept his distance just enough so that the women could not reach him. They moaned, bellowed, cried, and screamed obscenities as he walked past.

"Help me! God, please help me," wailed one of the women as she desperately reached toward Karen and the guard. She must have weighed under 100 pounds and looked as if she had been there for months.

"Shut the fuck up!" The man kicked the woman directly in the face. Blood sprayed onto Karen's cheek. "Walk!" he yelled.

As they continued forward, the smell became more putrid. The women were all yelling and screaming for help. Just as the guard was about to kick another woman, he was hit directly in the face by a wad of feces. He stopped in his tracks, removed a towel from his shorts, and wiped his face.

"You're a dead woman!" he snarled, as he pointed to a disheveled woman laughing at him. She had a crazy look on her face as she continued to taunt him with her laughter and smirks. Her hand was covered in feces.

The guard removed a billy club from his belt, walked up to the woman, and looked her in the eyes.

"You think that was funny, huh?"

Again, she didn't speak but, instead, laughed. Her loud, creepy cackle echoed off the metal walls and reverberated.

Without hesitation, the guard raised his hand and cracked the woman over the head with enough force to split her skull open. The sound was unlike anything Karen had ever heard. The woman collapsed like a ragdoll. Silence filled the room.

"Anyone else want their turn?" he grunted, scanning the room with his dark eyes. "I've got no problem beating the shit out of any of you skanks that fuck with me. Ya hear me?"

Aside from a few coughs, the room fell silent.

"That's what I thought!" He grabbed his billy club and tapped on the metal wall nearest to him. "And I want complete silence for the rest of the damn night. Not a peep. If I have to come back in here, I'm breaking faces."

He pushed Karen toward an empty area in the corner. Pulling out his billy club, he hit her on the back of her knees, forcing her to the ground. A chain with cuffs was already on the wall, and he quickly secured them on her. Karen winced in pain at his brutal treatment.

"Don't try anything stupid, Karen. This is your new home. Get used to it."

And with that, he turned around and disappeared behind the metal door. The loud clanking noise from it startled Karen, already an emotional mess. For a moment, she felt relief as the brutal guard was gone…at least for now.

Instinct drove her to attempt to stand, but the chain and cuff quickly tugged her back. The pain throughout her body became more intense. *Shit,* she thought to herself. *How in the hell did I get myself into this situation? This is where I'm finally going to die.*

"Pssst," came a voice near her. "Hey, what's your name?"

Karen's eyes were beginning to adjust to the softly lit ship and she could just make out the woman nearest to her. Too thin to be an adult but too tall to be a child. She was wearing nothing but a loincloth covering her genitals.

"Hey, you!" she said a bit louder. "I said, what's your name?"

"It's…it's Karen."

"Hey, Karen. I'm Tina. Where'd you come from?"

"Where the hell am I?"

"You're on the G.F. Thermond. Freighter. Beached years ago."

"Thanks. But where are we?"

"About twenty miles north of Sandusky. At least I think."

"Christ. Is there any way outta here?"

"Not that I know of. Even if you do make it to the door by some miracle, you'd be grabbed by one of the guards. And trust me, you don't want to piss anyone off here."

"How long have you been here, Tina?"

"Too hard to tell. Six months? Eight maybe."

A woman a few chains down moaned. The sound was disturbing, the noise amplified by the hollowness of the room.

"I've got to get out. I can't stay here," Karen cried.

"Relax. You're probably gonna be here for a while. Try and get some sleep." The woman flung a dirty blanket that smelled like urine Karen's way. "They ain't 800 thread count, but it'll do for now. Use it to keep your skin off the ground. You'll get terrible sores real quick."

"Thanks, Tina."

"No sweat. Things'll be better in the morning. They'll feed us at first light. If you're lucky, you'll get taken outta here by one of the men for a while."

"Taken out for what?"

"Don't worry about it now. Get some sleep and we'll talk in the morning."

But sleep wasn't coming anytime soon for Karen. The smell, the heat, the cries, and the moans kept her far from being in the mood for sleep. She was tired, beaten, thirsty, and starving. She wanted nothing more than to be back in the safety of the mines with her parents. She wondered why she always had to act as the hero. Always trying to be the tough one. Where did it land her? In the belly of a ship and too far from anyone she even remotely cared about. She dared not think about it, but what would they do to her in the morning? She knew it was only a matter of time before she'd be raped again. Or had they finally tired of her and she'd simply be shot?

She balled the dirty blanket up and tried to use it as a make-shift pillow, but the smell was too foul for her to stand. Instead, she simply rested her head against the metal wall and closed her eyes. She wondered what was going on in the mines. What had become of her sister, Lexie, and her family?

Just as she was starting to drift asleep, the clanking sound of the metal door jolted her back to reality. She had no idea if it was the middle of the night or morning. The footsteps of the guard walking on the metal floor were getting closer. No one spoke a word. She was silently praying that he would walk past her. Instead, the footsteps stopped right by her stall. He reached down and unlocked the restraints that bound her feet.

"You. Get up," the guard said as he poked her stomach with the club.

"Me?"

"Yes, you. Now shut up and do as you're told."

With his 9mm gun drawn and pointed at her, the guard led her through the door, over a metal scaffolding, and then down a narrow metal hallway. Walking on the metal floors caused a loud clanking sound with each step that then echoed throughout the hall. Right before she reached the very last door, the guard yelled for her to stop. He stepped around her and then knocked on the hollow metal door.

"Come in!"

He opened the door to find a tall, muscular, Hispanic man with a wild Mohawk, calmly sitting at an old wooden desk. Lying on the desk was a large silver gun.

"So, we meet again!"

"Singo! Of all people," Karen exclaimed.

"Guard. Leave us. You're dismissed."

The guard made an about-face and exited through the door, closing it behind him.

"Damn, girl, you look like shit."

"Screw you, Singo."

"Sassy as always, I see. Some things don't change."

"What am I doing here? What the hell do you want with me?"

Singo abruptly stood up and started to circle her, never breaking eye contact. With his gun in his hand, he stepped closer to her and began rubbing her breasts. She brushed his hand away before he could go any futher.

"So…you want to know what you're doing here…huh?"

"Yes! Yes, I do."

He let out a sinister chuckle and then, without warning, spun the gun around and cracked her on the back of the head with the butt. She screamed and collapsed to the ground.

"You've caused me a lot of trouble, bitch. Do you have any idea the kind of shit you've caused me?"

She tried to pull herself up as blood dripped from her head and onto the floor. She felt dizzy. Dazed. She tried to keep herself focused.

"Me? I've never caused you any trouble, Singo."

"Bullshit, woman! That's complete bullshit. First your sister and Doris come to my camp. Now I'm hearing that the Canadians are about to attack, trying to rescure you. We've had to move our entire operation because of your shit."

"That's out of my control. How am I supposed to do anything about that?"

"I've had enough. I don't have any use for you anymore. You look like shit. You smell like shit. And you're not worth a damn for labor."

"Good. Then let me go. Just drop me off somewhere and I'll find my way home."

"Let you go?" he said, laughing. "I don't think so, Karen."

He knelt down beside her and placed the barrel of the gun on her forehead. The cold metal pressed on her skin as panic overtook her body. She began to shake.

"Please, Singo. Please don't. I swear to God I'll just leave. You'll never see me again. I won't tell anyone where you are. Hell, I don't even *know* where we are. Please! I'm begging you."

"I fucking hate beggars. You're more trouble than it's worth. I kill people that are threats." He snorted through his nose, cleared his throat, and then spat directly on her mouth.

"Goodbye, Karen!"

She didn't have the strength to beg anymore. She was broken, dejected, and demoralized. Even if by some miracle she survived this ordeal, she'd simply be put back in the metal dungeon and raped. She knew she would never escape. She had nothing left to live for. Nothing to fight for.

She closed her eyes and prepared for the worst. At least, she thought, she would be free from the agony in which she was currently living. She would be at peace. To her own surprise, a sense of sudden calm came over her body. She thought of her parents. Her sister. She was saddened that she would not see Silas and Charlotte grow up. But, at the same time, she was ready to end her own suffering. She was ready.

She could feel Singo's hot breath on her face. She could smell his foul mouth. And then she heard the sound of the gun being cocked. She braced for what she knew was coming. It was inevitable. She closed her eyes as tight as she could…

Contact the Author

I sincerely thank you for reading this book and hope you enjoyed it. I would be extremely grateful if you could leave a review on Amazon.

I'd also love to hear your comments and am happy to answer any questions you may have, so do please get in touch with me by:

Email: drew.branham75@gmail.com

Facebook: www.facebook.com/drewanddjadoption

Website: www.andrewbranham.com

Twitter: @AuthorAndrewB

LinkedIn: www.linkedin-com/in/authorandrewbranham

To receive notification of my next book, please join my mailing list by visiting the contact section of my website www.andrewbranham.com.

I'd be delighted if you read my memoir, *Anything for Amelia,* the harrowing true story of one of the most difficult adoptions on record.

If you enjoy memoirs, I recommend you pop over to the Facebook group We Love Memoirs to chat with me and other authors there. www.facebook.com/groups/welovememoirs

I look forward to hearing from you.

Andrew Branham

Acknowledgments

Thank you to all of my friends and family that helped make this novel possible. Without their help and support, this project would not have materialized:

DJ McCann-Branham—husband
Jacky Donovan and Victoria Twead—Ant Press
Debra Ann Galvan—editor
Diane Day-Heaps—editor
Jay Ferguson—beta reader
Ed Branham—father and beta reader
All of my friends and family.

Ant Press Books

If you enjoyed this book, you may also enjoy these titles:

Chickens, Mules and Two Old Fools by Victoria Twead
(Wall Street Journal Top 10 bestseller)

Two Old Fools ~ Olé! by Victoria Twead

Two Old Fools on a Camel by Victoria Twead
(New York Times bestseller x 3)

Two Old Fools in Spain Again by Victoria Twead

One Young Fool in Dorset by Victoria Twead

Heartprints of Africa: A Family's Story of Faith, Love, Adventure, and Turmoil by Cinda Adams Brooks

Simon Ships Out: How one brave, stray cat became a worldwide war hero by Jacky Donovan

Seacat Simon: The little cat who became a big hero (children's version of the above book for age 8 to 11)

Smoky: How a Tiny Yorkshire Terrier Became a World War II American Army Hero, Therapy Dog and Hollywood Star by Jacky Donovan

Instant Whips and Dream Toppings: A true-life dom rom com by Jacky Donovan

Fat Dogs and French Estates ~ Part I by Beth Haslam

Fat Dogs and French Estates ~ Part II by Beth Haslam

How not to be a Soldier: My Antics in the British Army by Lorna McCann

Into Africa with 3 Kids, 13 Crates and a Husband by Ann Patras

Paw Prints in Oman: Dogs, Mogs and Me by Charlotte Smith
(New York Times bestseller)

Joan's Descent into Alzheimer's by Jill Stoking

The Girl Behind the Painted Smile: My battle with the bottle
by Catherine Lockwood

The Coconut Chronicles: Two Guys, One Caribbean Dream House by
Patrick Youngblood

Midwife: A Calling (Memoirs of an Urban Midwife Book 1) by Peggy
Vincent

Serving is a Pilgrimage by John S. Basham

Second hand Scotch: How One Family Survived in Spite of Themselves by Cathy Curran

Moment of Surrender: My Journey Through Prescription Drug Addiction to Hope and Renewal by Pj Laube

Made in the USA
Middletown, DE
03 April 2016